Longing for Her Kiss

Serpent's Kiss, Book 2

By

Sherri Hayes

Longing for His Kiss
Serpent's Kiss, Book 2
Sherri Hayes

Copyright 2017 by Sherri Hayes

This is a work of fiction. Names, places, characters and incidents are the product of the author's imagination and are fictitious. Any resemblance to actual persons, living or dead, events or establishments is solely coincidental.

Other Books by Sherri Hayes

Finding Anna series
Slave
Need
Truth
Trust

Daniels Brothers series
Behind Closed Doors
Red Zone
Crossing the Line
What Might Have Been

Serpent's Kiss series
Welcome to Serpent's Kiss
Burning for Her Kiss
One Forbidden Night: A Serpent's Kiss Novella
Longing for His Kiss

Single Titles
Strictly Professional
A Christmas Proposal: A Strictly Professional Novella

Acknowledgments

Writing a book is always a journey and I'm lucky to have had some wonderful people along for the ride on this one.

Thank you to my beta reader, Riane Holt. I'm not sure how she does it, but somehow she's able to find the littlest inconsistency within a story. Her eagle eyes never cease to amaze me.

Thank you to my two editors, Wyndy and Andrea, and to my proofreader, Angela, for helping make my book the best it could be.

A big thank you to Sara Eirew, my photographer and cover designer. Her beautiful pictures never cease to amaze me.

Although I'm writing fiction, I like for the stories to be somewhat believable and as true to life as possible. I want to thank Mack for reading through all the BDSM scenes in the book to make sure I got them right.

Dedication

This book is dedicated to all the men and women who serve, and have served, in the armed forces. Thank you for all you do and for the sacrifices you and your families make every day to protect the freedoms we hold dear.

Chapter 1

Lieutenant Colonel Alexander Greco sat in his vehicle, staring down at the envelope in his hand. Captain Kurt Martin had given it to him eight months ago. It was a letter to Kurt's wife, Grace. Life in a combat zone was unpredictable, which Kurt knew all too well. They'd both watched too many soldiers shipped home in a body bag. Because of this, it wasn't uncommon for a soldier to make a video or write a final letter to their loved ones back home. Just in case.

Most of the time, the letter was in the soldier's personal effects. Their next of kin would discover it upon going through their loved one's things. Kurt didn't want that. He'd made Alexander promise that if anything should happen to him, Alexander would deliver the letter to Grace in person.

A chill raced down Alexander's spine as he recalled the morning that had taken Kurt's life and left Alexander with an injury that would end his military career. There had been an incident in a nearby village. They'd needed a doctor, so Alexander had loaded up his gear and joined the convoy heading out.

Everything was going as planned until they were packing up to leave. Someone yelled and then all hell broke loose. An IED exploded, sending him and several others flying. He hadn't been hurt bad from that first explosion, but it had knocked the wind out of him. Before he could get up and move, however, another explosion hit.

Debris began falling from all directions. He couldn't move fast enough to get out of the way.

When the dust settled and the area secured, Alexander was pulled out of the rubble, his left leg crushed. A doctor who couldn't stand for more than an hour at a time was of no use to the Army.

Kurt hadn't been so lucky. One of the IEDs exploded right in front of him. He hadn't stood a chance.

For ten years Alexander had been an army doctor. Over that time he'd lost soldiers—men and women he considered friends. It was par for the course in a war zone. But nothing had prepared him for losing Kurt, a man he considered his brother.

Alexander closed his eyes and pinched the bridge of his nose to keep the tears at bay. Kurt was gone, along with six others in their squad.

An SUV drove past, the driver sending him a curious look. He'd been sitting in the same spot for twenty minutes with the windows rolled down letting in the breeze. Even so, the sun was beating down on his car.

Releasing a loud breath, he folded the envelope and tucked it into his shirt pocket before rolling up the windows and climbing out of the vehicle. His leg throbbed a little as he stood. He waited for it to subside as his body adjusted to the new position.

A car door slammed down the street followed by the sound of a kid laughing. Alexander shook his head, trying to clear his thoughts. After locking up the car, he crossed the street to the address he'd been given. He needed to keep his wits about him and not get distracted. He had a promise to keep.

Alexander ascended the steps of the beige two-story house. It had taken him over a month to locate Grace. By the time Alexander was released from the hospital and gotten his discharge papers, she was no longer living at the address Kurt had given him. She'd happened to mention to one of her neighbors that she was going home to be close to family. From his conversations with Kurt, he knew Grace was from St. Louis. That narrowed it down, but St. Louis was a big city. It had taken time and the help of a private investigator to finally locate her.

A wide porch ran the width of the house, but aside from an empty clay pot, it was bare. And although the yard was neat and well kept, it didn't look as if she spent much time outside. There were no flowers planted, no chairs or lawn ornaments.

He took in every detail, memorizing it. Alexander knew he was stalling. He also knew it wasn't going to get any easier the longer he put it off, and he owed it to Kurt. He'd given his word.

The sound of his knuckles against the old wood door bounced off the semi-enclosed space. He shifted his weight even though he knew it would do nothing to ebb the discomfort he was feeling. Or prepare him for facing his brother's widow.

Several minutes went by and no one came to the door. He was about to give up when he heard the sound of the deadbolt being unlocked. The door creaked open a few inches, and the small chain made a clinking sound as it moved and stretched. It was dark inside the house compared to the brightness outside, so the only thing he could see was a stray lock of blond hair.

"Can I help you?" a timid voice asked.

"Hello. I'm looking for Grace Martin. I was told she lived here." He used his most soothing doctor voice—the one he employed when he had to deliver bad news to a patient.

The woman on the other side of the door didn't respond. Maybe the private investigator had been wrong. Maybe Kurt's widow didn't live there.

"My name is Alexander Greco. I served with her husband and I was hoping to speak with her. I can come back if she's not home." His words trailed off as he heard the chain being released and the door opened wider.

"What did you say your name was again?" The woman's voice was a little stronger this time.

"Alexander Greco, ma'am. I was a doctor at the forward operating base where Grace's husband, Kurt, was stationed." He paused, his memories pulling him in a direction he didn't want to go. "We used to go on our morning runs together."

The woman opened the door wide, letting him get his first real glimpse of her. She was dressed in jeans and a faded Army T-shirt. He'd seen a picture of Kurt's wife. She was beautiful. The woman in front of him wore no makeup and had her hair pulled up in a messy ponytail. It didn't matter. Grace Martin was still stunning.

She tugged at the bottom of her shirt. "You served with Kurt." This time it wasn't a question.

"Yes, ma'am." Alexander wondered if Kurt had mentioned him

to her. From the change in her features, he was assuming he had.

Grace glanced over his shoulder and furrowed her brow as though she were deep in thought. "Would you like to come in?"

"If it wouldn't be any trouble."

She stepped back, allowing him to enter.

The inside of the house was much as he imagined. She was probably renting, which explained the stark white walls and lack of pictures.

He followed her down the hallway past what looked to be a modest living room to the kitchen. It was old with laminate countertops and cabinets that looked to have been painted several times over. Along one wall was a small table with three chairs. It wasn't overly stylish, but it had a homey feel to it.

"Can I get you something to drink?" she asked.

"I'm good. Thank you."

She glanced around before lowering herself into one of the wooden chairs.

Alexander pulled out a chair and sat down, making sure not to crowd her. The last thing he wanted to do was make her feel uncomfortable. "My apologies for not calling ahead of time, but I didn't have a working phone number for you."

Grace averted her eyes and swallowed. "That's because I don't have one."

He leaned closer out of pure instinct. "You don't have a phone?"

She looked down. "Not a landline. I have a cell phone for emergencies."

Alexander relaxed a little. He knew her family was from here, but a woman living alone should at least have a phone, some way to call for help should she need it. Maybe that sounded old-fashioned, but he didn't much care. He was who he was.

A heavy silence filled the air for several moments as he searched for how to start. While Kurt had talked about his wife, Alexander didn't really know her and she didn't know him. He and Kurt had gotten to know each other during their time overseas when Kurt had been injured a few days after Alexander's arrival at the base. They'd bonded over their love of baseball and good pizza. Of course, they'd had differing opinions on both.

She met Alexander's gaze for a second, and then looked away

again. "I'm okay."

The corners of his mouth lifted despite the seriousness of the situation. She obviously knew her husband well. Kurt had been a protector, just as Alexander was. It was probably another reason why they'd gotten along so well. "Kurt talked about you a lot."

Grace nodded. "He mentioned you in a couple of his emails. He said . . . he said you were a good friend."

"He was a good friend to me as well." Alexander paused. "He asked me to come see you. To find you should anything happen to him."

Alexander saw the moisture well up in her eyes and his heart broke. The urge to reach out to her was strong, but he held back. He didn't want her to be in pain, but he also knew it was inevitable. The letter Kurt asked him to deliver most likely contained his last goodbyes. Alexander didn't know how he'd handle seeing her break down in front of him, but he would do it for his friend. He owed Kurt that much.

"Were you there?" she asked, her voice barely loud enough for him to hear even sitting so close.

He felt the muscles in his throat constrict. "Yes."

She gripped the edge of the table, her fingers turning white under the pressure. "The men who came . . . they wouldn't tell me anything. Just that he . . . that he died in combat." She glanced up at him then, her eyes pleading.

As much as he didn't want to talk about that day, he would. He'd answer whatever questions she had. For Kurt. For her.

***

Grace's heart felt as if it would beat out of her chest as she waited for her guest to answer. Once his name had registered, she recalled Kurt talking about Lieutenant Colonel Alexander Greco several times. Her husband trusted him, which was what had led her to inviting him inside. If Kurt had trusted him, then she knew she could, too.

"We were in a village when we came under fire. There were explosions all around us." He paused and she held her breath waiting for him to go on. "It all happened very quickly."

Quickly. She closed her eyes as her chest constricted. It had

5

happened quickly. He hadn't lain there and suffered. "Thank you."

The pressure of a hand on hers caused her to open her eyes. "I have something for you."

She looked at him, confused. The men who'd come to tell her that her husband had died in combat had given her Kurt's personal effects.

"Your husband gave me a letter. He asked that I deliver it personally."

Grace resisted the urge to touch her collar—the one Kurt had placed around her neck before his last deployment. It had been her only comfort the day the soldiers had knocked on her door in full dress uniform to inform her that her husband was dead. She'd lain in bed for two days before a neighbor and fellow Army wife had come to check on her. It would be so easy to sink back into that black hole. She'd been tempted several times since that day. It was only her family that had stopped her.

She'd been so lost in her thoughts, her memories, that she almost missed the envelope Alexander held in his hand. He seemed to hesitate and then held it out to her.

Reluctantly, Grace took it and placed it in her lap. With a single finger, she outlined her name written in her husband's chicken scratch. A smile tugged at her lips but was swiftly followed by a gut-wrenching ache deep in her chest. She'd always teased him about his handwriting. She'd never . . .

"Kurt asked me to make sure you weren't alone when you read it, but I can go in the other room if you'd like some privacy." His words were soft, comforting.

She shook her head, or at least she thought she did. So many emotions were rolling through her she couldn't be certain. He didn't move, though, so maybe she had.

Grace had no idea how much time had passed before she garnered the courage to pick the envelope back up and turn it over. She carefully broke the seal and removed the two sheets of paper inside. Once they were in her hands, the words staring back at her, she froze. "I can't do this."

Alexander reached out again. He grasped her free hand in his and held on tight. It was as if he could sense how much she needed his strength.

She wiped the tears from her cheeks with the back of one hand

and held Alexander's fingers in a death grip with the other. He was the only thing keeping her grounded.

Her hand shook as she began to read.

My Grace,

I had dreams for us. Big dreams. We were going to go on a road trip across the country and stop at all the interesting towns along the way. We were going to go on that Alaskan cruise and watch the whales playing in the bay. Hike the Grand Canyon and make love under the stars. So many things we wanted to do together once my tour was up.

But if you're reading this, it means we aren't going to get to do those things together and I'm sorry about that. Something has happened to prevent me from returning to you and you know that only death would keep me away. You are my heart, my soul. You are everything good and beautiful in this world, my Grace.

When I sat down to write this letter, I knew in my mind what I wanted to say, but now the words won't come. I don't want to say goodbye to you, Grace. I don't want you to have to say goodbye to me, but you have to. I know it will be difficult at first, but you are strong, Grace. You always have been.

You have to move on. You have to live.

With that in mind, I am giving you my last orders, my sweet submissive.

I want you to move back home to St. Louis. Your family is there and you will need their support. Let them love and comfort you.

I know you will need time to grieve. I want you to take that time, but I also don't want you to hide inside yourself. You have to live, remember? Make new friends, travel. Do all the things that you and I talked about doing together.

And lastly, I want you to find a new Master. I know you'll most likely go home to St. Louis, so before my deployment I did some digging and found out about a local club there called Serpent's Kiss. It's run by a woman named Katrina Mayer. I think it will be a good place for you and she can help you and make sure you find a good Dom who will take care of your needs.

I know what you're thinking, Grace, but I'm asking this of you. I'm asking you to move on. To let me go. I will always love you. Never forget that. Never doubt that. But as much as I wish it weren't so, I can't be there to care for you anymore.

Alexander is a good man. If you need anything, ask him. I have no idea if he is in the lifestyle or not, but I trust him.

Please do not mourn for me too long, my Grace. You have a lot of life left to live.

Kurt

He couldn't mean it. He couldn't.

"Grace?"

She heard someone call her name, but it sounded far away.

"Grace."

This time the voice sounded louder. Closer.

"Grace!"

A hand shook her arm, causing the letter to fall to the floor. She reached for it without checking her balance. Only a set of strong arms wrapping around her torso kept her from face-planting onto the floor.

Those same arms helped her to right herself, but all she cared about was the letter. She had to read it again. Surely she had misunderstood. She couldn't . . .

Grace scanned over the words again, but they were the same as they had been the first time. Kurt wanted her to find another Master. The rest she could do, she was already trying to do as best she could, but that? How?

Something made her look up. Alexander Greco knelt beside her on the floor, deep concern etched into his features. He must have been the one who'd called her name.

"Are you all right?" he asked.

Chapter 2

Once he was fairly sure she wasn't going to faint, Alexander pried himself off the floor and went to get her some water. He found a handful of glasses in the cabinet to the left of the sink, grabbed one off the shelf, and filled it with water from the tap.

Grace hadn't moved. She was still sitting on the floor with a look of grief and what seemed to be an edge of panic on her face. The crying he'd been expecting, but not the other. What could have been in the letter that would cause such a reaction?

He bent down, careful not to change positions too quickly to allow his leg time to adjust, and handed her the glass.

It took her a moment, but she reached out and accepted the offering. "Thank you."

Alexander grinned. "You're welcome."

She took a sip of the water, and then eased herself back into the chair. Alexander followed her lead and retook his seat. He wanted to comfort her—the desire was almost overwhelming—but didn't want to crowd her either. They'd only just met and she didn't know him.

Several long moments passed before she cleared her throat. "Did my husband tell you what was in the letter?"

Her question made him more curious. "No. He only made me promise to deliver it to you and asked that I stay while you read it. He said he didn't want you to be alone."

Moisture filled her eyes once more, although he had no idea why. She was clearly upset. He needed to do something. "When was the last time you ate?"

Grace glanced up. She blinked several times before answering. "Um, I had a muffin this morning for breakfast and some soup for lunch."

It was after three in the afternoon. "Just soup?"

"I wasn't all that hungry." She averted her eyes, looking almost ashamed of her response. "I know I should be taking better care of myself. Kurt would be disappointed in me."

Her choice of words had him shifting his gaze to the necklace she was wearing. It was a silver chain with a heart that rested right above her collarbone. The heart had a keyhole in the center. Alexander had been practicing BDSM for close to fifteen years. Being a Dom was something that came naturally to him. He thought back to the conversations he'd had with Kurt. His friend had never said anything, but that didn't mean he and his wife hadn't been in a Dominant/submissive relationship.

"Grace." Alexander waited until she was looking at him. "Is there food in your refrigerator?"

She stared at him for a heartbeat, as if what he'd said hadn't registered. "Yes."

Alexander nodded, stood, and walked over to her refrigerator.

"I'm not—"

"You need to eat," he said as he went to open the door and take a look inside. He wasn't going to back down on this. She needed to take better care of herself. "Nothing's going to jump out at me, right?"

That brought a small smile to her face, which was what he'd intended. "No. At least I don't think so."

The inside of her refrigerator looked a lot like the one in his apartment, which wasn't saying much. It had the staples: milk, eggs, juice, some yogurt, and some leftover pizza. He pulled out the pizza since that would be quicker and less messy than the eggs. "You need to go grocery shopping."

"I know. I don't eat much at home."

He paused to give her a questioning look before putting some of the pizza in the microwave. Alexander knew he was probably charging through a bunch of boundaries he shouldn't, but if what he suspected was true, Grace hadn't only lost her husband. She'd lost her Dom. And since she was in a new city, chances were she didn't have anyone local she could share that loss with. She needed to be taken care of, and until she chose someone else for the job . . .

Grace looked sheepish again. "I work a café and I eat while I'm there most of the time."

"Good." At least she was eating. That made him feel a little better. "Your family is from St. Louis, right? Do they visit often?"

The microwave chimed and he took the pizza over to her at the table.

"Thank you." She gave him a grateful smile and picked up a piece. Apparently she'd decided not to fight him on the food.

"You're welcome." He sat down across from her, a little closer than before.

"I feel like I'm being a bad host," she said after swallowing her first bite.

He chose to ignore her comment. "Your family?"

"My sister stops by a few times a week to check on me, and I usually see my mom on the weekends." Grace took another bite, and then hesitated. "I feel like I'm being rude, eating in front of you like this."

"Are you forgetting who insisted you eat in the first place?" He quirked one eyebrow up in question, which made her grin again. It was good to see some of the sadness in her eyes fade, even if only for a moment.

"I can see why you and Kurt got along. You're a lot alike."

"I'll take that as a compliment."

She picked off a slice of pepperoni, seeming to examine it closely, and then whispered, "He was the best man I'd ever known."

This time Alexander didn't hesitate to comfort her when he saw the tears threaten again. He placed a gentle hand on her arm, letting her warmth seep through the tips of his fingers. "If I could have traded places with him, I would have. He talked about coming home to you all the time."

The next thing he knew, Grace leaned toward him and he pulled her into his embrace. He tucked her head into the crook of his neck and held her while she let go. Her entire body shook as she cried, and each time it was like a punch to his gut.

He let her weep, offering what comfort he could, and eventually her sobs quieted. "I'm sorry," she said, trying to pull herself together. "I shouldn't have—"

"No apologies needed." Without thinking, he reached up and brushed a tear from her cheek. "I'm more than willing to lend you my shoulder to cry on anytime you need it."

Her gaze met his and held for a moment before pulling away. "Excuse me for moment. I need to . . ."

"I'll wait."

Grace nodded and rushed out of the room. When she returned to the table, the only sign of her recent crying jag was the redness around her eyes.

He sat quietly across from Grace while she ate another two pieces of the pizza he'd warmed up for her. As much as he would have loved to continue talking to her, he wanted her to eat her food more. Everything else could wait.

"Did you want the rest?" she asked. "I can't eat anymore."

"Thank you for offering, but I had a big lunch. And besides, you might get hungry later." He smiled and went to put her leftover pizza away. "Is there anything I can do for you? Anything you need?"

He'd expected her to respond, but she didn't. She was looking back down at the letter, which was lying on the table.

Alexander was getting ready to ask again when she spoke. "Are you married, Mr. Greco?"

Her question threw him for a moment. "No, I'm not. And please call me Alexander."

"So you didn't have someone back home waiting for you?"

He had no idea where she was going with this. "No. I haven't had much time for relationships since I joined the Army, and even less since I was discharged."

Grace brushed her fingertips over the paper. She appeared deep in thought. "Thank you for bringing my husband's letter to me."

It very much sounded as if he was being dismissed. Alexander fished his wallet out of his back pocket and retrieved a business card with his cell phone number on it. One day he hoped it would also include information about his private practice, but until then it was an easy way to pass along his information when needed. "Take my number. If you need anything, call me. Day or night. I'm planning to stay in St. Louis . . . at least for a while."

For a second he thought she was going to refuse, but instead she took the card and nodded. "Thank you. For everything."

He climbed into his vehicle a few minutes later. With his errand accomplished, he should have felt a weight lifted off his shoulders, but he didn't. If anything, he felt more of an obligation now than he had before he'd met Grace Martin.

Pulling away from the curb, Alexander wondered if she'd use the number he'd given her. It would be easier for him if she didn't, but he'd never been one to take the easy road. If he had, he wouldn't have spent ten years serving in the Army. He would have put in his time and gotten out. But if he'd done that, he wouldn't have met Kurt Martin, and now Grace.

Alexander was reminded again of the necklace she wore. The necklace he was almost positive was a collar. Had that been the reason Kurt insisted Alexander be the one to deliver Grace the letter? Had he known Alexander was a Dom?

There was no way to know the answer to that question, but Alexander did know one thing. This wasn't going to be the last time he saw Grace Martin.

***

Grace stood by the window, behind the cover of the curtains, as Alexander drove away. He'd been reluctant to leave. Given the way she'd broken down, she really couldn't blame him. He probably thought she would fall apart again the moment he left.

He wasn't far off the mark. Once his car was out of sight, she made sure all the doors were locked before traipsing upstairs to her bedroom.

Her bed took up most of the space, but there was a small nightstand on one side with a lamp and a stack of books. She strolled over and turned on the light before kicking off her shoes and crawling onto the bed. Over the last month or so she'd started reading again. Her boss, Beth, had even lent her some of her favorite novels.

But tonight the only thing on Grace's mind was her husband's words. Sure, she could ignore her master's last command, but Grace had never been good at that. She'd always been a good little sub, and disregarding her Dom's last order wasn't in her.

Without much thought, Grace kicked the sheets down until she was able to burrow beneath them. Fall had arrived and the weather was starting to cool. She hadn't needed to turn on the air-conditioning for the last week. Still, most people probably wouldn't have wanted more than a sheet, let alone the comforter she kept on her bed, but she liked the weight.

She unfolded the letter and read it for the third time, hoping somehow that the words would have changed. They hadn't. It had taken years for her and Kurt to build the trust they'd had together, years to form the bond that gave her so much joy and pleasure. Even when he'd been thousands of miles away she could feel their connection.

He'd given her no timetable for finding another master. She could put it off, but in her heart she'd know she was disobeying.

Sliding farther down onto the mattress, she brought the sheet up until it was tucked beneath her chin, and rolled onto her side. Was she ready to start dating again? Find another master?

She had no idea how to answer that.

Somewhere along the line, Grace must have fallen asleep. It was dark out when she opened her eyes. She went to use the bathroom and get a drink of water before returning to her bed. There were so many decisions she needed to make and she'd never been good at that.

Grace lay there contemplating her options until her alarm went off at five thirty. It was Tuesday and she had to get ready for work. At least there she knew her place, what she needed to do.

Tommy was the first person Grace saw when she walked through the back door of the café. He was putting some of Beth's blueberry muffins into the oven. The thought alone made her mouth start to water.

"Morning, Grace."

She gave a small wave and went to put her purse on the shelf and grab her apron.

"How was your weekend?" he asked.

"It was good. How was yours?" It was the same way she answered every time he asked.

"Tommy had a date this weekend," Beth chimed in as she came around the corner and placed a large bag of flour on the counter. "Morning, Grace."

Grace went to the sink to wash her hands so she could help with the baking. "Morning."

They fell into what had become their normal routine. Beth and Tommy had known each other for years, since before Beth had opened the café, and you could tell by the way they teased each other. Grace never felt left out, though. They tried to include her as much as possible in their conversations and she appreciated it. The café was the one place Grace felt like she belonged these days.

The buzzer went off and Tommy went to get the muffins out of the oven to cool while Grace and Beth loaded the front counter with all the goodies they'd made that morning. Once everything was in place and ready to go, they each pulled a stool up to one of the prep tables and grabbed a muffin. It had become a morning ritual of theirs.

Beth said it was because she rarely was able to grab breakfast before she left for work anymore since her fiancé, Drew, had moved in with her. She said they tended to get distracted and food wasn't high on their list of priorities. While Grace could see where Drew could be a distraction, their morning muffin break hadn't started until after Beth had found out that Grace didn't always eat breakfast before coming to work.

"So have you and Drew set a date?" Tommy asked Beth as he polished off his muffin.

"We're still discussing it."

Tommy shook his head. "I don't know what you're waiting for."

"We've only been engaged for a month." Beth looked to Grace. "That's not long, right?"

Their discussion was cut short when the oven timer went off, letting them know that not only were the scones ready, but it was time to open the doors. Tommy hopped off his stool and took his plate over to the large stainless steel sink along the wall then he disappeared through the swinging doors that separated the front of the restaurant from the kitchen area.

"I guess that means it's showtime," Beth said, scraping some crumbs off the counter.

Grace tied a clean apron around her waist. "I'll get the soup started."

The day flew by and before Grace knew it, they were putting food away and wiping down tables. In the two months she'd been working for Beth, she'd gotten to know a lot of the regulars. They greeted her with a smile and always brightened her day. She felt like she'd found an extended family at Beth's Café. She owed her sister, Gabby, a huge thank you for pushing her to apply for the job.

"Any big plans for tonight, Grace?" Tommy asked as he cleaned the display case.

The first thing she thought of was her husband's letter. Of course, she couldn't say anything about that to Tommy. "I might swing by my sister's." It was a lie, but he didn't need to know that. Grace was planning to do the same thing she did most nights after work—go home to her lonely house and find a way to pass the time.

He poked his head up over the display case. "You should come out to dinner with us."

It took her a second to realize she must have missed something. "Dinner?"

Tommy chuckled. "Yeah. Dinner. Me. Beth. Drew. Nicole and Jeff. You could invite your sister, too. I'm sure Beth wouldn't mind."

"What wouldn't I mind?" Beth strolled into the dining room, carrying the vacuum.

He didn't miss a beat. "If Grace and her sister joined us for dinner tonight."

A smile lit up Beth's face. "Of course I wouldn't mind. Grace, we'd love for you and your sister to join us."

Grace felt backed into a corner. She wanted to make an excuse, to say no, but it wasn't in her. There was something about her that wanted to please. She'd always been that way. "I'll ask her."

"I can use my charm on her if you want," Tommy said. "I can be very persuasive when I need to be."

She'd seen it firsthand with their customers. All the regulars loved Tommy. He knew all of them by name and made each one of them feel special. It was something Grace envied, but she'd never have his outgoing personality.

Before she could think of something to say, Beth did. "I think she can handle it all on her own, can't you, Grace?"

A wave of gratitude for her boss washed over her. Beth seemed to understand her shyness even if Tommy didn't. "Yes."

Because she'd said she would, Grace called her sister and asked if she wanted to go out to dinner with Grace's coworkers and some of their friends. She'd no sooner gotten the question out when her sister told her she'd call their mom about watching Taylor and asked what time they needed to be there, which was how Grace found herself sitting at a table with her sister, Beth, Tommy, and a bunch of people Grace didn't really know all that well.

She knew Drew. Kind of. He'd stopped into the café a few times to see Beth, but given her timid nature, Grace hadn't said much more than hi to the guy.

The lack of knowing anyone didn't deter her sister. Gabby jumped right into the conversation. "Grace said you two recently got engaged. Congratulations."

"Thank you," Drew said, taking Beth's left hand in his. He kissed the ring on her finger. "It took me a while, but eventually I wore her down."

Beth rolled her eyes. "Maybe I just wanted to see how far you'd chase me."

He leaned in, his lips a breath away from hers. "To the moon and back."

Grace's chest constricted watching the exchange. The love Beth and Drew had for each other rolled off them in waves. It was a precious gift, one that had been taken away from Grace all too soon. She hoped they both knew how blessed they were and didn't take what they had for granted.

When their food came, the conversation turned to some outreach work Drew and his friend Shawn, who'd also joined them for dinner, were doing at a local school.

By the time she and her sister headed home, Grace was ready to drop. It had been almost a year since she'd socialized so much and it was exhausting.

"Are you okay over there?" her sister asked as they drove toward Grace's house.

"Yeah, I'm fine."

"You did well tonight. I'm proud of you."

Grace glanced over at her sister, her voice dripping with sarcasm. "Thanks."

Gabby laughed. "I didn't mean it that way. It's just . . . it was good seeing you get out of the house and enjoying yourself a little. You've been a bit of a recluse since you've been back."

"I get out of the house. I work five days a week."

Instead of responding to what Grace had said, Gabby went a

different route. "I know it was hard on you, losing Kurt. I can't say I know how you feel, but I know he wouldn't want you to be miserable for the rest of your life. He'd want you to be happy."

"I know," Grace said, looking out the window at the passing houses. If only her sister knew exactly what it was Kurt wanted her to do—how he wanted her to get on with her life. But that wasn't something she could share with Gabby. "I'm working on it."

Chapter 3

Alexander had plenty to keep him busy for the rest of the week. An Army buddy of his had made a call and got him an interview with a company that might be interested in having him do some consulting work. If he was going to stay in St. Louis long term then he was going to need a job.

Eventually he wanted to get back to seeing patients of his own, which meant filing all the paperwork through the state of Missouri for a medical license. It would take time—probably a year—before he'd be able to begin looking at opening a practice of his own or joining an already established one in town. Until then, he would be stuck reading through files and offering opinions.

But did he want to permanently move to St. Louis? It was the question he'd asked himself multiple times throughout the week. He could go anywhere. There wasn't anything holding him there anymore.

Except there was. He'd been in town for less than two months but he'd begun to feel settled in a way he hadn't in a long time. Growing up a military brat, and then joining the Army right out of med school, he hadn't put down many roots outside his years in college. The only time he'd ever felt he had a place was when he'd visited his grandparents. And it was thanks to them that he had some wiggle room financially to figure out exactly what he wanted now his military career was over.

On Friday evening Alexander hurried into the old brick building that housed Serpent's Kiss, trying to get out of the rain as swiftly as his legs would carry him.

Ali smiled when she saw him step into what they all referred to as the coatroom. He grinned as he ran a hand over the top of his head to brush away any water droplets. "How are you this evening, Ali?"

"I'm good, Sir. How about you?" Ali was always polite. She was a good sub. Why she didn't have a Dom he didn't know.

"Glad it's the weekend."

She smiled wider. "Long week?"

"You could say that." Long was one way of putting it.

"Well, I hope you enjoy your evening," she said.

Alexander nodded and headed into the main room of the club.

He'd been in his share of kink clubs over the years. They all were a little different. Some bordered on gentlemen's clubs but with a kinky theme. Others were wall-to-wall play areas. Serpent's Kiss was neither. The main floor was set up much like any other club. There was a bar, a dance floor, and sitting areas where people could gather and socialize. Although, that didn't mean things were kept vanilla. Not by a long shot. All around the room, subs—some more clothed than others—knelt at their Dom's feet.

As he made his way across the room toward the bar, he passed a Dom leading a female sub by a leash. They were headed upstairs to where the play areas were. The woman had a smirk on her face, which caused Alexander to chuckle. It looked as if someone was going to have some fun tonight.

"What can I get you?" Brandon asked from behind the bar. The man was in his mid-thirties, same as Alexander was, but Alexander could have passed for being ten years his senior. That was what war did to a person.

"Scotch on the rocks." He wasn't playing tonight, but it wouldn't matter. The club owner, Katrina Mayer, was a stickler for rules. Club members were only allowed one drink of hard liquor or two beers per night. It was a good rule and it ensured everyone came for the right reasons. This wasn't somewhere a person went to drown their sorrows.

With his drink in hand, Alexander scanned the room while Brandon moved down the bar to wait on someone else. Alexander had gotten to know many of the club members since he'd joined. Some he'd clicked with more than others. One of the Doms he'd gotten to know spotted him from halfway across the room.

"Rough week?" Daniel asked as he came up beside Alexander, tilting his head toward the glass in Alexander's hand.

"The longest." Alexander took a drink of his scotch before resting it on the bar. Between the interview and filling out all the paperwork required for his licensing, the week had seemed as if it would never end.

The other reason his week had seemed so incredibly long was because his thoughts kept drifting to Grace Martin. He'd done his duty: delivered the letter. He should be able to move on, but he couldn't. Something kept bringing her to the forefront of his mind.

A mischievous glint in his friend's eye gave Alexander fair warning of what was coming next. "I'm sure you could persuade one of the subs to play. Maybe even more than one. I've seen some of the looks a few of them have sent your way. Speaking of which . . ." Daniel nodded in the direction of the dance floor where a group of subs were dancing.

As if sensing Daniel and Alexander's gaze, two members of the group looked their way. One of them, Bridget he thought her name was, quickly lowered her gaze and blushed. Her reaction amused him, but did nothing to spark his interest. "I think I'm good."

"Suit yourself." Daniel ordered a bottle of water from Brandon, downed half of it, and then pushed away from the bar. "Missy asked if I would test out the newest addition to her toy bag. I'll find you later?"

"I'll be around."

Alexander finished his scotch, grabbed a bottle of water for himself, and went to find a seat. It had been a good day for him physically. So far his leg wasn't bothering him, but there was no sense in pushing his luck.

An hour later, Daniel had joined him and several others in one of the larger seating areas with Missy, who looked completely content after their scene. She sat quietly beside him wrapped in a blanket, sipping her water. The two weren't a couple, but they did play together from time to time. Then again, Daniel played with a lot of subs. He was a master flogger and the club's subs loved him for it.

"Did you ever track down the woman you were looking for?"

Beth, one of the club's Femdoms, asked him.

Alexander hadn't been paying much attention to the conversation, so it took him a little longer than it should to answer. "Yes, I did."

"Does that mean you'll be leaving town soon?"

The question came from Beth's fiancé and sub, Drew. "No. I'm thinking of sticking around for a while. See what my options are."

Katrina chose that moment to walk by. She stopped when she heard what they were talking about. "Did I hear that right? Are you staying in St. Louis?"

"It looks that way."

She rested her hip against the side of the couch and stretched one arm along the back. The position was casual, but the men in the area turned to look. Katrina had a body on her and every male in the room, Dom or sub, could appreciate it. "Good. I was kind of hoping I could talk to you about doing a medical scene demonstration. I know there are members who would appreciate exploring that area of play."

"Maybe you could get Bridget to help you," Daniel said.

Alexander ignored him. "Let me think about it."

"Just let me know. The invitation is there." Katrina's gaze went to the stairs. She stood and straightened the corset she was wearing. "If you'll excuse me, it looks as if I'm needed upstairs."

The rest of the evening dissolved into ideas for the scene Alexander had been asked to consider doing. It seemed Katrina wasn't exaggerating when she said members were interested. Role playing was the easy part. Knowing how to use the instruments properly and to maximum effect was where it could get tricky.

At eleven o'clock he said farewell to his new friends and drove back to the one-bedroom apartment he was renting. It was small but adequate. The space had come furnished, which had made things easier.

After tossing his keys onto the long kitchen counter that separated his living room from his kitchen, he strolled into his bedroom and stripped out of his clothes. The steam from the shower filled the bathroom as he stepped under the spray. He tilted his head forward, letting the water trail down his back and shoulders before reaching for the soap.

A jolt of pain streaked down his leg when he moved to rinse, and he knew he needed to hurry. Dealing with his physical limitations was part of his reality now. But he'd take it considering the alternative.

Of course his train of thought, as was so often the case this week, had led him to Grace. How was she holding up? Was she eating enough? Taking care of herself? He'd hoped she would call, but she hadn't.

***

Grace crawled out of bed Saturday morning and got ready for work. Her sister had come over the night before for a girls' night while their mom watched Gabby's daughter, Taylor, for a few hours. They'd watched a movie, eaten pizza, and downed about a dozen cookies. Gabby really was trying to pull Grace out of her shell, and in some ways it was working. For the first time since she'd gotten the news that Kurt had been killed, she hadn't needed to leave the room when the two people in the movie had kissed. The scene had still made her chest clench and caused moisture to well up in her eyes, but she'd held it together. Barely.

That didn't mean she hadn't shed more than her share of tears this week. She'd read her husband's letter over and over again and each time she ended up an emotional mess. Grace still had no idea how she was going to fulfill her Master's last command, but she would try.

The roads were practically empty as she headed downtown toward the café. During the week, people were already on their way to work at this hour, but on a Saturday most of them were still at home in bed. She appreciated the solitude.

After pulling up to what had become her spot behind the café, Grace made her way inside. She waved to Beth and Tommy and donned her apron before getting to work.

"The DJ was awesome," Tommy said as he helped her take the chairs off the tables and get them ready for customers. "We're going back tonight. You could come with us."

She flipped another chair and placed it on the floor before responding. "Thanks, but I think I'll pass."

He shook his head but didn't say anything more.

When Kurt was home, they would go out on dates, to munches,

or to play parties, but that was different than going out to a dance club. It was either only the two of them, or people in the lifestyle who understood her tendency to let her husband take the lead.

Beth strolled into the front room with a tray of fresh cherry Danishes. "Everything almost ready up here?"

"Yep. We're good," Tommy said, already making a beeline toward the back. He'd fully embraced the preopening muffin break.

Beth chuckled. "You'd think he didn't eat breakfast before he came."

Grace grinned at her boss. "Typical man."

This earned an even bigger laugh. "So true."

The breakfast and lunch rush came and went with them all rushing around trying to fill orders as quickly as possible. By the time things started to slow down, Grace was feeling it. So when Beth nodded toward a stool and pushed a sandwich her way, it didn't even cross her mind to object. "Thanks."

Normally, they all tried to take a break before lunch, but there hadn't been time for more than downing a slice of bread with a little butter on it. And even then, Beth had to run an order out to a table for her. Saturdays weren't typically so busy.

Beth moved a few things around before pulling up a chair across from Grace and picking up her own sandwich. Tommy could handle the customers, and if not he'd come get them.

"Any plans for tonight?" Beth asked between bites.

"Not really. I'll probably finish reading this book I've been working on." Grace didn't mind Beth asking about her plans. She wasn't as pushy as Tommy and there was something about her boss that made Grace think she kind of understood, at least maybe a little.

"Is it any good?"

"Yeah. It's pretty good." Grace really hoped Beth didn't ask her what the name of it was. She wasn't sure she could handle that. Given Kurt's wishes for her to move on, to find a new Dom, she'd been attempting to get herself into the correct mindset. In order to do that, she'd dug out some of her old novels, the ones that had made her interested in the lifestyle to begin with, and began reading them again.

"I might be interested in borrowing it. I'm always looking for a good read."

Grace swallowed. What would Beth say if she found out Grace

was a submissive? Or would Beth just think Grace enjoyed reading kinky romance novels? She had no way to know and Grace didn't want to lose this job.

The doors that led to the front counter pushed open and Tommy poked his head in. "I'm gonna go ahead and flip the sign."

Beth stood. "How many customers are still out there?"

"Just two tables. I've got it, B. You two finish eating."

Instead of sitting back down, Beth started filling the sink with water. One of the downsides to working in a restaurant of any kind was the dishes. Grace finished the rest of her sandwich, rolled her sleeves up, and went to help.

It was a little after three when she said goodbye to Beth and Tommy behind the café. Grace was ready to go home, but first she had to stop at the store. She was completely out of milk and she'd had to throw out the bread she had this morning because it had molded.

Everything was going fine—well, maybe not fine, but okay—until she was leaving the grocery store and her car wouldn't start. She tried to crank the engine but nothing happened.

Her first instinct was to call for roadside assistance, something Kurt had insisted upon since he was overseas, but then Grace remembered that she'd let the coverage lapse. It hadn't seemed important with everything else she was dealing with. Besides, she never went anywhere anyway. Why would she need it?

Fate was laughing at her now.

The only person she knew to call was her sister, although she had no idea what Gabby would do. Call a tow truck probably. And that was assuming her sister wasn't working today, which she often did on Saturdays. If not, Grace could be sitting there, milk spoiling in the back seat, for a couple of hours. Her mother was another option, but again all she would be able to do was call someone.

Alexander's words came back to Grace. *If you need anything, call me. Day or night.*

She hesitated for only a minute before digging his card out of her purse and dialing his number.

"Alexander Greco." His voice was strong and confident as he answered.

"Hi. It's Grace. Grace Martin." She felt silly calling him, but did she really have another option?

"Grace. I'm glad you called." He sounded genuinely pleased, which eased some of her tension.

"I'm sorry to bother you, but my car won't start and both my sister and my mom—"

"Where are you?"

Grace gave him her location and he said he'd be there in fifteen minutes. Knowing he was coming allowed her to relax. She rolled down the windows to let the breeze keep the inside of the car from getting too warm.

She spotted him first and got out of the car to get his attention. He grinned when he saw her and pulled his vehicle in a few spaces down from hers.

"Thank you for coming," she said when he approached.

"I told you to call me anytime. I meant it." He motioned toward her car. "Do you mind?"

"No, no. Of course not." She moved so he could get behind the wheel.

Alexander tried to turn the engine over twice but it did the same thing for him as it did for her—nothing. "Sounds like your battery's dead. How long have you had this one?"

She had to think. "I don't know. Four or five years, maybe."

"They usually only last about five years." He exited her vehicle, pulled out his phone, and started searching. "Surely there has to be a place nearby that sells batteries. We'll go get you a new one and get it put in. That should take care of the problem."

They loaded the few groceries she'd bought into his car, and then drove a few miles away to a place he found on his phone that said they sold car batteries. She followed him inside and waited while he told the woman behind the counter what they needed. It took them less than an hour to get the battery and for Alexander to switch the old one out with the new one. While he was replacing her battery, he even turned on his car's air conditioner to keep her groceries from spoiling.

"Thank you again," she said, sliding into the driver's seat, unable to convey how grateful she really was for his help. Her engine was running, good as new, once he'd replaced the battery.

"You're very welcome, Grace." She'd expected him to go, but he didn't. "Would you like to have dinner with me tonight?"

Grace knew she had to look as if she'd seen a ghost, but she hadn't been expecting his question. "Dinner?"

"I haven't had good Italian food since before I left on my last tour, and a friend told me about a restaurant here in town I've wanted to try. I'd be honored if you'd come with me."

It was on the tip of her tongue to say no, but her husband's insistence that she move on was there in the back of her mind. Going to dinner with Alexander would be a good test run to see if she could do this. "I need to take my groceries home first."

His answering smile had nervous butterflies dancing in her belly. "That's perfect. How about I pick you up at six? That will give me time to make the reservations and change."

"Sure," she said. The butterflies were fluttering away with no sign of stopping. "Six."

Picking her up at her house? Reservations? Whether it was supposed to be or not, it was sounding very much like a date.

Chapter 4

Grace checked her reflection in the mirror for the sixth time. She had no idea what to wear so she'd stuck with a dark blue skirt she'd had for a while and a simple white shirt. They were going to dinner and she wanted to look halfway put together on the outside even if she was feeling like a jumbled mess on the inside.

The thought of putting herself out there again scared the hell out of her. She'd only dated a few guys before she'd met Kurt in her freshman year of college. Even if she found a Dom who would meet her submissive needs and forget about the rest, she'd still have to open herself up to someone new and that wasn't something she'd done, at least not on such an intimate level, for over a decade. She also knew that wasn't what her husband had asked of her. He wanted her to move on, and she knew that meant more than just finding a new Dom.

But first things first. She'd go out to dinner with Alexander, talk, and try to have a good time. Baby steps.

The sound of her doorbell sent her heart racing. *Not a date,* she reminded herself.

After looking through the peephole to confirm it was Alexander, she unlatched the chain and opened the door. He was dressed in a suit and tie, freshly shaved—and in one hand he held a black cane.

"I'm a little early," he said, bringing her attention to his face once more. "I wasn't sure if you'd be ready, but I didn't want to sit out in my car like some crazy stalker."

She knew it was meant as a joke, but she was too anxious to laugh. "Let me grab my purse, and then I'll be ready to go."

Before he was able to respond, Grace hurried inside and snatched her purse from where she'd left it in the kitchen. He was still standing in the same spot when she returned, patiently waiting for her. She locked up and they headed out.

He held the car door open for her and waited while she slid into the passenger seat. "You look nice this evening."

Heat flooded her cheeks at the compliment. "Thank you."

Grace took several deep breaths as he made his way around the vehicle and climbed behind the wheel. It would make her look like a crazy person if she started to hyperventilate. This was not a date. They were . . . friends? Acquaintances? Two *people* having dinner together.

Alexander pulled away from the curb and headed toward downtown. "This is supposed to be the best Italian restaurant in St. Louis. Being of Italian heritage, it's hard to find places that live up to my standards." He glanced over at her, humor in his eyes.

"It's been a while since I've had anything besides spaghetti with sauce that came from a jar."

He gasped in mock horror. His gaze flashed in her direction, his eyes wide, before turning back to the road. "Blasphemy!"

A bubble of laugher built in her chest and escaped her lips before she could stop it. It felt good. But there was a little voice in her head that told her she should feel guilty about that.

When her laughter abruptly cut short, he noticed. "Feeling guilty?"

She had no idea how he'd known that. "How did you—"

"I'm a doctor, remember? And I was in the Army for ten years. I've seen survivor's guilt many times." He paused. "Too many times."

Survivor's guilt. That pretty much summed it up. Why should she be happy and enjoy life when Kurt couldn't?

She already knew the answer to that, too.

"You were happy and you felt guilty about it, right?" He didn't wait for an answer. "Like you shouldn't get to go on and be happy because he can't."

She pinched the fabric of her skirt with her fingertips and released it several times before answering. "Something like that."

Exactly like that.

"I've experienced it myself." He swallowed hard and she watched as he increased his grip on the steering wheel. "Sometimes it's difficult to rationalize why you're still here, living and breathing, and someone who has a family back home waiting for them isn't."

Grace could hear the underlying pain in his voice and it was strangely comforting. This man she didn't know very well understood, at least on some level, what she was feeling.

"How do you deal . . . get past it?" It was the unknown that had been lingering all around her.

"You don't."

That hadn't been the answer she was expecting.

He shot her a quick look before pulling up in front of the restaurant. She could already see a valet walking toward them. "It's one of those things you have to take one day at a time, Grace. I'm not sure it's something you ever really get over. It's just something you learn to deal with."

Alexander opened his door, and then a second later her door opened as well. Another valet was there to help her from the vehicle. When Alexander joined her he had the cane with him again. She tried not to be obvious, but he must have noticed her staring at it as they were going into the restaurant.

"You're wondering about my cane," he said once they were seated.

She averted her gaze, unable to look him in the eye. For some reason his observation embarrassed her.

"Grace." His voice was soft but firm, and she couldn't help but look up. "It's fine. I was wounded. My left leg was crushed, so sometimes I overdo it and have to use a cane." He paused. "All in all, I was very lucky."

"I'm sorry."

"There's no reason to be sorry. It is what it is. As I said, I was one of the lucky ones."

She didn't get the chance to respond as their server came up to their table to get their drink orders. "Do you like wine?" Alexander asked her.

"Yes, but it's been a while." The last time she had some was with Kurt. It was right before his last deployment. He'd taken her to her favorite restaurant, and then they'd come home, curled up by the fire, drunk an entire bottle of wine, and ended up making love on the couch.

The memory had tears prickling her eyes and she had to blink them away. When she had control of herself again, the waiter was gone and Alexander was staring at her. She reached for the water the waiter had brought and took a sip.

Grace was sure he would say something about her emotional state, but instead he said, "I ordered us some burrata to get us started."

"Thanks." She was grateful he didn't bring up her extreme reaction to his question about the last time she'd had wine.

"You're welcome." He smiled and picked up his menu. "Have you ever been to a restaurant like this before?"

She shook her head. The restaurant itself was fancy. White linens covered the tables and the waiters and waitresses were all in black and white tux-like uniforms. A single candle sat in the center of their table, creating a romantic ambiance. Grace could safely say she'd never been to a restaurant like this before.

"Traditionally there are five courses." He pointed to the sections on her menu.

It was then she noticed the prices. All the breath seemed to leave her lungs and she tried to find the right words so as not to offend him.

Once again, he seemed to know what was going through her mind. "Ignore the prices, Grace. I asked you to join me tonight." When she didn't comment, he added, "Would you prefer if I ordered for the both of us?"

Unable to get the words out, Grace met his gaze and nodded.

A few moments later their waiter returned with the wine Alexander had ordered. He presented the bottle for Alexander's approval, and then opened it and poured a sample for Alexander to taste. Once he approved the sample, the waiter poured them both a glass. Grace was almost afraid to drink it. She hadn't looked at the wine prices, but if it was anything like the cost of the food she didn't want to.

"Did you need a few more minutes with the menu?" their waiter asked.

"No, we're ready," Alexander said with what looked like a slight smirk on his face when he met her gaze. "For our second course we'll have penne filetto di pomodoro and spaghetti aglio e olio. Followed by chicken bruschetta and—" He turned his attention to Grace. "Do you like veal?"

"I don't know. I've never had it," she answered honestly.

He switched his focus back to the waiter. "Veal Sorrentino. Then a bronzini and gamberi fra diavolo."

"And for dessert, sir?" The waiter seemed unfazed by the long list Alexander had given him.

"Your tiramisu and your ricotta cheesecake with espresso con grappa."

"Very good, sir. I'll get this in for you right away and your burrata should be out shortly." The waiter took their menus and disappeared.

"Something wrong?" he asked.

Grace must have had a bewildered look on her face. "That's a lot of food."

He reached for his wine and held it up as if he were about to give a toast. "Didn't you know? Italians like to eat."

***

Alexander took a drink of his wine, never taking his gaze off her. He was enjoying the look on her face too much. She'd seemed genuinely horrified by the price of the food earlier. He was positive she'd been doing calculations in her head. He wasn't rich by any means, but he could afford to splurge on a good meal once in a while.

Gradually, a grin began to pull at her lips. "I guess I didn't realize how true that was."

"I promise all your doubts will be gone by the end of the evening."

She started to say something, but then stopped when their waiter approached the table with their burrata and bread. Once he stepped away again, Grace seemed in no hurry to continue with whatever had been on her mind.

He cut open the burrata and motioned for her to help herself. "You said you worked in a café."

"Yes." After several long moments, she seemed to realize he wanted her to elaborate. "It's not far from here, actually. The woman who owns it, Beth, she's really nice." Grace paused. "Working there has really helped me, with . . . you know."

The wheels were turning in Alexander's head as the pieces began slipping into place. He pushed them out of the way for the moment and reached out to lightly touch the back of her hand. "I do."

A moment passed between them, one that those around them wouldn't understand. It was one of understanding, grief, and of picking up the pieces when life threw you a curveball that knocked you flat on your ass.

She caught him slightly off guard when she flipped her hand over and rested her palm against his. "Thank you."

Alexander gave her hand a slight squeeze and grabbed the bread, offering her some more. "I meant what I said the other day. If you need me, all you have to do is ask."

Grace nodded.

For the rest of their dinner he tried to keep things light, although he was dying to ask more about Beth and the café where Grace worked. Surely it couldn't be a coincidence? Beth was a common name and St. Louis was a big city, but how many Beths could there be in St. Louis who also owned cafés? And if it was the same Beth, did she know that *his* Grace was her employee?

Calling her *his Grace* seemed wrong somehow. She wasn't his. She was Kurt's. And even though Kurt was gone, it still felt like she belonged to him.

His gaze traveled to the necklace she wore. Maybe that was it. If it was in fact a collar and she still wore it, then she still belonged to him.

Which was completely irrelevant when it came down to it because Alexander wasn't looking to start anything with Grace Martin. He was there to watch over her—to be her friend. That was it.

At least that's what he kept telling himself.

Hours later, with their bellies full, they pulled up in front of her house, the last rays of the sun casting an almost orange glow on everything it touched. He turned off the engine and made his way to the passenger side of the vehicle to open her door. His leg was throbbing and he was having to lean on his cane, but he'd been taught you always walked a woman to the door and that's what he was going to do.

"Thanks," she said, pulling her skirt down as she stood.

"It's me who should be thanking you." Alexander closed the door. "I quite enjoyed the company. It gets boring having dinner with just yourself every night."

She chuckled and there was a slight redness in her cheeks. He felt that pull to her again he couldn't explain and he didn't want to examine too closely.

As the evening wore on, Grace had begun to relax. He wasn't sure if it was solely that she felt more comfortable with him or if the wine had something to do with it. Since he was driving, he'd limited himself to two glasses with dinner. Grace had polished off the rest of the bottle, but she wasn't unsteady on her feet. That could have had something to do with the amount of food she'd eaten. He was sure it had been a while since she'd consumed that much in one sitting.

Alexander began walking toward the house and, as he'd hoped, Grace followed him. He noticed she kept glancing at his leg again, which made him realize how much he must be leaning on his cane.

"I'm fine." She didn't respond, so when they reached her door he stopped to face her. Her brow was furrowed and the edges of her mouth were turned down into a slight frown. He didn't like it. Especially since only moments before she'd been in such a good mood. "Really, I'm fine. I worked out this morning, that's all, and I'm paying the price for it now."

Grace met his gaze as if searching to see if he was really telling her the truth or only saying that to make her feel better. Whatever she saw, it must have satisfied her. "You should take better care of yourself."

Her reprimand was so out of character with the shy woman he'd known up to this point that he could barely contain his amusement. "I'll keep that in mind."

They stood there, unmoving, as if waiting for something. If this had been a date then this was when Alexander would have either been kissing her good night or seeing if she wanted to invite him in.

But it wasn't a date and this was Kurt's widow. "Good night, Grace."

"Good night."

Alexander waited until she unlocked the door and went inside before heading back to his vehicle. He debated for about two seconds before deciding to drive to Serpent's Kiss. It was still early—only nine thirty—and even though his leg needed rest, something more important drove him. He needed to talk to Beth, and going to her place of business wasn't an option at this point.

He barely acknowledged Bridget sitting at the coat check as he passed by her to enter the club's main room. If he was being honest, he barely noticed her. The pain in his leg was getting worse the more he stood on it. He knew he should have gone home and waited to talk to Beth, but he wasn't willing to wait a week to find out if what he suspected was true.

As he scanned the room looking for Beth, he grew more irritated, both that he didn't see her and because of his leg. He limped over to the bar, feeling like a man twice his age, and took a seat.

"What can I get you tonight?" Brandon asked.

He wasn't looking for a drink, but the bartender might be able to help him anyway. "I'm looking for Beth. Is she here tonight?"

"Yeah." He looked over Alexander's shoulder. "They were here a few minutes ago to get some waters. I think . . . there they are," he said.

Alexander turned. Beth was in a midnight blue corset, a matching thong, and a pair of boots that came halfway up her thigh.

"I think they are heading upstairs to play."

By the looks of it, Alexander would have to agree. "Thanks."

Forcing his legs to move, he crossed the room to where she was waiting at the bottom of the staircase. She was facing away from him as he approached, so she didn't see him until he was almost on top of her.

"I didn't realize you were here tonight." She was relaxed and smiling, ready to have some fun with her sub.

"I need to speak to you about something." His tone must have alerted her something was off because he saw some of her good mood disappear.

Drew chose that moment to come out of the locker room. His feet were bare and all he was wearing was a pair of jeans. He walked up to them and stood beside his mistress.

Beth placed a hand on Drew's naked chest and met his gaze.

"Go upstairs and get into position. I'll be up in a minute."

He didn't move right away, and she gave him a look that let him know it hadn't been a request.

"Yes, Mistress."

Once they were alone again, she was all business. "What did you need to talk to me about?"

Alexander needed to sit down, so without saying anything he made his way over to a chair a few feet away.

She followed and took the seat opposite him.

"It's been a long day and I'm not going to beat around the bush. Does Grace Martin work for you?"

Beth didn't blink. It was almost as if she'd expected his question. "Yes."

"You knew she was the woman I was looking for." He hadn't meant it to come out as an accusation exactly, but he knew that was the way it sounded.

She nodded. "A few weeks ago you mentioned her name was Grace. And before you'd said she was the widow of an Army friend of yours who'd been killed."

He took some time for that to sink in, not wanting to lash out at her because of his pain. Besides, if she'd said something to him earlier, would it have really made a difference? If he recalled correctly, Alexander had mentioned Grace's name to their group of friends at the club only days before he'd gone to see her that first time.

"Grace told me you make sure she eats while she's at work."

Beth relaxed the set of her shoulders, but didn't sit back in her chair. Alexander knew he needed to let her go so she could join her sub.

"She tried to brush off lunch one day. When I asked her what she'd had for breakfast that morning she told me she'd had half a banana and a few bites of toast," Beth said.

He thought back to the huge meal he and Grace had eaten earlier and, despite the pain he was in, he instantly felt better. "Thank you for looking after her."

Beth hesitated. "She needs someone to look after her."

Did Beth know?

Of course, as soon as the thought crossed his mind, Alexander pushed it away. He didn't even know. Not for certain.

Still, it seemed Beth had picked up on some of the same things he had. "Yes, she does."

They shared a look before Beth stood, her boots making her taller than she usually was. "Let me know if I can do anything to help."

"Have fun with your sub," Alexander said.

The twinkle in Beth's eyes was back. "Oh, I plan to."

Chapter 5

"Could you hand me that glass, Grace?"

It was Sunday morning and she was over at her mom's, helping her go through some boxes. Caroline Lewis was a force to be reckoned with when she got something in her head. She was convinced some papers she needed were stashed in the attic, so she'd asked Grace to come over and help her find them. Two hours into the search and they hadn't turned up much besides some old receipts and a lot of dust.

"Are you sure you remember putting them in one of these boxes and not in the filing cabinet?" Grace asked.

The sound of the back door opening was swiftly followed by her sister's voice. "Knock, knock. Anyone home?"

"In here," their mother yelled.

Gabby strolled into the living room, her three-year-old daughter, Taylor, in tow, dragging a stuffed animal. "What's all this?"

"Mom has a meeting with a guy to talk about her retirement this week—"

"Yes, and I need to find the paper that has all the information about your father's pension." Her mother scowled and reached for another box. "Otherwise I'll just have to go back again."

Her sister shot her a look and Grace shrugged. Their dad had been a meticulous record keeper. Their mother . . . not so much. She tended to throw things in boxes and worry about it later.

Gabby sat down next to Grace and settled Taylor on the couch beside her. "I thought maybe we could all go out for lunch."

She hadn't even finished her sentence and their mother was shaking her head. "I can't go anywhere until I find this." Licking the tip of her index finger, she began riffling through the stack of papers she had resting on her lap. "You three should go, though. Grace never eats enough these days."

Grace's cheeks heated with embarrassment. "Mom!"

"You know it's true," her mother said without looking up from her task.

"We can bring you something back," Gabby said as she gathered her daughter onto her lap.

"That's all right. I have leftovers I can warm up when I get hungry."

Gabby stood. "Grace, you ready?"

Instead of answering her sister, Grace addressed her mother. "Mom, are you sure you don't want me to stay and help?"

"Go with your sister. I'll be fine."

Ten minutes later they were sitting at a booth in a chain restaurant she'd frequented a lot growing up. It was one of those places that pretty much stayed the same no matter how much time had passed. They'd changed the carpet to a slightly darker shade of gray and the walls looked as if they'd received a new coat of paint recently, but other than that it hadn't changed.

Grace reached for a menu and was surprised to find she was actually hungry. Considering the amount of food she'd consumed the night before, she figured she'd be good for most of the day.

"So I swung by your place last night," her sister commented as she perused the menu.

Grace hummed, hoping her sister would move on to other things.

She should have known better. Once they'd given their order to the server, Gabby made sure Taylor was occupied with the placemat and crayons the restaurant had provided, and then leaned in toward her sister. "It was after seven and you usually don't go out that late."

If she made a big deal of hiding her evening out, it would only make things worse. "I was invited to dinner."

Gabby's eyes lit up. "With?"

"An Army buddy of Kurt's stopped by the other day. He gave me his number and told me to call him if I needed anything. I had some car trouble yesterday, so I called him. Afterward, he invited me to have dinner with him."

Her sister's eyes looked as if they were about ready to bug out of her head.

"What?"

"What, she asks. What?" Gabby shook her head in disbelief. "You got asked out on a date and you didn't tell me?"

"It wasn't a date."

Gabby sat up straight and folded her hands in front of her on the table. "Did he pick you up?"

"Yes."

"Did he pay for dinner?"

"Yes." Grace didn't like where this was going.

"Did he walk you to the door afterward?"

"What does that matter?" She was deflecting and she knew it.

"I guess that answers my question." Her sister leaned forward again, lowering her voice as if she were sharing some big secret. "I know you're a little rusty at this, sis, but that's what we in the modern world call a date."

"He's new in town," Grace said, trying to convince her sister. "He just wanted some company."

"Uh-huh."

"Fine, don't believe me. But it wasn't a date."

Her sister chuckled, but let it go. Their server brought their lunches a few minutes later and conversation turned to their mother's impending retirement. "She's going to go stir-crazy."

"Maybe she's looking forward to slowing down," Grace said without much conviction.

Gabby snorted. "Yeah, right."

Although the thought had crossed Grace's mind as well, she'd chosen not to dwell on it. "Maybe she could babysit Taylor more. Free you up to, you know, do other . . . stuff."

A wicked smile bloomed across Gabby's face. "Are you suggesting I need to get laid?"

"No," Grace barely managed to spit out through her shock. Her sister had always been blunter than she was. "I just meant you'd have time to . . . to go out. That's all."

The gleam in her sister's eyes hadn't lessened. She was enjoying Grace's discomfort. "Date."

"Sure," Grace said, looking anywhere but at her sister. "If that's what you want."

Her sister opened her mouth to say something that would no doubt embarrass Grace more, but she stopped short when Grace's phone rang.

There weren't very many people who had Grace's cell phone number and one of them was sitting across from her. As she opened her purse to retrieve the phone, her first thought was that it was her mother ringing to say she'd changed her mind and to ask if they'd bring her something back. But when she looked at the screen she knew it wasn't her mother.

Grace hesitated for a second, debating whether or not to answer. She recognized the number from when she'd called it yesterday. It was Alexander, but she had no idea why he was calling.

"Aren't you going to answer it?" her sister asked. If she didn't answer it, her sister would have more evidence that her dinner with Alexander last night had been more than simply two people sharing a meal.

"Hello." Her voice sounded shaky to her own ears as she answered the call.

"Grace, it's Alexander Greco."

That brought a small smile to her lips. "I know. I recognized your number."

There was a slight pause before he said, "I hope I'm not interrupting anything. I wanted to make sure you weren't having any more issues with your car."

"I drove it to my mom's this morning and it started right up." Grace could feel her sister's stare from across the table, but she was trying her best to ignore it.

"Good." She heard a door opening in the background. "Remember that battery has a warranty on it, so if it gives you any trouble we'll take it back."

"All's good so far."

There was a prolonged silence. "Sorry. I was trying to do two things at once." He laughed. "Probably not the best move. I'm not as agile as I used to be."

"Is your leg bothering you today?" Grace had a feeling he'd

been downplaying how much it was hurting last night.

"No. It's much better today. Thank you for asking." She heard another noise in the background, but this time she couldn't tell what it was. "The other reason I called was that I wanted to see if you'd like to join me for dinner again sometime this week. I was thinking maybe Tuesday or Wednesday? I'm flexible." He paused. "In some ways at least."

A giggle escaped before she could stop it. She knew her sister was sitting there listening to every word and that once she ended the call the gloves would come off. Still, she owed Alexander an answer. "Sure. I don't have any plans."

"Tuesday, then?"

"Okay."

"I'll pick you up. Say, around six?" he asked.

Once the time was agreed upon, she told Alexander she needed to go. He didn't keep her, but reminded her to call if she needed anything before Tuesday.

She avoided looking in her sister's direction until her phone was safely tucked back into her purse. When she did finally chance a glance, Gabby had a knowing smirk on her face. "Want to try telling me again it wasn't a date?"

Grace swallowed. There would be no deterring her sister now. If Grace had thought Gabby's questions had been bad before, they were nothing compared to what was coming. All Grace could do was brace for impact.

***

Alexander arrived at Grace's house with five minutes to spare. He'd made sure to take it easy that day so there wasn't a repeat of the discomfort he'd been in on Saturday evening, even using his cane when he'd swung by what was to be his new office to sign some paperwork. Sitting behind a desk wasn't how he wanted to spend his days, but it would have to suffice for the time being.

He was halfway up the walkway when Grace stepped out onto her front porch. She must have been watching for him.

The dress she wore teased her legs as the wind whipped around the hem and she held tight to the shawl draped over her shoulders as she came toward him.

"Hungry?"

A blank look crossed her face momentarily before it changed to a look of shy embarrassment. "I wanted to save you from having to walk up the steps."

While he was touched by her gesture, it was unnecessary. He had limitations, but nothing that would keep him from picking a lady up at her door. "You didn't have to do that."

She must have heard something in his tone because her expression shifted again. "I didn't mean to offend you."

Alexander didn't want her to feel bad about what she'd meant as a courteous gesture. "You didn't." He turned. "Shall we?"

Grace hesitated for a second before nodding.

He decided to keep things more casual this time around, so he chose a barbecue restaurant he'd heard a few people talking about. When they pulled up in front he noticed her eyes light up. "I take it you've been here before?"

"Pappy's? Of course. They have the best barbecue in town."

Alexander chuckled as he turned off the engine. "That's what I've been told."

The restaurant was busy when they made their way inside. He had to move to one side more than once to allow someone to pass. It was a good sign. Between the amount of people there on a Tuesday night and Grace's endorsement, he was hoping the food would be good. It had been years since he'd had good barbecue.

A petite woman stood behind the register. She smiled as they approached. The time they'd had to wait in line had given him the opportunity to decide what he wanted.

After placing their order, they went to find a seat. He spotted an empty booth along the far wall and pointed it out to Grace. She followed his line of sight and maneuvered her way across the room. Alexander followed close behind.

"Has the place changed much since the last time you were here?" he asked when he noticed her looking around.

She grinned and shook her head. "Not at all."

He smiled back.

Their food arrived and he had to admit it was good. Really good.

"I'll definitely be back," Alexander said as he finished the full rack of ribs he'd ordered. "That was amazing."

"Everything here is so good."

"Maybe we can make this a weekly stop." He'd said it as a joke, but she didn't laugh. "What's wrong?"

She picked up her fork, not looking at him. "Nothing."

"Grace."

He saw her swallow. "It's just something my sister said, that's all."

"What did your sister say?"

Grace pressed her lips together and met his gaze. "She said I shouldn't be going out to dinner with you because you're going to get the wrong idea."

"I see."

Shifting in her seat, Grace set her fork down. "I don't—" She sighed. "I don't think I'm ready to . . . date yet."

"Is that what we're doing?" he asked, not taking his gaze off her.

"I don't know. Is it?"

He chose his words carefully. "I'm new in town and I don't know many people I would like to spend an evening out with, and I enjoy your company."

She was quiet for a long minute. "Okay."

They finished up and headed back to his vehicle. There was still some unease floating in the air around them and he knew he needed to defuse it. He didn't want Grace to feel awkward about going out to dinner with him. Although, he didn't quite understand his desire to hang out with her either. Maybe it was only because she was a connection to Kurt. Maybe it was because he felt an obligation to look after her, having seen her reaction to reading her husband's letter. "Do you know anywhere around here we could get some ice cream?"

Grace clicked her seat belt in place before looking in his direction. "There used to be a place down by the Arch."

He pulled out into traffic and made his way across town, the Arch already poking out through the buildings. She sat beside him, looking out the window, not saying anything. For some reason he still felt as if something was bothering her. Alexander had no idea if it was her fear that she was misleading him or something else.

"Kurt told me you were from St. Louis. Did you grow up here?"

It took her a few moments to answer. "My parents moved here

when I was three. Dad got a job offer he couldn't pass up." She paused. "The ice cream shop is right there."

Alexander nodded and parked behind a black SUV. As he climbed out he recognized a few of the nearby buildings. He'd driven down this way when he was looking for Serpent's Kiss.

By the time he made it to the sidewalk Grace was already there waiting for him.

The shop was small. It only had a handful of tables, so after getting their ice creams they took them outside so they could people watch.

"Can I ask you something?"

He scooped up some of the chocolate fudge ice cream he'd ordered and nodded. "Grace, you can ask me anything."

"If we're not on a date, why is it that you always insist on paying?"

Alexander smiled. "Habit, I suppose." He paused while he took a bite of his ice cream. "Or I guess you could just say I'm old-fashioned."

She didn't say anything.

He waited for several minutes, hoping maybe she'd ask another question. When she didn't, he turned to look at the Arch figuring that would be a safe topic. "Have you ever been up?"

"What?" she asked, distracted.

"The Arch. Have you ever been up to the top?"

"Oh. Yeah, once. When I was little. Ten, I think. Everything down below looks really tiny."

Her gaze was on anything but him. Not in a way to make him think she was engrossed in what was going on around them, but more as if she was avoiding eye contact with him. So much so he felt he needed to ask, "Do you want me to take you home?"

That made her look at him.

"You seem uncomfortable tonight and I don't want you to be uncomfortable. This was meant to be fun. For both of us."

A look of guilt crossed her face and it made him regret his words.

"It's not you," she said. "I have a lot on my mind."

"If you need someone to listen, I'm here. I know we don't know each other all that well, but—"

"Kurt wants me to move on."

Her statement caused his mind to go completely blank.

Before he could recover himself, she continued. "The letter you brought me. Kurt said he wanted me to move on, find someone else, and . . . well, I'm trying to figure out how to do that. I'm not sure that I can."

Things were beginning to fall into place. "Is that why you asked me about this being a date?"

Grace nodded.

Alexander set his ice cream aside and turned to face her. He was still trying to process what she'd told him with what he knew about his friend. "If you don't feel you're ready, then you're not ready."

"But what if I'm never ready?" she asked, pleading in her eyes.

"I think you will be. Eventually." She opened her mouth to say something, but he went on anyway, cutting her off. "I know it may not feel that way now, but you even told me yourself that you've gotten better since you started your job at the café."

She started to say something else but then seemed to change her mind. Instead, she nodded.

They went back to eating their ice cream in silence, watching the cars go by. Hearing the anguish in her voice reinforced Alexander's determination to be there for her and help her in any way he could.

Chapter 6

Grace ran her hands over her hair in a nervous gesture. As she reached her neck, she felt her collar still around it. She went to the mirror and took a long look at herself.

Again, her gaze zeroed in on her collar. If she was going to do this, Grace knew she needed to take it off. She couldn't truly move on if she was still wearing another man's collar.

Her hands shook as she eased them beneath her hair at the nape of her neck and her fingers grazed the clasp. It took her several attempts, but finally it came free. She held it in both her hands, staring at it for what felt like forever before closing her eyes and forcing herself to breathe.

Once she was fairly sure she wouldn't lose it, Grace crossed the room to her closet. She lifted a small cardboard box from the shelf and placed it on the bed. Inside were several of Kurt's things, things she wasn't willing to part with, including a dried flower from their first date.

Grace opened the box and was immediately assaulted by memories. It took everything in her not to say fuck it, put her collar back on, and stay home. But that wasn't what Kurt wanted for her.

Before she could talk herself out of it, she placed her collar inside the box along with her wedding ring, closed it, and put the box back in the closet. She ran out of the house, needing to get away before she changed her mind.

***

Grace took a shaky breath, opened her car door, and placed her feet on the pavement. Each step she took toward the brick building felt heavier than the one before. She felt naked. Exposed. And utterly terrified. It was the first time she'd been without her collar for almost ten years.

It had been over a month since Alexander had delivered her husband's letter to her. A month that she'd spent preparing for today—the first step in fulfilling her master's last command.

When she reached the door, a little voice in the back of her head told her she still had time to turn around and leave. Seconds before she followed that voice, the door opened and a woman appeared. "You must be Grace."

"Yes." Her voice sounded shaky to her own ears, but maybe Katrina Mayer, the owner of Serpent's Kiss, couldn't hear it. At least that's what she was hoping.

"Come. We'll go to my office."

Grace followed Katrina inside. They walked through a small foyer, then a larger one. Then they stepped into what had to be the club itself. It was empty, of course—it was the middle of the day, after all—but Grace could still picture what it would be like full of people. She swallowed and clutched her purse tighter to her chest.

They went down a short hallway before reaching Katrina's office. There was a large wooden desk in the center of the room, two chairs, a love seat, and some filing cabinets. It looked like any other office.

"Please, have a seat."

"Thank you," Grace whispered, lowering herself down into one of the chairs.

Katrina leaned back in her chair and Grace tried not to fidget. She hadn't known what to expect from the club mistress. Katrina had been nice enough on the phone when she'd called and explained who she was and why she was calling, but people weren't always the same in person as they were on the phone. When Grace had spoken with her, she would have guessed Katrina to be around Grace's age, but if Grace had to guess, she'd say the club's mistress was closer to fifty.

"Are you sure you're ready for this, Grace? You said it's been less than a year?" She was surprised at the level of sympathy she heard in the woman's voice.

The best thing to do was be honest. "I don't know if I'm ready. I don't think I'm going to until I try."

Over the last two weeks, she'd been out to dinner with Alexander several more times and each time it had gotten a little easier. They'd formed a friendship of sorts. He didn't know many people in St. Louis and she needed to start living again, something she hadn't done much of since moving back home. Alexander seemed to understand that. He'd helped her get ready for this next step even though he didn't fully understand what that next step was.

Katrina stared at her from across the desk for a long minute before speaking. "Did you bring your paperwork with you?"

"Yes." Grace pulled the papers from her purse and handed them to Katrina. One was an explanation of the club's rules, which Grace had to sign. The rest were her test results. All club members had to be tested for STIs every six months.

The club mistress took her time scanning over the documents, making sure everything was in order. She laid the papers on the desk. "Do you have any questions for me before we take a tour of the club?"

Grace shook her head. "I don't think so."

They headed down the hall back to the large room. "The club is open Friday and Saturday from six in the evening until two in the morning. There's no attendance requirement, however, the more often you come the more comfortable you'll get with the club and its members." She stopped and held Grace's gaze. "I know this is a big step for you."

"It is." Grace started to reach for her collar, but then remembered it was no longer there. If she was going to find a new Dom, she couldn't be wearing her husband's collar.

Another wave of sadness and anxiety rolled through her.

Katrina gave her a minute, and then they continued on. The first floor had plenty of seating, a bar, a dance floor and a stage. Katrina explained that the stage was used for demonstrations.

"Would you like a water before we head upstairs?" Katrina asked, moving behind the bar.

"Yes, please." Grace felt parched and she had no idea why. Probably nerves.

After handing Grace a bottle of water, Katrina led the way over to the staircase up to the second floor. "Over there," she said, pointing to a hallway behind the stairs, "are the locker rooms. We don't have a dress code here. You can dress how you feel comfortable." Katrina's eyes lit up. "Or however your Master or Mistress desires."

It was strange, but listening to Katrina talk about things eased some of Grace's fears. What she was seeking was normal in this place. No one would think it odd or crazy for her to be there looking for a Dom. In fact, it would be expected.

The second floor was a long hallway with a series of rooms. Each had a large window giving those in the hallway a front seat view to whatever was going on inside. She'd seen most of it before. These were the playrooms and whether her mind was ready or not, her body was. It had been almost two years since she'd felt the sting of a crop on her backside.

But was she ready for a man who wasn't her husband to wield it? That was the question. A question she wasn't sure she had the answer to.

After taking a look at each of the rooms and explaining how they handled the use and care of the toys, Katrina led Grace back to her office. "Do you still wish to join Serpent's Kiss, Grace?"

She knew she could say no, walk out that door, and go on with her life as she had been, but she trusted her master. He knew better than anyone what she needed. "Yes. I still want to join."

Katrina nodded. "Wait here. I'll go get your membership card ready. You'll need it to get into the club."

The time passed slowly, even though Katrina was only gone for a few minutes. During that time Grace wondered how she was going to go about finding a new Dom. She'd been to clubs before, but never on her own.

"Here you are."

The suddenness of Katrina's reappearance startled Grace.

Katrina chuckled. "Sorry. I didn't mean to sneak up on you. Here is your membership card."

"Thanks." The card was a dark gray with a red *S* and a black *K*. She tucked it into her purse.

"The main door out front is always unlocked if the club is open, however, you'll need to swipe it to get into the main lobby, and then again to enter the club. If you have any trouble, call me. I'm always here if the club's open."

Grace nodded.

"Before you go," Katrina said, moving back to the other side of her desk, "I've been thinking. Given your situation, I'd like to assign you a protector."

"A protector?"

"Yes. One of our Doms would stay with you, show you around, introduce you to some of our club members. Answer any questions you have. At least for your first night."

To be honest, that sounded wonderful. If she was on her own, she'd probably sit in a corner all night and not interact with anyone. "Thank you. I think that would help."

Katrina grinned. "Did you have any other questions I can answer?"

"Do I need to bring my limits list with me?"

"You can, if you'd like, but it's not necessary. I'm assuming you've negotiated a scene before?"

She had, but it had been a while. "Yes."

"If you decide you'd like to play, just let your protector know what kind of play you're looking for and he can help guide you to a Dom who might be able to meet your needs. But that's up to you. If all you want to do is observe and meet a few people, that is fine, too."

The more she talked to Katrina the better Grace felt. Some kink clubs were all about play, but that didn't seem to be the case with Serpent's Kiss.

"The goal is to enjoy yourself. There's no pressure."

She thanked Katrina again as she walked Grace to the door.

"We're glad to have you. I think you'll make a great addition to the club."

Grace said goodbye, promising she'd be there Friday night around six thirty. Katrina thought it would be best if Grace arrived before the club got busy. She couldn't disagree and to Grace's surprise, as she pulled away from the club and drove home, she wasn't filled with dread about Friday night. Maybe this wouldn't be so bad after all.

***

On Friday during her shift at the café Grace was a mess. She almost dropped a handful of orders and managed to spill soup on her shirt. Luckily, Beth had a change of clothes in her car. The shirt was a little big on her, but considering the alternative of wearing one with a huge tomato soup stain down the front, she'd taken it.

She'd been nervous all week, so much so that she'd bowed out of her dinner plans with Alexander on Thursday night saying she wasn't feeling all that great. He'd offered to bring her something instead, insisting she needed to eat. Grace hadn't been able to say no, so he'd brought her chicken soup and a large baguette. His generosity made her feel guilty for lying.

"Any plans for the weekend?"

It took her a moment to realize Beth had been talking to her. "Um, I don't know yet."

"Drew and I are thinking about driving to Chicago after we close on Saturday. He's never been."

Grace grinned. Even talking to Beth had become easier over the last month. "It's been years since I've been to Chicago. I'm sure it's changed."

Beth threw a dirty towel into the laundry bin and removed her apron. "I haven't been there in about five years myself, but he surprised me last week with tickets to a show." Her eyes lit up as they both grabbed purses and walked to the back door. "I'm excited about getting away more than anything. Just the two of us. Alone in Chicago."

As happy as Grace was for her boss, she couldn't shake the sadness she felt. But it was slightly different this time. Before when she'd listened or watched the obvious signs of another couple in love, she'd felt such a pang of loss for her husband that it was almost debilitating. Grace still felt the loss to an extent, but she also felt a longing as well. She missed that feeling. Maybe that meant she really was ready.

She was on her way home when her phone rang. Since she was driving, she let it go to voice mail. It could only be one of three people. Her sister. Her mother. Or Alexander, which was most likely. They were the only three people to ever call her besides Beth, and considering Grace had seen her less than ten minutes ago, it was highly unlikely it was her.

Once she made her way into the house and took off her coat—the weather had finally begun to turn two days ago—Grace checked her phone. She'd been right. It had been Alexander. She'd call him back, but not before she took a shower. Even with the fresh shirt, Grace could still feel the remnants of soup on her.

Twenty-five minutes later, Grace headed downstairs in her robe to heat up dinner. As her food was warming in the microwave, she called Alexander back.

"I was starting to get worried." His obvious concern made her feel bad for not returning his call as soon as she'd gotten home.

"Sorry. I was driving home when you called and I really needed to take a shower. I was a bit clumsy today and managed to spill a full ladle of soup on myself." She still couldn't believe she'd done that.

"Did you burn yourself?"

"No, but my shirt didn't fare so well. Beth had a spare in her car that she let me borrow." Speaking of which, Grace made a note to get Beth's shirt washed this weekend so she could return it to her on Tuesday. She'd do it tonight, but there wasn't time before she needed to be at Serpent's Kiss and she didn't want to be late.

"Maybe you should have stayed home and rested." She knew he was referring to her not feeling well the night before, which only made her feel worse since it had been a lie.

"It wasn't that. I was just distracted and not paying attention to what I was doing." The microwave beeped, letting her know her food was ready. Grace tucked the phone between her ear and her shoulder as she retrieved her dinner. She took extra special care not to spill anything on her way to the table. Taking another shower before getting ready would only put her in a crunch for time.

"What's for dinner?" he asked, and she knew he must have heard the microwave.

"The rest of the chicken soup you brought over." She paused before taking another bite. "Thank you again. You didn't have to."

"That's what friends are for, right?"

They talked until she was finished eating her soup, making plans to go out to dinner the following week. Twice, he said, in order to make up for her canceling on him on Thursday.

By the time she trekked back upstairs to get ready, she was feeling more relaxed. That was until she went to her closet and pulled out her outfit for the evening. Katrina had said there wasn't really a dress code, but Grace had been in the lifestyle long enough to know what was expected and what wasn't. Especially if the goal was for her to find a new Dom.

The black corset showed off her curves, as did the tight black skirt she was wearing. Grace chose a black thong to go with the outfit. She wasn't planning to play with anyone tonight, but she still needed to look the part. That was the whole point of going, right?

Her anxiety increased as she drove toward downtown St. Louis, and skyrocketed when she pulled into the small parking lot alongside the club.

Sitting alone in her car, engine off, she tried to give herself a pep talk. Grace had never searched for a Dom before. She and Kurt had discovered the lifestyle together. It had been fun and revealing. They'd learned so much about each other.

Was she ready for that with someone else?

Grace turned to look at herself in the rearview mirror. "You can do this," she muttered to herself.

Before she could talk herself out of it, Grace got out of the car. She clutched her coat tighter to her body as she hurried across the parking lot— or hurried as much as she could in heels. The wind had kicked up, blowing from the north. It was going to be a chilly night.

She stepped into the small foyer, out of the wind, and removed the membership card Katrina had given Grace from the small purse she'd brought with her. With shaky hands she swiped the card. There was a soft clicking noise, letting her know the door was unlocked. She turned the knob and stepped inside.

The room she walked into was exactly as she remembered it with one exception. Tonight there was a woman sitting in the alcove at the far end of the room. She looked up when she heard Grace enter.

"Are you Grace?" she asked.

Grace nodded.

"Katrina told me you'd be coming tonight. Welcome to Serpent's Kiss."

"Thanks."

The woman smiled. "I can take your coat and purse if you'd like. You won't need it in the club."

It was only then that Grace realized she had a death grip on her coat and purse. The woman probably thought she was crazy.

Crossing the room, Grace removed her coat. She handed it to the woman, followed by her purse.

"Do you need something to keep your membership card in while you're inside? We have little ID holders with wristbands if you need one."

"No, thank you. I have a pocket in my skirt."

"Perfect." She grinned and turned to hang up Grace's coat and purse. "I'm Ali, by the way."

"Nice to meet you." Ali was dressed similar to Grace except she wore tight leather pants instead of a skirt.

"Katrina should be here any minute."

"Oh. Okay." Was that normal or had she done something wrong already?

Ali chuckled. "Don't look so worried. Katrina does this with every new member. I think she likes to see their first reactions, but in your case she also wants to introduce you to Justin."

Grace didn't get a chance to contemplate that before the door to their right opened. Katrina strolled into the room in a midnight blue corset and black pants that looked as if they'd been painted on. She finished off the outfit with black boots that came up to her knees. She looked every bit the Domme she was.

"Good evening, Grace."

Without conscious thought, Grace's gaze lowered. "Good evening, Mistress Katrina."

There was a pause before Katrina responded. "I think you're going to do just fine here, Grace. Come on in. I want to introduce you to your protector, Justin. He'll be sticking with you tonight while you get used to things."

Grace followed Katrina over to the door where she'd entered.

"Make sure you keep your membership card with you. You'll need to swipe it here." She pointed to the card reader on the wall next to the door. "And you'll also need it for any drink purchases at the bar." When she didn't move, Katrina tilted her head toward the card reader. "Go ahead and swipe your card and we'll get started on finding you a Dom."

Swallowing, Grace took her membership card and swiped it through the reader. Just like with the other door, she heard a click. It was time.

Chapter 7

The music was the first thing that caught Grace's attention when she followed Katrina into the club. It wasn't as loud as she'd thought it would be. While its beat did fill the room, the volume was at a level where it didn't impede conversation.

"Doing all right?" Katrina asked.

Grace hadn't realized she'd stopped moving until Katrina said something. "Yeah. Just . . . taking it all in."

Katrina chuckled. "You haven't seen anything yet."

They walked farther into the large room. There weren't a lot of people there, but it was early. Even so, there was already a sub sitting in her Dom's lap while he talked with another club member. The sub looked on edge, but then again that could be because she wasn't wearing much and her Dom was playing with her breast with no sign of stopping or taking things further anytime soon. Her legs were also clenched together more so than was natural. If Grace had to guess, the sub had a vibrator somewhere.

Seeing the scene made Grace's internal muscles pulse. It had been so long since she and Kurt played. Sure, he'd given her commands to follow via email and through their random phone calls, but it wasn't the same as him being there—being the one who slipped the vibrator in her pussy or in her ass.

Grace was so distracted by her memories that she almost ran

into Katrina, not realizing she'd stopped. Luckily, she'd caught herself in time before she embarrassed herself by tumbling into the club mistress.

A tall man with broad shoulders stood a few feet in front of them, looking down at Grace. "Grace, I'd like you to meet Justin. Justin, this is Grace."

The man nodded in her direction. "It's nice to meet you, Grace."

"You, too, Sir," Grace said, wanting to be polite and respectful. Still, it felt strange. She hadn't called anyone *sir* besides Kurt for years.

Katrina ignored any awkwardness. "Justin will answer any questions you have. If you'd like him to introduce you to some of our members, he can. If you'd rather strictly observe, that's fine, too. It's entirely up to you."

"Thank you, Mistress Katrina."

Katrina grinned and glanced over her shoulder. "If you'll excuse me, there are some things that need my attention. Come find me if you need anything."

Justin wasted no time once they were alone. "The club will get quite busy in an hour or so. Would you prefer to be on a leash or are you good staying at my side without one?"

The look on his face was one she knew well. He appeared indifferent, but he was fully expecting an answer to his question.

"I think I'm good without the leash," Grace said. "I'll stay by your side, Sir."

He nodded. "Very well, then. Let's get you something to drink."

Grace didn't object. In fact, she realized she was quite parched. She'd been too full of nerves before to notice.

Moments after approaching the bar, the bartender was there in front of them. "What can I get you two this evening?"

Justin turned to her. "What would you like?"

While alcohol sounded really good right about now, she didn't really know Justin or Katrina or any of them. She needed to keep her wits about her tonight. "Water, please."

"Just two waters for now, Brandon."

Brandon opened a small refrigerator behind the counter, retrieved two bottles of water, and placed them both on the bar in front of Justin. "Here you go."

Justin picked them up and handed one to her. It was kind of

crazy, but something as simple as that eased some of her tension.

"Brandon, this is Grace. Grace, Brandon. He tends the bar most nights, but occasionally Katrina lets him have an evening off."

Brandon shook his head as he wiped the counter in front of him, removing two water rings from the bottles he'd set down. She hadn't even noticed. "Welcome, Grace."

"Thank you." She was tempted to add *sir* to the end, but she had no idea if Brandon was a Dom or a sub. Sometimes it was hard to tell.

"Did Katrina explain to you how the bar works?" Justin asked.

"Yes." It was one of the first things Katrina had told her during their tour.

Brandon tossed the towel behind him and turned his attention back to them. "Justin showing you around tonight?"

"Yes." Grace swallowed. She was still thirsty and yet she hadn't taken a drink of her water.

Justin must have realized because he looked down at her water and then at her. "There's no limit on water, or soft drinks."

Without a word, she twisted the cap off her water and took a sip. The cool liquid coated her throat. When she glanced over at Justin, he had a smirk on his face. She wished she understood how Doms knew stuff like that.

"You're lucky you have Justin here showing you around tonight. He'll make sure you're taken care of. It can be a little overwhelming for newbies," Brandon said.

Grace looked around the room. In the time they'd been at the bar at least ten more people had entered. She could only imagine what it would be like in another hour or so.

One of those new people stepped up to the bar, needing a drink, and Brandon excused himself to help them.

Justin turned to her. "Let's take a walk upstairs before things get crazy."

He didn't wait for her to agree, but she followed anyway.

When she'd been upstairs with Katrina the place had been empty, of course. As soon as they reached the top of the stairs, it was clear that was no longer the case. The sound of someone moaning was impossible to ignore. A man stood, arms crossed, in front of a large window. She remembered it from her tour. He was staring into one of the playrooms. The same room the moaning was coming from.

Justin didn't appear to be fazed by whatever was going on in the room. "Grace, I'd like you to meet Cooper. He's one of the club's dungeon monitors." To Cooper he said, "Grace is a new member."

The man had half turned as they approached to give her a once-over before returning his attention back to the room.

Justin looked into the playroom and she followed his gaze. A woman was lying spread-eagled on a bed. She had a dildo between her legs while the man stood above her, a flogger in one hand and a magic wand in the other. The woman's eyes were closed, her head thrown back in what looked to be pleasure. Again, Grace's body reacted.

"He's brought her to the edge a half dozen times." Cooper's voice was even, businesslike, but Grace didn't miss the bulge in his jeans.

"I wonder how long she'll last."

It was more of a rhetorical question, but Cooper answered Justin anyway. "If the sounds coming out of her are any indication, not long."

Another loud moan tore from the woman's throat as the man pressed the magic wand against her clit. She arched her back off the bed, her breath coming in rapid pants. It was completely mesmerizing and Grace found that she couldn't look away.

The man bent down, not removing the magic wand, and whispered something in the woman's ear. Every muscle in Grace's body clenched a split second before a long cry erupted from the woman as finally she was allowed to orgasm. Grace remembered that feeling. The feeling of finally being granted release.

A mixture of longing and sadness rushed over her. She missed that. She wanted that. But at the same time, Grace knew she'd no longer be able to experience it with her husband, the man she'd loved and served for most of her adult life.

When she finally tore her gaze away from the scene, Grace realized both Justin and Cooper were staring at her. She couldn't read the expression on Justin's face, but there was no mistaking the one on Cooper's. He knew what watching the end of that scene had done to her.

Grace felt the heat rise to her cheeks and lowered her gaze to the floor. As much as she craved to submit again, she didn't think she could handle a scene as intense as the one she'd just witnessed. She wasn't even sure she was ready to submit to another Dom at all.

Movement inside the room caught her attention again. The man had released the woman and climbed up on the bed with her. He held her against his side while he stroked and kissed her. The sight caused a knot to form in the pit of her stomach. Would she ever experience that deep connection with a man again?

She barely noticed as another couple walked past the three of them down the hall. Or when Cooper excused himself to go help the other couple.

Justin was patient with Grace. He let her stand there immersed in what was going on in her head without comment. It made her wonder how much Katrina had told him.

She had no idea how much time had ticked by before she met Justin's gaze.

"We should head back downstairs. Give them some privacy." Justin didn't wait for her agreement. He placed a hand on her lower back and guided her toward the staircase.

They were halfway down the stairs when Grace gasped.

Justin noticed right away and turned to see if she was okay. "Do you need to sit down?"

No. She didn't need to sit down. She didn't know what she needed.

All the air left her lungs as she saw Alexander lower himself onto a couch about thirty feet away.

She needed to get out of there. She needed to leave. Now. Before he . . .

It was as if some cruel turn of fate caused Alexander to look in her direction. His gaze settled on her and his eyes went wide. So much for running away.

***

Alexander couldn't believe his eyes. All afternoon he'd wanted to go check on her, but he'd stopped himself, opting for a phone call instead. Grace had come out of her shell quite a bit since their first meeting, but he hadn't wanted to crowd her. There were times he still saw the sadness in her eyes. He hated seeing it, but he also knew she needed the time to grieve.

It was because of that he was sitting there staring at her in shock. The expression on her face said she was as surprised to see him as he was to see her.

The urge to cross the room was almost overwhelming, but he resisted. She was with Justin. Alexander didn't know him well, but he was one of the club's Doms and often acted as a protector to new subs. He didn't have a sub of his own and he'd been in the lifestyle for several years, from what Alexander had heard. The subs at Serpent's Kiss, and more importantly, Katrina, trusted him. That didn't, however, change the irritation Alexander felt seeing him hovering over Grace.

"Everything all right?" Daniel's question jarred Alexander back to the present, but he didn't take his gaze off Grace. She'd frozen in place halfway down the staircase. Justin was saying something to her and she shook her head.

"Not sure," Alexander said to his friend.

Grace tore her gaze from Alexander's and turned to Justin. She said something, lowered her head, and rushed the rest of the way down the stairs, Justin keeping pace with her as she made a beeline for the door.

Alexander stood and took an automatic step to intercept her. Then stopped. If he pushed himself, he'd be able to catch her, but to what end? They needed to talk and this wasn't the place for it.

"Do you know her?" Daniel asked, obviously figuring out who had captured Alexander's attention.

Grace almost collided with another couple as she rushed out the door. Only Justin's quick reflexes prevented the impending disaster. She mumbled something, probably an apology, and then disappeared into the coatroom.

Alexander sat back down. "Yes. I know her."

His friend looked confused by his tone. "I take it that's not a good thing?"

"I don't know yet."

After Grace left, the night seemed to drag on. He couldn't relax and enjoy himself. Daniel had tried to engage him in conversation a couple of times before giving up and leaving Alexander to his thoughts.

The temptation to swing by her house nagged at him during his drive home. It wasn't that late and he was almost certain she'd be awake. But he forced himself to go to his apartment instead.

As he crawled into bed that night, Alexander replayed that handful of minutes when they'd locked gazes across the room. She hadn't been wearing her necklace, the one he'd never seen her without. It only reinforced his notion that it was her collar. The collar Kurt had given her.

He ran a hand over his face in frustration and released a deep sigh. While he'd suspected she was a sub, that didn't explain what she was doing at Serpent's Kiss. Grace had told him more than once she didn't think she was ready to move on. Yet, if she'd joined the club, surely that would mean she was ready. Didn't it? And if so, what had changed?

There was also the question of what he was to do with this new nugget of information. Over the last month he'd come to care about Grace. Their friendship meant something to him. Aside from Daniel, she was his only real friend in St. Louis. If she needed a Dom, Alexander could be that for her.

But did he want to be? That was the real issue. Did he want to cross that line? Could he? Even if it meant she really wasn't ready to fully move on and only wanted to relinquish control?

That, of course, didn't even take into consideration the guilt he was experiencing for what he was already feeling when it came to Grace. She was his brother's widow. He was supposed to look out for her, not take her into his bed. And yet as the thought took hold in his mind that's exactly what he wanted to do.

Grace was sexy, smart, kind, and now he knew for certain she was submissive. All of that together had his lower half waking up. He hadn't been with a woman since before his last deployment. Until then, that had been perfectly fine with him.

Shaking his head, he tried to push the thoughts out of his brain. Fantasizing about something that might never—and maybe shouldn't ever—come to be was only going to add to his frustration. As much as he didn't like it, the ball was in her court now. She was the one who'd changed the game by showing up at the club. The next move was hers.

Chapter 8

Grace didn't sleep that night. Or the next. She kept seeing Alexander's face every time she closed her eyes, that look of shock and disbelief. What was he doing at Serpent's Kiss?

Okay, she knew that was a stupid question. If he was there that meant he was in the lifestyle. And instinctively, Grace knew he was a Dom. She remembered Alexander bringing her water that first day after she'd read Kurt's letter. He'd taken charge and made sure she was all right, or as all right as she was going to be given the circumstances.

She'd thought for sure he'd call on Saturday, or show up at the café, but he hadn't. The silence from him was worse than if he'd confronted her.

As she gathered up her dirty laundry on Sunday morning, she moved about in an almost robotic fashion, unable to turn off her mind. Friday night was supposed to have been a chance for her to feel things out—to see if she could fulfill her master's last request. And if so, to take those first steps in trying to find a man she was comfortable enough with to submit to. Everyone she'd met had eased her nerves about this new mission she was on, and Grace had begun to believe that maybe she could do this.

Then she'd spotted Alexander and her instinct to flee had taken over.

Grace groaned as she tossed her clothes into the washer. Although Alexander hadn't called her on Saturday, Katrina had. She wanted to make sure Grace was okay given her quick exit the night before. Justin was worried something had happened, but had no idea what.

It occurred to her that she should probably apologize to Justin. When she'd frantically told him that she had to leave—now—he must have seen the crazed look in her eyes because all he did was nod and offer to walk her out. If not for him, she would have bowled over a couple while attempting to leave as quickly as her feet would carry her.

In retrospect her reaction seemed over the top and irrational. She'd apologized to Katrina for her rash behavior even though the club mistress had been understanding about it. At the time it felt as if running had been Grace's only option.

All it had done, however, was delay the inevitable. There was no way she'd be able to avoid Alexander forever. Sure, she could try, but somehow she knew he'd only tolerate that for so long. Sooner or later he was going to want answers and she felt she owed them to him. Kurt might have asked Alexander to deliver the letter to her, but after that, he could have left her alone. He'd done his duty.

Thinking about the time Grace and Alexander had spent together in the last month had her feeling nauseous. Not because it was bad in any way. On the contrary. If not for him, she might never have called Katrina. The reason her breakfast was disagreeing with her was because on some level she felt as if she'd betrayed him somehow.

She owned him an explanation. No more running. The next time she came face-to-face with him she needed to be prepared. Grace knew he would have questions. After the way she'd insisted she wasn't ready to move on, he had to.

Grace was still trying to figure out what she was going to say to Alexander when she arrived at her mom's. Before she could turn the car off, her sister was striding toward her. "You're late."

Grace glanced at her watch. It was five minutes past twelve. "Not that late."

Her sister linked her arm with Grace's as they made their way into the house. "Tell me it was because you were doing something fun—preferably with that doctor you've been hanging out with—and not something mundane like doing laundry."

Embarrassment at how well her sister knew her had heat rising in her cheeks. "I had to put a load in the washer before I left. It took longer than I expected." She didn't mention that the reason it took her so long was because she'd been distracted.

Gabby wrenched open the door and shook her head. "What am I going to do with you?"

It wasn't as if her sister hadn't made her thoughts on the subject crystal clear. If Gabby had her way, Grace would be spending her nights being ravished by Alexander.

She opened her mouth to tell her sister she just wasn't ready, like she had in the past, but the words died in her throat. A thought began to form, one she really needed to think through and not when her sister and mother were close by, so she put on the best smile she could manage and headed inside. Her sister followed, not appearing to be bothered at all by Grace's lack of acknowledgement.

"There you are," her mother said the moment they crossed the threshold into the kitchen. "I was beginning to think we'd have to send out a search party."

Grace crossed the room and gave her mom a hug, making sure to sidestep the spoon in her hand. "Sorry I'm late."

"Why don't you grab some glasses from the sink and take them to the table? Everything's almost ready," Caroline said.

While Grace gathered the glasses, her sister began carrying food to the table.

"Taylor with her dad this weekend?" Grace asked when she didn't see her niece.

"Yeah." Gabby twisted to the side, getting out of the way of the hot plate their mother was carrying. "Jax called Friday night. His folks came down for the weekend and wanted to spend some time with her." She shrugged. "I couldn't say no."

Grace filled their glasses with the iced tea their mom had made, and then sat down. "I'm sure they appreciate it."

"I have no doubt she'll come home with at least a half dozen new toys."

"Less you have to buy," their mother pointed out. "Besides, it's a grandparent's right to spoil their grandchildren."

Both Grace and Gabby rolled their eyes. Most of the toys Taylor owned had come from Caroline.

After that the conversation turned to Caroline's impending retirement. She'd found the paperwork she needed. All that was left was for the date that was circled on her calendar to get there.

"Any idea what you're going to do with all your new free time?" Gabby asked.

"I was thinking of doing some volunteering."

The conversation took off from there with Gabby and her mother sharing different ideas on where Caroline could volunteer. Grace was only half listening. Every now and then she'd contribute to the conversation, but for the most part, she sat quietly and let Gabby and her mom talk. Grace had too many other things on her mind. Besides, the last thing she wanted was for her sister to bring up Alexander in front of their mother. As far as Grace knew, Caroline didn't know about him, and at the moment Grace wasn't up to answering questions.

After spending most of the afternoon with her mom and sister, Grace drove home. She glanced at the clock when she walked into the kitchen. It was still early. Plenty of time to follow through with what had been rattling around in her mind the entire time she was at her mom's.

But could she do it? Should she?

Grace chewed on the end of her thumb as she stared at her purse like it held some sort of great wisdom. It didn't, of course. This was a decision she had to make for herself.

"What should I do?" she asked the empty room.

As she stood there, Grace realized she really did want an answer and the person she wanted the answer from was Alexander. She was in a place where she didn't know which way to turn.

More than anything, the way she was feeling in that moment, the desire for his guidance, was what compelled her to move her feet. She found her cell and scrolled until she saw his name pop up on her screen.

Seconds ticked by as Grace waited for him to pick up.

"Grace?"

"Hi. I was wondering—" She swallowed. "I was wondering if you'd like to come over for dinner tonight."

There was a long pause. "What time?"

Her mind went blank for a second. "Seven?"

"I'll see you at seven, then."

Grace hung up the phone and clutched it to her chest. Even though she was nervous, she was also certain she was doing the right thing. All she could do was hope that Alexander agreed.

***

Alexander pulled up in front of Grace's house at six fifty-six. The porch light was on, welcoming him, even though sunset was still almost an hour away. He took his time getting out of his vehicle, even though his leg wasn't bothering him tonight, and made his way up the walkway. It had been almost forty-eight hours since he'd watched Grace scurry out of Serpent's Kiss. To say he was anxious to hear what she had to say was a vast understatement.

He rang the doorbell and within seconds she was there, framed in the doorway. She looked small and unsure of herself. Over the last month he'd seen her begin to come out of her shell, some of her shyness melting away. However, the more lighthearted Grace he'd gotten to know was nowhere to be seen.

"Good evening, Grace."

"Hi." She tucked a lock of hair behind her ear and took a step back, inviting him inside. "Dinner's almost ready."

Alexander stood off to the side as she closed and locked the door, before following her into the kitchen. This was her show, and as tempting as it was for him to demand answers, he was going to wait her out.

She busied herself with finishing dinner but every now and then he caught her shooting glances in his direction. When she finally did join him at the table, she kept her gaze on her plate. She didn't make a move to start eating, so neither did he.

"Aren't you hungry?" she asked in a shaky voice.

"I am." He paused before reaching for the serving spoon she'd placed on the table and handing it to her.

"I'm not sure if I can eat."

He didn't budge. "You invited me to dinner."

There was a moment's hesitation before she took the spoon and scooped some of the casserole onto her plate. He waited until she was done before getting his. The meal was awkward. She picked at her food more than she ate it. The temptation to order her to eat was strong, but he bit back the urge.

Her fork slipping from her fingers and clattering onto her plate drew his attention.

"I'm sorry," she whispered.

Alexander wiped his mouth with his napkin and placed it next to his plate before speaking. "What are you sorry for?"

She released a loud breath and for a second he thought maybe she was crying, but then she looked up to meet his gaze. "I told you I wasn't ready, and then I went to the club."

He waited for her to continue.

"I didn't lie. I still wasn't sure I was ready, but . . ." She looked down at her lap. "I told you about Kurt's letter. About how he wants me to move on." When he didn't respond, she glanced up. "You've probably guessed that Kurt and I . . . we . . . he was my Master."

Alexander had suspected as much after seeing the necklace she wore the first time they met, but hearing her say it out loud had him putting what she hadn't said into perspective. "When he said he wanted you to move on, he didn't just mean for you to start dating again, did he?"

She shook her head. "No."

It made sense. Kurt would want his sub's needs to be taken care of. "So you were at Serpent's Kiss to find a Dom."

"Yes."

He was still digesting this new information when she slid to the floor, kneeling next to his chair. She placed her hands on her thighs, palms up. He knew that pose. Knew what it meant.

Placing a finger under her chin, Alexander made her look at him. He raised an eyebrow, silently asking her to explain herself.

"I would like for you to be my Dom, Sir." Her gaze didn't waver.

As the moments ticked by, Alexander couldn't resist the opportunity to tease her. "How do you know I'm a Dom? Maybe I'm a submissive."

Grace's eyes widened for a second before the look of panic in them faded. "I don't think so, Sir."

"Why's that?"

She took her time thinking about her answer. "I guess it's a lot of things. The way you carry yourself. The way you've looked after me, even when you didn't have to."

He dropped his hand and seriously considered her assertion. She wanted him to be her Dom. And if she'd gone to Serpent's Kiss then she was probably looking for someone to play with. A part of him was screaming, *"Yes!"* But the more logical side of his brain wondered if that would be altogether smart. He was beginning to have feelings for her, and adding a power exchange relationship to the equation was only bound to enhance those feelings. He was opening himself up to heartache.

"Take a seat." Seeing her kneeling before him wasn't helping his brain function properly.

Grace stood and retook her seat next to him at the table.

The look on her face made him want to say fuck it and to hell with the consequences. He had to keep his wits about him, however. This wasn't a time for being impulsive.

"Tell me what it is you want, Grace." She opened her mouth to speak, but he cut her off. "Not what Kurt wanted. What *you* want."

She didn't answer right away. "When I read that Kurt wanted me to find a new Dom, I didn't think I could do it. I wasn't in a place mentally where I felt I could give that much of myself to anyone. I know what it takes to be a sub. Letting go and trusting. Giving up control."

Her voice shook slightly, but there was determination behind it as well. She was braver than she was giving herself credit for.

"Then you started coaxing me out of my shell . . . getting me out of the house and back into the world." The edges of her mouth rose in a small smile. "You gave me the confidence to believe that maybe I could do it. Contacting Mistress Katrina and going to Serpent's Kiss was a test."

"And what did you find out?" he asked.

"It made me realize Kurt was right. Being submissive is part of who I am and I can't pretend it's not just because he's not here anymore."

Alexander had to ask. "When you saw me you couldn't get out of there fast enough."

"I hadn't expected to see anyone there I knew. And when I did, I panicked." She met his gaze. "I didn't know what to do, so I ran."

What she said swirled around in his head. If he said no to being her Dom, there was a good chance she'd go back to Serpent's Kiss and find another Dom who'd be more than willing to take her on. Grace was beautiful and she was an experienced submissive. He had no doubt someone would be happy to step up and fill that role. The thought turned his stomach.

"Are you sure, Grace? There's no rush. You have time."

"You don't want to be my Dom?" An air of sadness came over her.

He placed his hand over hers, unable to resist touching her. "I didn't say that."

She looked down at their hands then back up at him. "I trust you, Alexander. If I'm going to do this, I want it to be with you."

That simple assertion was what broke him. How could he say no? "We'll need to go over your limits and what your expectations are."

A look of pure, unadulterated relief crossed her face. He still had no idea how he was going to deal with his developing feelings for her, but he'd cross that bridge when he came to it.

Chapter 9

Grace couldn't articulate how grateful she felt that he'd agreed. "Thank you."

One side of Alexander's mouth quirked up in a half smile. "Maybe you should wait until we compare lists before you thank me."

She chuckled.

"You never know. I might be a wicked sadist." He wasn't even trying to hide his grin.

This was the Alexander she'd gotten to know over the last month. The one that made her laugh and feel as if there was still life to be lived. "Maybe I'm a masochist."

"Are you?" he asked, amusement lighting his eyes.

Grace considered fibbing for the sake of drawing out their back and forth, but thought better of it. Even if a spanking wouldn't be an altogether bad thing. "Not really."

He released her hand and sat back in his chair. "Had to think about that for a minute, did you?"

"No. But . . ."

When she didn't continue, he leaned forward again. This time he didn't touch her, but that didn't mean she wasn't highly aware of him. She felt the dynamic shift even though they were still sitting at her kitchen table. "But what?"

She glanced down at her lap again, unable to look him in the eye as she admitted her thoughts. "It's been a long time, and I considered fibbing a little so that maybe you'd realize I wasn't being completely truthful and think I deserved a spanking."

Alexander was quiet for so long that she tilted her head up to see his face. He appeared to be studying her.

"But I decided against it." Her words died in her throat as he stood.

Without saying anything, Alexander held out his hand. She only hesitated for a second before placing her palm in his.

He led her into the living room, walked over to the couch, and sat down. After releasing her hand, he patted his leg twice.

Grace's heart rate kicked up a notch. She knew what he wanted her to do. Knew what he wanted and she was unable to deny she wanted it, too.

On less than stable legs, she closed the distance between them and lowered herself so she was lying stomach down across his lap, her ass on display for him.

The feel of his hand on the curve of her back made her tense. Grace took a deep breath and tried to relax.

He gave her some time to settle in, not rushing anything. It gave her even more confidence that she was making the right decision.

"What's your safeword?" he asked.

She hadn't even thought about safewords. That's how much she wasn't thinking at the moment. This was a man she'd never played with. Of course there needed to be a safeword. Even for something as basic as an over-the-knee spanking. "Mushroom."

His hand twitched and she wondered if he was grinning. "Mushroom?"

She nodded, or at least tried to, considering her position. "Kurt hated mushrooms."

Alexander's entire body vibrated before he ran his hand down over her backside. "Mushroom it is."

Even though she was wearing pants she still felt the heat of his hand as he rubbed his palms over her ass. With every caress she relaxed more, giving herself up to the moment. Then with a quick flick of his wrist she felt the sting she'd been waiting for . . . longing for.

He landed another smack to her other cheek, then another and another. Heat spread from where his hand was making contact up her spine and throughout the rest of her body. It was almost as if something in her let go a little more with each blow he landed to her flesh. She felt settled. Grounded. As if things that hadn't made sense for so long did in that moment.

It wasn't until Alexander began stroking her back and whispering, "It's okay. Let it out," that Grace realized she was crying. And not quiet tears. No, these were loud, gut-wrenching sobs that seemed to come out of nowhere. Everything she'd been holding in was spilling out. She couldn't have stopped it if she tried.

At some point she rolled over on her side, curling in toward him. Alexander helped her to sit up but didn't let her go. He held her on his lap, continuing to comfort her as her tears subsided.

"Feel better?" he asked, brushing the hair away from her face.

Grace nodded. "I don't know what that was."

"Endorphins."

She didn't argue. She didn't have the energy. All of a suddenly she felt very tired. Her lack of sleep over the past two days was catching up with her.

"Tired?"

"Yeah. I didn't sleep very well the last couple of nights."

He helped her to sit up and wiped the moisture from her cheeks with his thumbs. "Why don't you go upstairs and get ready for bed? I'll clean up down here."

Grace didn't want to move, but she knew he was right. As appealing as the thought was, she couldn't stay in his lap all night.

Alexander stayed on the couch as she made her way out of the room and up the stairs to her bedroom. As she changed her clothes, Grace could hear him moving around downstairs. It should be her doing the dishes and putting things away, but when he'd suggested she get ready for bed it hadn't even crossed her mind to protest. She was too tired. Just keeping her eyes open was a challenge.

Once she was changed, she debated whether or not to go downstairs or crawl into bed. The latter was tempting, but somehow she knew Alexander wouldn't leave without saying goodbye.

He was waiting for her at the bottom of the stairs. When she reached the last step, some of the awkwardness from before returned. Grace started to look down, but his finger caught her chin. "There's no need to be embarrassed with me, Grace. Not ever."

"Thank you. For earlier, I mean."

Alexander traced the line of her jaw back and forth several times. "I imagine I enjoyed it as much as you did."

His comment brought a different kind of embarrassment flooding through her.

This only seemed to amuse him. "I already checked to make sure the back door was locked and everything is turned off. All you have to do is lock up behind me. Then I want you to head to bed and get some rest. I'll call you tomorrow and we'll set up a time when we can go over everything."

She knew by *everything* that he meant their lists and what kind of arrangement they would have. It was something she hadn't given much thought to. It hadn't seemed real. Until then.

He held her gaze for a moment longer before dropping his hand and backing toward the door.

Grace locked the door behind him and watched through the window as he climbed into his vehicle and drove away. Once she could no longer see the lights of his car, she slowly headed back upstairs. Like a good little sub, she made a pit stop in the bathroom, and then slid into bed.

Her ass still tingled a little from the spanking she'd received. If she closed her eyes she could almost feel the impression of his hand lingering. It was comforting.

She released a contented sigh, turned on her side, and wrapped her arms around her pillow. There was a lot she needed to think about, but it was going to have to wait until tomorrow. Sleep was slowly pulling her under and she didn't want to fight it.

***

On Monday morning Alexander woke up with Grace at the forefront of his mind. Granted, this wasn't the first time she'd dominated his thoughts. He often found himself remembering something she'd said or done when he'd least expect it. This morning, however, his mind was more focused. He'd agreed to be her Dom without knowing anything about her limits or what she wanted from him. It wasn't the smartest decision of his life, but he couldn't bring himself to regret it. This was Grace. He'd be what she needed him to be.

Yeah, he knew that made him a sucker or a sap or whatever, but at least he was man enough to admit it. If only to himself. She was special and he planned on doing everything he could to help her realize it.

His workday dragged. It wasn't that he hated his job exactly, but he'd be lying if he said he loved sitting behind a desk all day looking over various malpractice complaints. On the plus side, he was learning what not to do with his future patients. Most of the things that crossed his desk were simple cases of lack of communication. Many doctors, it seemed, took for granted how much their patients knew and understood. He'd read over the patient's issue, and then the doctor's response. He could see the disconnect.

At five o'clock, he rubbed his eyes with the heels of his hands. He'd never been happier to be done with a day's work.

"Long day?" Jewel, one of the paralegals, stood in front of his desk, clutching a stack of folders.

He set the folder he'd been working through off to the side and pushed away from his desk. "Little bit."

"Some of us are going to BJ's for drinks. You're welcome to join us."

"Thanks," he said, grabbing his jacket. "But I have some things to do tonight."

She didn't seem upset by his declining the invitation. "Maybe next time."

"Sure."

Jewel wished him a good night and strolled into the file room.

The first thing Alexander did when he got in his car was check his cell to see if he had any messages from Grace. He'd been half expecting her to call or text him at some point saying she'd changed her mind, but there was no such message. That meant she either hadn't changed her mind or she was too scared or nervous to say she had.

While her changing her mind might make things easier for him, it wasn't what he wanted. After having her sprawled across his lap the night before, that had been painfully obvious to him. *Painful* being the operative word. He'd played with a sub once since being discharged from the Army. It had been a very basic scene at Serpent's Kiss about two weeks after he joined. A way to get his feet wet again, as it were.

He hadn't, however, had sex for close to two years. Between his deployment, and then his recovery, there hadn't been all that many opportunities. And grabbing a quickie, locked in a latrine in the middle of the desert hadn't really been an option. At least not for him. Seeing Grace like that, touching her—spanking her—had sent all his blood rushing to his groin.

Remembering had his problem rising to the surface again. Alexander groaned and tried to focus on the task at hand. He needed to call Grace like he promised.

The phone rang three times before she answered. "Hello."

"Hi." Hearing her voice brought a smile to his face. "How was your day off?"

"Good. I slept in, and then did some reading." She paused. "I also spent some time updating my limits list."

He hadn't known if she'd bring it up first or not, but he was glad she had. "I did that about two months ago after I joined Serpent's Kiss."

"Mistress Katrina mentioned it when I met with her." She let her words hang in the air.

Alexander understood. Grace wasn't the type to jump into playing with someone she didn't know, and if she wasn't playing then there was no reason to update her limits list. "Are you having any second thoughts?"

She responded quicker than he thought she would. "No."

Someone walked in front of his vehicle, but he barely noticed. He was entirely focused on his conversation with Grace. "I'd like to take you out to dinner tonight."

"All right." She paused. "Should I bring my list?"

"I think that would be a good idea."

They made arrangements for him to pick her up in an hour before hanging up. He needed to get home, shower, change, and figure out where they would go. While he wanted to keep things casual, he also wanted them to have at least some privacy. That would be difficult if they were seated in the middle of a busy restaurant. Plus, he wanted the night to feel important because it was. This was a big step for Grace, and Alexander understood that.

She was ready and waiting for him when he arrived. Her blond hair was loose and it made him wonder what it would feel like to run his fingers through it. He resisted the urge. It wasn't his right. Yet.

"I like your hair down like that," he said as he opened the passenger-side door for her to get into the car.

Grace lowered her gaze, but she didn't comment. He was pretty sure he saw the telltale signs of a blush creeping up her neck.

As they drove to the restaurant, she sat with her purse in her lap and her hands folded on top. She looked at the road ahead, her shoulders back. It was very proper and very non-Grace-like.

"There's no need to be nervous."

He saw her glance over at him out of the corner of his eye. "I know. It's . . . been a long time since I've done this."

"Had dinner?"

Her soft giggle was exactly the reaction he'd hoped for.

Reaching for her hand, he gave it a gentle squeeze. "It's just dinner, Grace. The same thing we've done twice a week for the last month. The rest? We'll figure it out. There's no pressure."

Out of the corner of his eye he saw her nod. She didn't say anything more and he didn't push.

They pulled into the restaurant parking lot and he went to open the door for her. She took his arm as she had many times before and they headed inside.

The place was small. There were maybe ten tables in the whole place, which in Alexander's opinion was perfect. That, coupled with the fact that it was a Monday night, meant there were only a few other customers.

Once they were seated at a booth in the back corner and the server had taken their order, Alexander figured maybe it was time to get down to business. She wasn't going to relax until things were out in the open. "Did you bring your list?"

Grace nodded and reached into her purse. She held it out to him.

There were several pages. He recognized it as the template Katrina had on the Serpent's Kiss website. One of the nice things about it was that it was detailed. There were even obscure kinks listed, some of which he hoped to never witness. He understood and supported the *my kink is not your kink* assertion, but as a doctor there were some things he couldn't get behind.

Alexander scanned what Grace had marked and was pleased to see that most of their kinks lined up. There were a few exceptions, there always were, but nothing they couldn't work with. What did give him a little pause was that she had marked oral, vaginal, and anal sex as 'love.' Not that he'd expected her to hate it, but he figured there'd be a note or that they would be listed as soft limits. Did that mean she was ready to jump into a sexual relationship?

He turned the papers over and placed them on the table off to the side. Their server had brought their drinks and their appetizer while he'd been reading over her list. It didn't escape his notice that Grace had yet to touch any of it. "Help yourself."

With a little reluctance, she picked up some bread, tore off a piece, and dipped it into the hummus. He followed suit, watching as she placed the pita into her mouth and swallowed. After reading her limits list, he couldn't help that his mind went in the direction it did. He grabbed his water and downed half of it.

She picked at her napkin a few times. "Was there something wrong with my list?"

"Not at all. Why would you think that?"

Grace shrugged. "You look uncomfortable."

He couldn't help but snort. She wasn't far off, but not for the reasons she was thinking. He leaned in and lowered his voice. "I just read a breakdown of all the things you'd like me to do to you." Alexander stopped to let that sink in. "Let's hope I don't have to get up from the table anytime soon."

Her eyes widened with shock, and then with what he thought might be interest. He held her gaze until their server came with their food. The spell was broken, but that was okay. Interest he could work with. He was determined to make sure Grace didn't regret asking him to be her Dom.

Chapter 10

Grace concentrated on her food and attempted to ignore the way her body reacted to his words. Her lower half pulsed with anticipation. It had no issue jumping headfirst into this arrangement with Alexander.

And that's what it was: an arrangement. He was agreeing to be her Dom, not her boyfriend. It wouldn't be the same type of relationship she'd had with Kurt. She knew that. Which was why there was a little voice in the back of her brain asking if she was really sure she wanted to do this. That voice, however, wasn't very loud and it was easily overtaken by her need to open up and let go of everything she'd been dealing with for the last nine months.

Her thoughts drifted back to the night before when she'd been draped across his lap, feeling his hand make contact with her backside. The sting had been gone when she'd woken up that morning and she'd missed it. Grace wondered how long she'd have to wait before he would do it again. Or she could ask. Maybe . . .

"How's your dinner?"

She looked up to find him staring at her. "It's good." As if to prove her point, she took a bite and grinned.

He waited for several seconds. "Grace, if something's bothering you, you need to tell me."

"No. It's . . . I was thinking about last night." She felt the blush start to rise on her cheeks. "On the couch."

"Ah." Alexander chuckled. "Yes. I can see why that would have you distracted."

His response in no way helped with her blush. She tucked her head down and dug back into her food.

Of course, he wouldn't change the subject to something more mundane like the weather. She should have known better. He was a Dom after all. "I'd like to take you to the club with me this weekend."

She swallowed and met his gaze. Wasn't it too soon for that? "You do?"

He nodded. "I think it will be an excellent way for me to gauge where we should begin. Plus, I think it will be good for you to be around other subs."

That made sense. She and Kurt had known each other for over a year before they'd started playing and they'd done a lot of experimenting at first to see what they both liked. This was a different situation entirely. "I guess that's probably a good idea. I need to apologize to Justin anyway."

"Yes, you do." He took another bite. "Running away isn't the answer. What's going to happen the next time you see someone at the club you know?"

Grace had a hard time swallowing down the food she'd been chewing. She hadn't thought about that. "I don't know."

"You should know that as your Dom, I won't let you run away again. Being a sub isn't something you should ever be ashamed of."

"I know." She laid her fork down on her plate. "I just don't know how to react. Kurt and I mainly played in our house, and the few times we did go to clubs, we didn't know anyone else there."

Alexander seemed to take that in but didn't comment. At least not right away. He waited until their server cleared their plates and brought dessert. "Did you have any questions for me?"

She thought about all the things she could ask him. "How long have you been in the lifestyle?"

He appeared pleased. "I started experimenting in med school."

A part of her didn't want to ask the next question for some reason. The answer didn't really matter, but something compelled her to ask it anyway. "How many subs have you had?"

"How many have I played with or how many have I had a

relationship or agreement with?" he asked.

"Um . . . both?" She knew how unsure she sounded.

He picked up a piece of baklava before answering. "I've played with twelve women over the years, only two of whom I've had any sort of formal arrangement with."

That wasn't so many. Not if he'd been in the lifestyle for ten years and was single. Of course, he'd also been in the military, which meant deployments.

Her silence must have been a lot louder than she thought. "Does that seem like a lot?"

Grace shook her head. "No, I suppose not."

He moved on. "I want to talk to you a little about my expectations."

"Okay." All of a sudden the baklava tasted very dry in her throat as she tried to swallow.

"I don't know how things worked with Kurt, but when we're playing I expect you to obey me. You'll have your safeword, but unless you choose to use it, I expect compliance."

She nodded. "Yes, Sir."

"Good." He retrieved the papers she'd given him at the start of their meal, looked them over again, and then met her gaze across the table. "Now, we have just a few more details to go over."

They stayed at the restaurant for almost another hour going over specifics on her list. Nothing too graphic. They kept their language vague in case someone was listening, but still there were times she wanted a hole to open up beneath her and suck her in.

As he drove her home, Grace tried not to read too much into Alexander's insistence that they continue their dinner dates during the week. They wouldn't be playing then. He'd said he wanted them to have some downtime where the rules didn't apply.

He'd also asked her about sex, which had been the most embarrassing topic of conversation to have in the middle of a restaurant. They were alone and most of the other customers had cleared out. Neither of those facts mattered as she turned beet red.

She'd known the subject would come up given what she'd marked on her list, but she hadn't expected him to bring it up then. Mortified, she'd told him that she wasn't sure. That her body was more than ready, but she didn't know if she was actually ready to have sex with someone who wasn't her husband.

To her relief, Alexander understood. He assured her that they would take things slow in that regard and figure it out along the way. It was the perfect response, and yet it wasn't. She should have been grateful he wouldn't push her into jumping into bed with him, but she couldn't deny that she was a little disappointed.

He parked in front of her house and walked her to her front door.

"Did you want to come in?" she asked. He'd come in sometimes after their dinners, and to be honest, she wasn't sure she wanted to say good night to him yet even though it was already after nine.

"I don't think that's such a good idea."

She was a little confused until she saw the look in his eyes. Their conversation earlier had had an effect on him, too.

Before she could think of anything to say, he reached up to brush the back of his fingers against her cheek. "It's not that I don't want to, Grace."

The air around them felt heavy and she felt herself leaning into his touch.

He placed his hand under her chin and tilted it up until she was looking at him. "I'll email you a list of rules and requirements tomorrow."

That had been the last thing she'd thought he'd say.

Alexander released his hold on her and dropped his hand down to his side. "How about I take you to dinner Thursday evening and you can let me know if you'd like to make any changes before Friday?"

Friday. The club. She'd almost forgotten.

"Grace?" He had one eyebrow raised and was waiting on an answer.

"Sounds good," she managed to choke out.

"We'll go as slow as you need. I promise."

A sort of peace came over her. She released a deep breath and smiled. "I know. I trust you."

He held her gaze for a long moment and she saw something in them change. She knew that look. It made her insides flutter. "Go inside, Grace."

She took out her keys and opened the door, sending one last look at Alexander. "Good night."

"Good night."

***

As promised, Alexander emailed an outline of their arrangement along with his limits list to Grace first thing Tuesday morning. He knew she was at work, so she most likely wouldn't get a chance to look it over until later that night, but that didn't help the bit of anxiety he felt. She'd never played with anyone but her husband, whom she'd known for a decade. It was going to be different for her, an adjustment. He could only hope she would embrace it.

Her assertion the night before that she trusted him had almost sent common sense out the window. He wanted to take her up on her offer to come inside, but he knew that wasn't wise. They needed to do this right. He wanted to do it right for her. And even she had admitted she didn't know if she was ready for sex yet.

Scrubbing a hand over his face, Alexander ignored the growing discomfort in his groin. He'd taken care of things when he'd gotten home the night before, but it didn't feel like it. Thinking about Grace and all the things he wanted to do to her, with her, was enough to have his libido soaring out of control. He really did need to get laid. The only problem with that was the only woman he had any interest in taking to his bed was Grace.

He had a meeting over lunch that ran well into the afternoon. Over his ten-year military career he'd had a few commanders that liked to chatter on instead of getting to the point, but the man who was currently standing at the far end of the conference room took the cake. He'd been rambling on about medical billing procedures for almost forty minutes. It might not have been so bad had he been sharing some sort of new way of doing things, but he wasn't and Alexander wasn't the only one in the room who looked as if he were about to fall asleep.

The man finally sat down and another man took over. There was a collective sigh of relief in the room when the new speaker began talking about an upcoming case involving an experimental drug.

By the time the meeting let out, it was nearly three thirty. Almost everyone went to their desks to check their email and voice mail. They'd been in that dreaded meeting for close to four hours with only one bathroom break. He would rather have run ten miles.

Given his job, he doubted he had any important emails waiting for him at his desk, so after making a quick stop at the bathroom he headed downstairs to the patio for a little air. He took a seat on one of the benches and scrolled through his phone. There was no way to know if Grace had opened his email or not. She was most likely home by then, but that didn't mean anything.

Alexander hated that he was so anxious. It wasn't like him at all. But this was Grace and there was so much that could go wrong.

His thumb hovered over the screen as he debated whether or not to send her a text. He was still debating when his phone dinged.

Got your email. – Grace

It was crazy how something so simple could bring a smile to his face.

Have you opened it yet? – Alexander

It took a minute for her to answer.

Yes. Just now. – Grace

Okay. Let me know if you have any questions. – Alexander

He waited for another few minutes to see if she would send him another message before he went back inside, but she didn't. Tucking his phone back into his jacket pocket, he stood and made his way back inside. As much as he didn't want to, he needed to get back to his desk. There was a stack of papers that needed his attention.

Grace didn't contact him again that night or the next day. If he was being honest, it worried him a little. Had she read something that put her off? Had she changed her mind? The rational part of his brain told him that he'd sent her a lot of information to go over and that she still had work. It wasn't as if she could sit in front of her computer all day dissecting what he'd sent her.

On Wednesday morning he'd been tempted to swing by the café and see her, but he hadn't wanted to seem like a stalker. Instead, he'd gone to work as usual and kept his phone close by.

He was sitting at his desk that afternoon when he got a text from her.

Can you come over tonight? – Grace

His heart sank.

Sure. What time? – Alexander

Six? I'll make dinner. – Grace

I'll be there. – Alexander

He set his phone aside and tried not to jump to conclusions. It was entirely possible that she wanted to go over some things and either didn't want to wait or didn't want to talk about whatever it was out in public. He hadn't missed how uncomfortable she'd gotten during various parts of their conversation on Monday evening.

With as much optimism as he could muster, Alexander rang the doorbell at exactly six o'clock. A gust of wind whipped around the corner, reminding him that he needed to get a heavier jacket before winter. Although it didn't get as cold in St. Louis as it did in DC, he would still need something more substantial than the windbreaker he was sporting.

Grace answered the door with a smile on her face. It gave him hope that she hadn't changed her mind and decided she didn't want him as her Dom. "I'm glad you came."

"Of course," he said as he stepped over the threshold into her home.

"Can I take your jacket?"

He shrugged out of his coat and handed it to her. "Thanks."

Grace had the table already set and there was a bowl of salad at each spot. She stood by her chair and waited. It took him a moment to realize she was waiting for him.

Pulling out her chair for her, he gestured that she should sit. She'd obviously read over his rules.

Alexander joined her at the table, picked up his napkin, and placed it over his lap. "I see you've read over what I sent you."

"Yes, Sir. I have."

"Is that why you asked me to come over tonight?" While he was always happy to see her, it did concern him that she hadn't wanted to wait until tomorrow night.

"Yes. I wanted to talk to you about some things and . . . well, I didn't want to talk about them at the restaurant."

He put some dressing on his salad, picked up his fork, and gestured for her to go ahead.

"I would like for us to play tonight."

His fork stopped halfway to his mouth.

"If it's all right with you, Sir."

Alexander laid his fork down, wiped his mouth, and placed his napkin on the table before giving Grace his full attention. While he had no issue with them playing tonight, he needed to understand her reasoning. "Why?"

She worried the bottom of her lip with her teeth before glancing up at him with those wide eyes of hers. "I've been thinking about it and thinking about it, and when I do I get more and more nervous."

"Maybe you're not ready." He reached out to touch the back of her hand. "It's okay if you're not."

Grace shook her head. "That's not it. I just keep thinking of all the what-ifs. I mean, I've never played with anyone but Kurt. What if it's different with someone else? What if I can't . . ."

"What if you can't what?"

"What if I can't submit to someone else?" she whispered.

This was a real fear. He could see it in her eyes.

Resituating his napkin, he picked his fork back up. "Eat," he said, motioning toward her salad.

She hunched her shoulders in what looked to be defeat and reached for her fork. "I'm sorry. I didn't mean—"

"If you want us to play tonight, you'll need your energy. Eat."

Grace froze, and then a sly smile tugged at her lips.

"That's right. You're getting what you want, *gattina*. Don't get too used to it." He winked at her, letting her know he wasn't upset.

If truth be told, she'd probably get away with more than she should in this relationship—arrangement—or whatever it was you wanted to call what they were about to embark upon. He was hard-pressed to deny her much of anything. There was something about Grace that called to him whether she wanted it or not. Somehow he doubted it would take long for her to steal his heart. He only hoped she didn't rip it out and stomp on it.

Alexander knew she wouldn't do it on purpose, but he wasn't naive. He knew she was still in love with her husband. Knew that the only reason she was doing this was because Kurt had asked it of her. But that didn't change how he felt. Grace needed someone to take care of her—love her—and he was more than up for the job as long as she would let him.

Maybe that made him a sucker, but he could live with that.

Chapter 11

He worked beside her to clean up after their meal before saying they should head up to her bedroom. It was really going to happen. They were going to play.

Grace tried to control her breathing as they climbed the stairs. With each step she took she counted her blessings that Alexander had agreed to be her Dom. As nervous as she was about tonight, she knew it would have been ten times worse with someone else.

When they reached her room, she paused outside the door. This was it.

Grace took a deep breath in and let it out slowly before crossing the threshold. She stood off to the side as Alexander strolled into the room and took a look around. He ran his fingers over the comforter on the bed before glancing at the items on top of her nightstand. She saw his brief hesitation before he picked up one of her books.

During one of their dinners, she'd mentioned how much she liked to read. What she hadn't told him was the type of books she preferred. Grace stood by helplessly as he flipped the book over and read the back.

After several moments, he placed the book down and moved on without comment. A small part of her was disappointed. At least if they talked about her books she could focus on something other than the scene they were going to do tonight.

"Do you have a toy bag?" His voice came out of nowhere and startled her. When she met his gaze across the room he had a smirk on his face. He'd known what he was doing.

"It's a chest," she said. "It's in the closet. It's locked."

When she didn't move, he raised an eyebrow.

"Oh. Yes. Sorry." Feeling a bit silly she hadn't realized he was asking her to get the toys out in the first place, she rushed to her nightstand to get the key.

She and Kurt had picked up the chest years ago at a town market. At the time it had been overkill for what they had, which wasn't much outside a small crop, a flogger, and a few vibrators. Grace pulled the chest from the closet, unlocked it, and lifted the lid. Their toy collection had grown over the years.

With a little extra care than what was normal for someone of Alexander's age, he knelt down in front of the chest.

"I can get you a chair, Sir."

He looked up, meeting her gaze. "Thank you, but I'm fine. Is everything in here clean?"

"Yes, Sir."

Without saying anything more, he went back to inspecting her toys.

They stood there for several minutes as he looked things over. Every now and then he'd pick something up to move it, but for the most part he seemed to be taking an inventory of what she had. With each passing second she grew less sure of herself.

Without selecting any of the toys, Alexander stood. He looked her up and down before staring her in the eye. "There is no shame if you need to use your safeword tonight."

"Yes, Sir."

He held her gaze for a moment longer before speaking. "Remove your shirt and pants."

Grace swallowed and reached for the hem of her shirt. She could do this.

Cool air hit her skin as she lifted the shirt over her head. It wasn't that cold in the room, so she imagined it was the situation itself that had her so sensitive.

She reached for the button of her jeans, pushing it through the material, and then lowered the zipper. Grace had stripped many times for her husband, but this was different. Alexander had never seen her naked. What if he didn't like what he saw?

Her nerves started to get the best of her and she froze.

"Is there a problem?"

Grace shook her head. No, there wasn't a problem. Only her own insecurities. "No, Sir."

Before she could overthink it anymore, she wiggled the jeans lower, letting them drop to the floor. She bent down to pick them up, but Alexander's voice stopped her. "Leave them."

She felt incredibly exposed standing there in nothing but her bra and panties, but she knew from experience that this was only the beginning. It was what she'd asked for and on some level needed. Already, despite her nerves, she felt her body responding.

Alexander took a step forward, closing the distance between them. She could feel the heat from his body even though he wasn't touching her. It felt as if he were six inches taller all of a sudden.

He moved to stand behind her, still close. The hairs on the back of her neck stood at attention, anticipating. He leaned in, his breath ghosting over her ear. "You're a beautiful woman, Grace."

"Thank you, Sir." She wasn't sure what to think about the way the muscles in her belly clenched at the sound, the feel of his voice vibrating against her skin. It had been so long since she'd felt anything like this.

"Remove your bra, Grace." The command was spoken as softly as his compliment regarding her body, but she knew it was a command nonetheless.

With shaky hands, she reached behind her back and unclipped her bra. The straps slid down her shoulders and she let them fall, pulling the cups away and exposing her flesh. She knew without looking that her nipples were hard.

She heard him hum behind her and knew he'd seen the state of her nipples. The sound sent another wave of anticipation through her.

"Cup your tits with your hands."

What? Why wasn't he—

"I won't ask again. Do it, or use your safeword."

Using her safeword hadn't even crossed her mind. It was only not understanding the reasons behind what he was asking that had her hesitating. But it wasn't her job to understand. She trusted Alexander and she knew he'd take care of her.

Grace cupped her breasts, holding their weight in her hands. It wasn't as if she'd never touched herself before. She had. A lot, actually.

As if he could read her mind, Alexander's breath brushed her ear again. "Take your thumb and forefinger and pinch your nipples."

This time she didn't think about it. She just did what he asked.

"You know I'd do it harder than that, Grace."

She pinched harder and felt a zing race down her spine.

"Harder."

A gasp left her lips and warmth rushed between her legs.

"That's better." She could hear the smile in his voice. "Do you pinch your nipples like this when you masturbate?"

"Sometimes." Questions like this shouldn't bother her. Especially since she fully expected Alexander to not only pinch her nipples himself at some point but have sex with her as well.

"Does that embarrass you?" he asked, still not touching her. Was that his plan? To tease her all night?

"Yes." She paused. "A little."

"Then you might turn as red as a beet before we're finished."

The shock of his statement caused her to lose concentration and release her hold on her nipples for a second.

He chuckled. "Oh, *gattina*, I'm going to have so much fun with your shy nature."

She didn't respond. What was she supposed to say to that? Besides, it hadn't been a question.

Her nipples were growing more sensitive the longer she stood there pinching them. The feel of him standing behind her, towering over her, watching was also making it very hard to concentrate on anything outside the two of them. She wanted him to touch her, but didn't know if she should ask him to.

"What are you thinking, *gattina*?"

Grace didn't want to lie and knew she shouldn't. "I was thinking how much I want you to touch me, Sir."

"We have plenty of time for that." He moved a strand of her hair out of the way so he could see better. "Take your right hand and slide it inside the front of your panties. I want you to touch yourself."

Her nipple throbbed when she released it, sending pulses down to her sex. Of course, part of that could have been anticipation as well. It had been almost two years since she'd masturbated in front of a man. She was equal parts nervous and excited. And completely turned on.

The feel of her damp flesh hit her fingers, showcasing how aroused she truly was. Grace was never able to get this wet when she was by herself. Even though Alexander hadn't touched her, he was there, and every cell in her body knew it.

"Are you wet, Grace?"

"Yes, Sir."

"Is your clit swollen?" Every word he said sent tingles down her spine and seemed to have a direct line to her sex.

Without thinking about it, Grace ran her middle finger over her clit and gasped. "Yes."

"That's good." She heard the smile in his voice again. "Now take your panties off and go lie on the bed."

***

Alexander would have given about anything to read Grace's mind when he'd ordered her to remove her panties and get onto the bed. The look on her face had been enough to let him know he'd caught her completely off guard, which was what he wanted. If she didn't have time to think too much about things, she wouldn't have the chance to second-guess herself. He knew what this meant to her and that it needed to go well.

Throughout dinner, he'd been contemplating their scene. While he'd put a scene together on the fly before, it had never been with a sub such as Grace. She wasn't new to the lifestyle, which had its advantages. He wasn't worried about her not saying her safeword should she need to use it. There also wasn't the issue with her not knowing her hard and soft limits.

No, with Grace the problem was a lot more complicated. He needed something that would test the waters, get them used to each other in these new roles yet allow her to set the pace without having her top from the bottom. It was a delicate balance and one that was sure to leave him needing a long cold shower when he got home.

Grace pushed her panties over her hips and down her legs, revealing her amazing ass. It had taken considerable effort for him to keep his hands to himself. Alexander knew what it felt like against his hand when he'd spanked her, but that had been with her clothes on. He wanted to feel her soft skin against his palm as it turned a lovely shade of pink.

A groan nearly escaped his throat when she climbed onto the bed, ass in the air. Luckily, he stifled it. Tonight wasn't about him. He'd get his needs taken care of another time. Tonight was about what she needed.

He waited until she was lying face up on the bed. She'd spread her legs without being asked, a sure sign this wasn't the first time she'd been told to do something similar. The tips of her nipples were dark pink from where she'd been pinching them. It really was a beautiful sight.

Once she was in position, Alexander went to the toy chest. When he'd looked it over earlier he saw a few things he felt would be perfect for their scene.

There were a few crops in the chest, but one looked to be more worn than the others. He removed that, along with a small flogger, a lifelike dildo, and a bullet vibrator.

When he turned around, he found Grace was watching him. Her brow was furrowed a bit and she was breathing a little harder than normal. Other than that, she remained still. Her legs were still spread and her hands were flat on the bed.

Alexander placed the toys on her nightstand next to her books. When Grace had told him she liked to read romance novels, he hadn't given it much thought. Being in the military for ten years he'd known there were kinky romance novels out there, but for some reason he hadn't pictured Grace reading them. Maybe it was because she was so shy. Then again, before Friday he hadn't known she was a submissive.

He stood next to the bed, looking down at her. "How are you doing?"

"Good, Sir."

"Are you ready to continue?" he asked.

There was still a bit of uncertainty behind her eyes, but she answered anyway. "Yes, Sir."

"Place your hands above your head and press your palms against the headboard. I want those gorgeous tits of yours up in the air."

Grace had to use her feet to scoot herself higher onto the bed in order to reach the headboard, which made him grin. The position naturally arched her back slightly, thrusting her breasts up.

He picked up the crop and used it first to nudge her legs apart. When she'd moved, she'd closed her legs a little more than he liked. She opened up, giving him a great view of her pussy. He took the time to really look at it for the first time. As of tonight that pussy belonged to him.

That thought did nothing to help the growing problem in his pants, but he had no desire to stop the train of his thoughts. He trailed the crop up the inside of one of her thighs, across her belly button, and then down the inside of the other thigh. Like a good little sub, she held perfectly still.

Alexander flicked his wrist twice, landing a single sting to each of her inner thighs. She closed her eyes and pressed her lips together.

He did it again, higher up. This time he saw the muscles of her sex clench. She liked that. He also noticed that most of the tension in her body had disappeared. Grace was in the moment and he wanted her to stay that way.

Running the tip of the crop over her clit caused a whimper to leave her throat. It wasn't a sound of distress in the least. She was turned on and she wanted more.

All in good time.

Alexander took his time exploring her body with the crop. Everywhere he wanted to touch with his hands, his lips, he kissed with the crop instead, lingering where he wanted to linger. Grace had an amazing body. When he'd first met her she'd been too skinny, most likely from not eating the way she should. Between Beth's efforts and his own, they'd managed to put some meat back on her bones, and he was enjoying the results.

When he got to her breasts, he circled them several times making sure to cover every inch before zeroing in on her nipples. She arched her back, silently begging for more as he teased her. When he lifted the crop and snapped it back against the tip, she moaned. The sound went straight to his cock.

Before he threw all common sense out the window and starting sucking on those pretty tits of hers, he returned the crop to the nightstand and reached for the dildo. He held it up at an angle she could see. "When was the last time you used this?"

Her eyes fluttered open and she blinked several times as if she were coming out of a fog. She probably was. He saw the muscles in her throat move as she swallowed. "It's been a while, Sir."

He nodded. "Open your mouth."

She did as instructed and he placed the dildo between her lips. Grace didn't need to be told what was expected of her. She began sucking and licking the dildo as if it were a real cock. If she kept it up, he was liable to come in his pants.

When he couldn't take it anymore, Alexander removed the dildo from her mouth and placed it between her legs. He sat on the edge of the bed and pressed the head against the entrance of her pussy. With shallow movements, he began working it deeper. He was entranced by the way her body swallowed up the fake cock.

His plan had been to insert the dildo into her pussy, and then leave it there while he used the flogger and vibrator on her, but plans changed. He pulled the dildo halfway out before pushing it back in with a little more force. Grace's reaction made him want to do it again, and again. She was doing her best not to move, but she wasn't completely succeeding.

Her breathing became more labored and her fingers pressed against the headboard. He could tell she was close.

He teased her for several more minutes, alternating between deep hard thrusts and faster, shallower ones. She seemed to like the deeper, harder ones best, which was good to know. He looked forward to testing her reactions when it was him instead of a flexible piece of silicone.

Stretching, Alexander grabbed the bullet from the nightstand and turned it on. He placed it against her clit.

Grace's mouth fell open and she tilted her head back. He thrust the dildo into her hard and fast several times and her hips came up off the bed. It was obvious she wasn't thinking straight anymore. He was honestly surprised her hands were still on the headboard. It was no doubt the result of her previous training.

He turned the speed up on the bullet and that was all it took. An almost strangled sound erupted from deep within her throat as she came.

Alexander removed the bullet and the dildo, putting both on her nightstand before taking the blanket at the end of the bed and placing it over her. Forgetting about everything else, he lay down on the bed beside her and pulled her into his arms. He wanted to kiss her, but settled for brushing his lips against the top of her hair. "You did good, *gattina*. You did good."

Chapter 12

It took Grace a moment to realize she wasn't alone and why. Her eyes had drifted closed after their scene and before she knew it, she was asleep. She'd felt safe, relaxed, and a little pleased with herself. Despite her fears, she'd done it. But more than that, she'd enjoyed it.

As soon as that realization popped into her head, guilt began to creep in. She knew it wasn't logical. Kurt had told her to move on, to find another Dom, and she'd done that. He'd want her to be happy and she was. Mostly.

Grace couldn't ask for a better man than Alexander to help her with this. The way he'd handled the scene was exactly what she'd needed.

Thinking about their scene had her blushing. He'd seen every inch of her, made her come. She could still smell a hint of sex in the air.

His arms tightened around her as he shifted his weight. The blanket covering her naked body slipped lower on one side, exposing one of her breasts.

She went to pulled it back into place, but he beat her to it. "Are you cold?"

The sound of his voice, the feel of his body next to hers, had her temperature rising again. She was far from cold. "No."

"How are you feeling?" he asked as he ran a gentle finger from her elbow to her wrist. It was distracting.

She tried to ignore her body's response. "A little sleepy, but good."

"I wasn't expecting you to conk out on me." Grace could tell he was smiling. It helped lighten the mood.

"Sorry."

"It's fine. Just don't make a habit of it." He gave her a gentle squeeze, letting her know he was only giving her a hard time.

Neither of them moved as several minutes ticked by. It wasn't awkward or uncomfortable. In fact, Grace felt more at ease than she had in a really long time. "Thank you."

"You're welcome." He brushed his thumb along the inside of her wrist. "Although, I should probably be the one thanking you."

Grace didn't agree, but decided to let it go. Alexander was happy. The scene had gone well. Great, even. She was now relatively sure she could accompany him to Serpent's Kiss and not embarrass him or herself.

"We need to talk about the scene," he said a while later. She'd been close to drifting off to sleep again. Being in his arms felt more right than anything had since her world fell apart.

"Okay."

He seemed to sense she was waiting on him to start. "Was there anything you didn't like?"

"No, not really."

"That doesn't sound definitive."

He shifted again and she wondered if his leg was bothering him. She began to pull away.

"Where do you think you're going?" His Dom voice was back, slightly deeper than his normal voice. It made her heart rate kick up a notch.

"You keep shifting your weight. I thought maybe your leg was hurting. I wanted to give you some space." She saw his frown and knew he wasn't pleased.

"Let me worry about my leg." He tugged her back against his side. "You're avoiding the question. Was there something about the scene you didn't care for?"

"No. There wasn't anything you did I didn't like." That was the truth. She'd loved it all. And she'd wanted more. That's the part that had her feeling the guiltiest. If he'd wanted to have sex with her tonight she would have let him.

Alexander knew there was something she wasn't telling him. "But?"

She glanced down at her hands where they rested in her lap. Honesty. "You didn't touch me."

When he didn't respond, she looked up. He appeared to be amused.

"What?" she asked, confused.

"I used a crop on you and shoved a dildo inside your pussy."

At that moment, she wanted to crawl under the covers. She'd never been good at talking about this stuff and Alexander wasn't mincing words. "I know."

He placed a finger under her chin and forced her to meet his gaze. "But you wanted my hands on you."

She nodded.

Alexander cupped the side of her face, his fingers tickling the hairs at the base of her neck. He leaned in closer. She could feel his breath on her face. Was he going to kiss her?

"There are so many things I want to do to you, Grace. So many ways I want to touch you. But tonight wasn't about that. Tonight was about you letting go of your fears and realizing that you are still a woman who has needs, wants, and desires. A woman that needed to see that she could let go again and trust that I would catch her."

Grace felt the moisture prick her eyes and tried to hold back the tears. He'd seen her cry enough already.

He pressed his soft lips against hers for a brief moment before pulling back. "You need a bath, and then bed. You have work tomorrow."

Without waiting for her to reply, he eased himself out of her bed. He held out his hand for her and she took it. The blanket fell away, leaving her naked in front of him.

Alexander didn't even pretend he wasn't looking. His gaze lingered on her breasts before he headed lower. If she'd ever wondered if he was attracted to her, she now had her answer. The look in his eyes told her everything she needed to know.

For a second, she thought he was going to kiss her again, but then he turned and led her into her bathroom. Grace had to admit she was disappointed. She'd wanted him to kiss her.

He drew her a bath and helped her into the tub. "Relax and enjoy your bath then get some sleep. I'll make sure the house is locked up when I leave."

She wasn't sure why, but she'd been hoping he'd stay. It was silly. They both had work tomorrow and he had no clothes there. Plus, it wasn't as if he was her boyfriend or anything. They weren't dating. He was her Dom. It was an arrangement.

"What's wrong?"

"Nothing." She tried to smile, but it must have fallen flat because his frown was back.

"This doesn't work if you lie to me."

"I'm not." His skeptical look had her backtracking. "I'm just not used to this kind of . . . arrangement."

He leaned back again the doorframe and crossed his arms over his chest. "What kind of arrangement is that?"

"You being my Dom. Me being your submissive."

"You've had a Dom before," he said, obviously not understanding what she was getting at.

"Yes, but I was married to him." She sighed, frustrated that she was having trouble explaining herself. "We were . . . I mean . . . it was just different, I guess."

Alexander took a moment before answering. "Grace, I'm not sure what you think this arrangement is or isn't, but maybe I need to spell it out for you. As my submissive, you belong to me. And as your Dom, I belong to you."

Grace nodded. She knew that.

But he didn't stop there. "I won't be playing with anyone else while we're together. I won't be dating anyone else either."

She felt her mouth fall open.

He pushed off the doorframe and turned to go. "Finish your bath and get some rest. I'll text you in the morning and I expect you to text me back as soon as you're able. Do you understand?"

"Yes, Sir."

Alexander exited the bathroom, leaving her pondering what he'd said. Did that mean they were dating? Exclusive? She had no idea, and to be honest, she didn't know how she felt about it. Not that she was planning on going out and dating anyone else, but dating implied there was an emotional element to their relationship.

Grace could hear him moving around downstairs, making sure

her doors and windows were locked. The sound of the front door opening and then closing had her sliding down lower into her bath. Did Alexander want their arrangement to be more? It certainly sounded like that. The question became could she give him that if it was in fact what he wanted?

She didn't know the answer and that frightened her even more than the thought of going to Serpent's Kiss again, this time as Alexander's submissive.

The water began to cool, so Grace got out and reached for a towel. She'd do her best—try to be the best sub she could be for him. Hopefully, that was enough.

***

Alexander sent Grace a text before he left for work asking if she'd slept well last night. He knew she was most likely busy at the café, but he expected her to get back to him before lunch. They'd texted back and forth during the day before and it never took her more than an hour or so to get back to him. He hoped what had happened last night between them didn't change that.

To his surprise, his phone dinged as he was getting into his car.

Yes. – Grace

There was a pause.

I hit the snooze three times this morning. – Grace

He chuckled. Grace wasn't exactly a morning person, but she was used to her schedule and she enjoyed her job. They'd talked about how she always had to hit snooze once in the mornings before she could drag herself out of bed. Three times meant she really hadn't wanted to get up.

I'm glad you got some rest. – Alexander

Have a good day at work. I'll pick you up at 6. – Alexander

When she didn't respond right away, he went ahead and drove to work. Halfway there he heard her message come in. Unfortunately, he had to wait until he arrived at work to check it.

Okay. I'll be ready. – Grace

His day went by quickly. There'd been a mountain of new folders on his desk that required his attention and at lunch he'd had to run to the post office. The state licensing board had sent him another form they needed to be filled out and sent in. He wanted the

100

process of getting his license to practice in Missouri completed as soon as possible. That meant staying on top of whatever the licensing board required. He sure as hell didn't want to be sitting at a desk for the rest of his days going over malpractice suits.

Jewel asked if he wanted to join her and some others for drinks again. He felt bad that he had to keep turning her down, but there was no way he was giving up the evening with Grace. He also didn't think she'd feel comfortable tagging along with him while he hung out with his coworkers. The new terms of their relationship alone had her leery.

He hadn't missed the look on her face when he'd told her there would be no one else as long as he was with her. She'd lost a little color in her face and her jaw had dropped. Alexander had thought he'd been clear before about exactly what he expected, but apparently he'd not been clear enough. He didn't want to scare her, but she needed to know he wasn't going to be playing, or dating, anyone else as long as they were together.

Thinking about seeing Grace again had him whistling on his way to his vehicle. He got a few strange looks, but he didn't care. In less than an hour he'd see Grace again and tonight he planned on pushing her boundaries a little more.

As promised, Grace was ready and waiting when he showed up at her house. She had her hair pulled back and a little makeup on. The makeup was new. And while she looked nice, he preferred her natural beauty.

"Shall we?" he said, offering her his arm.

She locked the door and hooked her arm through his.

It didn't take long to get to the restaurant. They'd been there before and had both enjoyed the food. That was good since he was starving. He'd skipped lunch in favor of going to the post office.

"Good evening. Two?" the hostess asked.

Alexander nodded. "Yes, and a booth please, if you have it."

She grinned and picked up two menus. "Right this way."

The booth was along the wall in the center of the room. Not as private as he'd like, but he could work with it.

He motioned for Grace to have a seat. Instead of taking the seat opposite, he slid in beside her.

Grace scooted closer to the wall, making room for him. One they were both settled and the hostess had left them alone, he rested his hand on her knee as he picked up his menu. He was very glad she'd chosen to wear a skirt tonight.

She sucked in a breath.

"Problem?" he asked.

"No, Sir."

"Good." He smiled. "Hopefully you know what you want because I could eat a horse."

Careful not to move her lower half, Grace picked up her menu.

When their server stopped by their table, he ordered their drinks and an appetizer, giving Grace a few more minutes to decide what she wanted. He was being good, keeping his hand still while she looked.

Their server returned with their drinks and a basket of bread. She jotted down their orders and told them she'd return shortly with their appetizer.

Once they were alone again, he decided it was time to have some fun. He pushed the hem of her skirt up a little and began tracing small circles on the inside of her leg a few inches above her knee. Grace tensed.

He turned and whispered in her ear. "Relax. No one is going to know I'm doing anything unless you act as if something's wrong."

He saw her swallow.

"If I'm doing something you don't want me to do, all you have to do is say the word." Grace knew exactly what word he was talking about.

She remained silent.

He picked up a piece of bread and handed it to her. "Did you eat lunch today?"

"Yes." She was trying hard to keep still. "A sandwich and some soup."

Alexander was glad to hear Beth was still taking care of her. "Good. I expect you to eat three full meals a day, no exceptions."

When she didn't answer, he gave her leg a light pinch. "Yes, Sir."

"I'm going to make sure you take care of yourself, *gattina*." He inched his fingers a little higher. "That's part of my job."

Grace nodded.

He removed his hand and reached for a piece of bread for himself, leaving her on edge. That was good.

Their appetizer came, a fondue. The interactive nature of the food lightened the mood a bit and he was pleased to see her release some of her tension. He dipped some of the bread into the melted cheese and held it to her lips.

She opened her mouth and he watched as her lips sucked the food inside. It was almost as bad as watching her give that fake cock a blow job the night before. He wanted to feel those lips around him, sucking him into oblivion.

Shaking the thought from his mind, he skewered another piece of bread and dipped it into the cheese. Pushing Grace was one thing, but jumping into bed with her was another. He wanted her to feel completely comfortable with him and what they were doing before he went there. This wasn't just about him getting laid or getting her off. At least not for him. He didn't want her to regret anything they did together. Ever.

Their meal came and he steered things to safer topics, all the while continuing to touch and caress her beneath the table. He asked about her mom and how things were going with her upcoming retirement. By the time they finished their meal, it almost felt like it had before he'd seen her at the club. She'd giggled at his jokes and even snorted when he'd suggested maybe her mom could take up juggling as a hobby.

Grace was smiling as he drove her home. A real, genuine smile. Throughout dinner she'd gotten more and more used to his touch. His heart felt lighter and heavier all at the same time.

She hugged her jacket against her as they stepped onto her front porch. Fall had definitely arrived in St. Louis. "Do you want to come in?"

Want had nothing to do with it.

He walked forward, backing her up against the door. Grace looked up at him, her eyes sparkling in the evening light.

"I don't think that's a good idea," he whispered, his lips hovering an inch above hers.

Grace licked her bottom lip. "Why?"

He stifled a groan. She didn't make this easy.

Instead of answering with words, he closed the distance between them, wrapped his arm around her waist, and pulled her against him. She let out a tiny squeak before his mouth covered hers.

It was the first time he'd kissed her. Really kissed her. Sure, he'd brushed his lips against hers a few times in the past, but this was different.

Her lips gave under the gentle pressure of his mouth. He sucked her bottom lip into his mouth, remembering how her tongue had moistened it moments before. She was so soft in his arms, molding her body to his.

Alexander dug his fingers into her hip, needing her closer. He slipped his tongue into her mouth, exploring, tasting. It wasn't enough, and yet he knew it had to be. For now.

Breaking the kiss, he rested his forehead against hers as he met her gaze. She was breathing hard, her chest rising and falling, making it that much more difficult to do what he knew he needed to.

"Good night, Grace."

She blinked as if she were waking from a daze. His male pride soared at having been the one responsible.

Even though he knew she'd heard him, Grace didn't move.

"Grace?"

"Hmm?"

"You need to unlock the door and go inside." He released her and took a step back—the cool air helping to bring some sanity back to the situation.

It seemed to do the same for her. Grace dug her keys out of her purse and turned to unlock the door. She looked over her shoulder before going inside. Several strands of her hair were loose and her lipstick was almost completely gone, even though she'd gone to the bathroom before they'd left the restaurant and reapplied it. Alexander was most likely wearing the other half of it himself. He couldn't care less.

"Good night, Grace."

A light pink tinted her cheeks. "Good night."

Chapter 13

Friday morning dawned and Grace had to drag herself out of bed. It had taken her a while to get to sleep the night before. Her mind and body had been too worked up from the kiss she'd shared with Alexander. He'd kissed her before. A few times. But even she knew last night had been different. His kisses before had been innocent. Chaste. There'd been nothing innocent about what happened on her porch.

She went to work, happy for the distraction. That was until Alexander texted her at noon to remind her he'd be picking her up at six. After that, she hadn't been able to think of anything else. They were going to the club and this time around he would be her Dom and she would be his submissive.

Beth noticed she was distracted. "Any big plans this weekend?"

Grace debated how to answer her boss. "I sort of have a date."

It was the easiest way to explain her and Alexander's plans for the evening. Especially to someone who didn't know anything about BDSM. She could only imagine Beth's reaction if Grace told her she was going to a kink club with her Dom.

"That's great." Beth paused. "Right? I mean I'm assuming you like the guy. You agreed to go out with him."

"Do you remember me telling you about Kurt's friend, the Army doctor?" Grace asked as she put the food Beth had prepared onto a tray.

Her boss' eyes lit up. "Really? That's great." She put the finishing touches on another sandwich and handed it to Grace. "But haven't you been out with the guy before? I mean maybe not on an official date or anything, but out to dinner and stuff?"

"Yeah." Grace didn't know exactly how to explain it without going into detail. "I guess it's just that things are changing."

Beth studied her face. "Is that not what you want?"

"No. I do." Grace released a frustrated sigh. She wasn't doing a very going job explaining. Then again, how could she? The only one who knew the whole story was Alexander. "It's just . . . new."

"Now, that I can relate to." Beth laughed. "My advice? Don't worry so much. Things will work out the way they're meant to."

Grace picked up the tray full of food feeling a little better after talking to Beth. She still had no idea what to expect from tonight, but her boss was right. Things would work out the way they were meant to, good or bad.

At three thirty Grace said goodbye to Beth and Tommy and made her way to the store before heading home. She had a lot to do before Alexander picked her up. After showering and shaving, she went to her closet to find something to wear. She didn't want to disappoint her new Dom.

Grace tried on a handful of outfits before settling on the same fitted leather skirt she'd worn the week before and a white top that dipped low in both the front and the back. Because of how it was made, Grace wouldn't be able to wear a bra. If Alexander was anything like her husband had been, he would like that.

The doorbell rang a little before six and she raced downstairs as fast as her three-inch heels would carry her. Figuring it was Alexander, she opened the door without looking, only to find her sister staring back at her with her eyes about to bug out of her head, holding her niece. The look on her sister's face had her wanting to cover up.

"What are you doing here?"

It took Gabby a moment to answer. "I tried to call, but you didn't answer." She gave Grace a long once-over. "Now I know why."

This wasn't a conversation Grace wanted to have standing in her doorway, so she took a step back and let her sister inside. "Sorry. I was probably in the shower."

Her sister scanned her surroundings, and then met Grace's gaze with a smirk on her face. "Are you waiting on your doctor?"

She started to say he wasn't hers, but stopped herself. He was hers. At least for the time being. "He's taking me to a club."

"Oooo. Dancing. Fun." Her sister placed a single finger in the center of her top and pushed down, revealing more of Grace's skin. "No bra. Nice. Someone's hoping to get lucky tonight."

Grace batted Gabby's hand away. She could already feel her blush starting. "You said you called?" She really needed to get her sister's attention away from what she was wearing and how she was going to be spending her evening.

Gabby repositioned her daughter on her hip. "When I picked Taylor up tonight, her babysitter told me she had a death in the family and won't be able to watch her tomorrow or Monday. Mom said she can watch her tomorrow while I'm at work, but I was hoping you could cover Monday." A sly grin appeared. "That is if you're not spending your day off with your new man."

"I can watch her Monday." Grace chose to ignore the rest of what her sister said.

"Great! We'll talk more Sunday." Gabby gave her a swift kiss on the cheek before heading toward the door. "I'll get out of your hair so you can finish getting ready, but I'll expect details."

Grace tried not to groan, and waved goodbye to her sister. Every time Gabby had asked her about Alexander in the past, Grace kept insisting there was nothing going on between them, that they were just friends. It wasn't as if she could claim that anymore. They were definitely more than friends now. He was her Dom. Everything else? Grace wasn't sure about that herself. She had no idea how she was going to explain it to her sister.

With Beth it had been easier. Beth wasn't going to ask for a blow-by-blow, as it were. Gabby would want to know when things changed and why Grace had been holding out on her. It made her want to call her mom and tell her she wasn't going to make it over this week. Of course, that would only put off the inevitable.

She heard Alexander's footfalls on the porch and opened the door before he had a chance to ring the bell. He was dressed in black slacks and a greenish-blue shirt that buttoned down the front. Her heart rate picked up at the sight of him.

It wasn't until he came inside that she realized he had his cane with him. "Is your leg bothering you?"

He raised an eyebrow and she realized her mistake. Not a great way to start the evening.

"Sorry, Sir." She lowered her gaze to the floor as he closed the door.

Grace wasn't sure what she was expecting his reaction to be, but she nearly jumped out of her skin when she felt his hand on the back of her thigh. "Easy, *gattina*."

She bit down on the inside of her cheek and told herself to breathe.

He gave her a moment, and then eased his hand up under her skirt and ran his fingers along the seam of her thong. "Very nice."

"Thank you, Sir."

His hand remained on her ass as he moved to stand in front of her. He lifted her chin with his free hand, his cane dangling only an inch from her breast. "I approve of your top as well."

She swallowed, not saying anything as he ran the back of his hand down her neck to the hollow between her breasts where the material of her shirt pooled. But unlike her sister, he didn't tug at her shirt to confirm she wasn't wearing a bra. Then again, he didn't have to. Grace could feel her nipples pressing against the silky fabric, trying to get free.

Grace was so focused on her body's reactions she almost missed his next words. "It's going to be a big night for you, and as I said before, there will be no running. You will be by my side as my submissive and you will conduct yourself as such. If there is a problem, you will tell me immediately."

"Yes, Sir."

They stopped to have dinner. He'd sat beside her again, but this time he kept his hands to himself. She didn't know if that was due to the fact that the restaurant was crowded or if it was because he could tell how nervous she was.

When they arrived at the club, he helped her out of her coat and handed it to the woman behind the desk in the lobby. "Thank you, Ali."

"You're welcome, Sir," the woman said. "Have a fun time tonight."

He placed a hand on Grace's lower back and guided her into the club.

***

Alexander paid close attention to Grace's reaction as they walked into the main room of the club. He kept his hand on her lower back as he guided her through the crowd and over to the seating area. Daniel was already there chatting with Nicole and Jeff.

Daniel saw them first. His gaze fell on Grace, and then back to Alexander. "And who do we have here?"

It was then he saw Nicole's expression change. She recognized Grace. And from the looks of it, so did her sub, Jeff.

A moment later, he knew Grace had recognized them, too. Alexander had been so concerned about her reaction to seeing Beth that he hadn't considered she'd also know Nicole and Jeff. He knew Nicole and Beth were best friends, but he wasn't aware Nicole and Grace had ever met.

Alexander circled his arm around Grace's waist and pulled her closer to his side before answering Daniel's question. He wasn't about to have her take off on him. "This is my submissive, Grace."

His friend raised one eyebrow in silent question, but didn't comment.

Turning to Nicole, Alexander said, "I think you may already know each other?"

"Yes. Grace works at the café with Beth."

He edged Grace closer to the couch, sat down, and tugged her onto his lap. "I didn't realize you frequented the café."

Nicole shrugged. "I drop by every now and then."

Alexander also heard her unasked question lingering behind her words. Did Beth know Grace would be at the club tonight? He subtly shook his head and saw her frown. While he could understand her concern for her friend, it wasn't Beth he was worried about. Grace had been in the lifestyle with her husband for years. She wouldn't out her boss. She might, however, try to run again.

"Well, clearly I'm the odd one out here," Daniel said. The two Doms had hit it off right away due to them both having a military background even though Daniel was almost twenty years older than Alexander. Then again, there were days when Alexander felt twenty years older than he actually was. Daniel leaned toward Grace. "It's nice to meet you."

Nicole appeared mildly irritated at the casual way Alexander was handling the situation. Jeff, on the other hand, looked somewhat bored. This new development didn't seem to bother him. Daniel took another long look at Grace. Alexander could only imagine what his friend was thinking.

But the reaction he was most focused on was Grace's. Her breathing had picked up and her fingers were white from pressing them as hard as she could into her legs. He pried her fingers up and laced them with his.

"How did you two meet?" Nicole asked.

Alexander slipped his thumb under the hem of Grace's shirt and began rubbing back and forth. He needed her to relax. "Her husband and I served together."

It was as if a light bulb went off in everyone's head.

"So this is the woman you spent so much time searching for," Daniel said.

Alexander grinned, not breaking the rhythm of his touch against her skin. "She made herself difficult to find."

Grace let her shoulders sag a little. She was paying attention to the conversation even though she hadn't said a word. He hadn't given her any speaking restrictions for tonight other than letting her know that she owed both Justin and Katrina an apology for running out last Friday. Her silence thus far, however, didn't surprise him. His Grace was shy.

Daniel chuckled, either unaware or ignoring Grace's reaction. "I remember."

Conversation turned to a new piece of equipment Katrina had acquired for the club. Alexander was only half paying attention. Grace was still stiff in his arms.

Several more minutes passed and the topic of conversation shifted again, but Grace's posture hadn't changed. He lifted their linked hands and brought them to his lips. She met his gaze. "Would you like something to drink?"

"No, thank you, Sir."

Alexander released her hand and cupped the side of her face. "Tell me what's bothering you."

Her bottom lip trembled. "What if Nicole tells Beth and I lose my job? I don't want to lose my job."

"You're not going to lose your job."

"You don't know that," she whispered.

He stared back at her, both eyebrows raised.

She lowered her gaze. "Sorry, Sir. I didn't mean—"

He tipped her chin up so she was looking at him again. "I'm not upset with you, *gattina*. I do, however, want to understand why you think your boss would fire you for being a member of a kink club when her best friend is one."

That, at least, had her thinking. "I just don't want Beth to think less of me."

"Why would I think less of you?" They hadn't heard the couple approach, but it was obvious at least part of their conversation had been overheard.

Grace stiffened once again in his arms.

"Good evening, Beth. Drew," Alexander said to the new arrivals.

The look on Grace's face was priceless. Her eyes were as big as saucers and her mouth was parted in an *O* shape. He could see the wheels turning in her head. If Beth was here, that meant she was a member as well.

"Alexander." Beth took a seat beside Nicole and tossed a pillow onto the floor near her feet. Without any further instruction, Drew lowered himself down onto the pillow.

A few seconds passed before Alexander brushed his thumb over Grace's lips, drawing her out of her thoughts and back to the present. "I do believe Beth is still waiting on an answer."

Grace swallowed before twisting slightly so she didn't have her back to Beth. "I don't know. I just . . . you never know how people will react." She paused and glanced down at her lap. "I didn't know you were . . ."

"A Domme?" Beth looked mildly amused.

Grace looked at Beth and he saw the beginnings of a smile. "Yeah."

"I was wondering if you were a submissive," Drew said from Beth's feet. It had been interesting watching their relationship evolve over the last two months. "It's good to have another sub to balance things out."

Beth ran a single nail along the back of Drew's neck. Alexander was grateful for Drew's levity. He'd made Grace feel as if she was part of the group.

"Were you and your husband in the lifestyle?" Beth asked Grace.

Grace nodded. "For about ten years."

"That's impressive," Nicole said.

Alexander had to agree. Keeping up any relationship while overseas came with challenges. He couldn't fathom the difficulties of balancing a D/s relationship when one partner was in a war zone.

"It just worked for us." He felt Grace shrink against him and knew she was ready for the spotlight to be off her.

Patting her leg, he indicated he wanted her to stand. "Excuse us. We're going to get something to drink, and then we need to find Katrina and Justin." He used his cane to help him to stand even though he really didn't need it tonight. He'd only brought it as a precaution.

They made their way across the room to the bar. There were several people waiting on drinks, so it was a few minutes before Brandon got around to serving them. "What can I get you?"

Alexander looked at Grace. She was nervous, but he didn't think she was about ready to bolt so that was progress. "What would you like?"

"White wine, please."

He nodded. "One white wine and a water."

Brandon grinned and headed toward the opposite end of the bar.

Once he returned with their drinks, Alexander surveyed the crowd until he located Katrina coming out of the back rooms, most likely from her office.

Alexander placed a hand on Grace's back and began heading in Katrina's direction.

Chapter 14

Grace felt as if everyone was staring at her. They weren't, of course. Most of the club members were engrossed in their own conversations and play. The only person who was focusing on her was Alexander as he eased her across the room toward Katrina.

The club mistress stopped to talk to a couple as they strolled by. She smiled and seemed to be in a good mood.

As the other couple walked away, Alexander picked up their pace and closed the distance. Katrina noticed. She acknowledged Grace, but posed her question to Alexander. "How are you this evening?"

"We're good. You?"

"I can't complain." She chuckled. Then her gaze landed once again on Grace. "I wasn't aware the two of you had been introduced."

"Grace is the one who brought me to St. Louis."

Katrina looked Grace over again as if seeing her with new eyes. "I see."

Did everyone at Serpent's Kiss know about him searching for her? It was beginning to sound like it. And did they know about the letter, too?

Grace didn't get a lot of time to ponder the questions running through her head before Alexander spoke up again. "We've been getting to know each other for the last month, but until I saw her at the club last week, I didn't know she had any interest in BDSM."

The club mistress' mood shifted and she was all business. "I'm guessing you two have come to some sort of an agreement?"

Alexander nodded. "Yes."

He didn't go into any details and Katrina didn't ask. Grace tried to recall if the club had any specific policies when it came to couples who had a negotiated contract but her mind was completely blank.

Pressure against her back had her meeting Alexander's gaze. He looked down at her as if he was waiting for something.

It only took her a few seconds to realize what exactly he was waiting on. She turned to Katrina and lowered her gaze to the floor. "I wanted to apologize again for running out last Friday. It was rude of me."

After a brief interval, Katrina responded. "I accept your apology, Grace." She paused. "I assume the reason for your swift departure had to do with Alexander?"

Grace nodded. "Yes, Mistress. I saw him and panicked."

"Seeing people we know from the outside world inside the club can be jarring. We are making ourselves vulnerable."

"Yes, Ma'am." Grace shifted her weight. "I need to apologize to Justin as well."

"I'm sure he would appreciate that. I do believe he's upstairs helping Cooper tonight."

"Thanks."

Less than a minute later they were heading up to the second floor. A few steps from the top she began to hear sounds of play. They were all muffled, but unmistakable.

Alexander took her hand and led her down the hallway. "We'll kill two birds with one stone while we're up here. After you apologize to Justin, we're going to watch some scenes."

She knew that was part of the plan for tonight, for him to see firsthand what she liked, but being there surrounded by the sounds and the smells of the dungeon had her pulse racing. It didn't mean she wasn't still nervous, but her nerves were being overshadowed by an energy that had her excited to see what the rest of the evening had in store. She just had to get through her apology to Justin first.

The man in question stepped out of one of the rooms with a toy bag in his hand. He walked in the opposite direction, opened a door at the end of the hall, and placed the bag inside. Grace didn't think the door went to a playroom.

Justin saw them when he spun around. He seemed to breathe a sigh of relief at seeing Grace. "I'm glad you came back."

She decided to jump in with both feet. That was why they'd sought him out, after all. "Sir, I wanted to apologize for running off last week. I know I caused you worry and that was not my intention. I saw Alexander and I didn't know what to do, so I ran."

The two Doms exchanged a look. "Thank you for explaining, Grace. And I am glad you're back. I would hate for you to miss out on the fun because of your fear."

"Somehow I don't think that will be permitted anymore, Sir."

"No, *gattina*. It won't," Alexander said.

Justin glanced over his shoulder. "Did you two want a room? There's one down the hall that's available."

"Thank you," Alexander said. "But we'll just be observing tonight."

"Let me or Cooper know if you need anything," Justin said before going to assist someone in room number five.

Alexander didn't give her any time to let her mind wander. He headed in the opposite direction Justin had gone and stopped in front of the large viewing window of room number one. The couple inside looked to be finishing up a scene. She lay curled up on her side with him holding her from behind. It was such a tender moment. Grace felt as if they were intruding.

After a few moments, they moved on to room three. A man was chained to the ceiling, his cock and balls covered in clothespins. She'd had clothespins attached to various parts of her body before and she could see the tension in the man's arms as the woman placed weights through tiny holes in the clothespins that were attached to his balls.

They didn't stay in front of that room for long. Although watching a scene like that didn't really bother her, it didn't do anything for her sexually either. Alexander seemed to realize that.

It took them two more tries before they came across a scene that had the muscles in her abdomen clenching. The woman was on her knees, clamps with a long chain attached dangling from her nipples, while she sucked on the man's cock. He had her hair gathered into a ponytail and used it to guide her movements. It was so erotic that

Grace felt herself getting wet.

Alexander moved to stand behind her, but Grace barely noticed until he reached up under her skirt and ran his thumb over her clit through the thin material of her panties. She couldn't help the moan that escaped her throat. "You like that, don't you? Seeing her suck his cock?"

There was no point in denying it. "Yes."

He brushed his thumb against her clit again. And again. Her breathing began to pick up and she almost spilled her wine.

Alexander removed it from her grasp and placed it on the window ledge before returning his attention to her. "This is what you wanted, wasn't it? For me to touch you?" he whispered in her ear as she continued to watch the scene in front of her.

Before she knew it, she could feel her orgasm approaching. Alexander had the front of her skirt pulled up and wasn't doing anything to hide what he was doing to her. Something inside her said she should be embarrassed, but it did nothing to curb her arousal.

"Come for me, *gattina*. Let go and come."

She closed her eyes and imagined that it was her in there on her knees with Alexander's cock in her mouth. A fresh wave of arousal leaked out and her breath hitched. She wanted to know what he tasted like—what he felt like—between her lips.

He moved her panties out of the way and stroked her clit without any barrier. Between that and her imagination, she was a goner. Her orgasm rippled through her, causing her knees to buckle.

Alexander steadied her, his arm wrapped tight around her waist.

It took her a few minutes to recover and when she did, she realized they had an audience. Justin, Cooper, and two other couples were watching. The embarrassment took up residence in her cheeks and she buried her head in Alexander's chest.

He kissed the top of her head and removed his fingers from her panties, ignoring the onlookers. "That was beautiful, *gattina*. You have no reason to be embarrassed. In fact, you should be quite proud of yourself. Every man who witnessed that is having to adjust himself to make more room in his pants."

His statement did nothing to curb her discomfort. In the moment, it hadn't mattered, but now that her arousal had faded, she couldn't believe she had done that. "Are they gone?"

Alexander chuckled. "Everyone except Justin and Cooper, yes."

Grace groaned. She was not an exhibitionist.

Then she remembered how hard she'd come.

Maybe she was an exhibitionist. Or maybe it was Alexander. He brought things out in her, had her thinking of things she hadn't before.

He reached for her wineglass and handed it to her. "Let's head back downstairs. I want to talk to Daniel before we call it a night."

***

Grace spent the rest of their time at Serpent's Kiss sitting on his lap. He kept his hand on her leg, tracing little circles with his fingers. Every now and then she would squirm when he would inch his way a little higher. He wasn't sure if she was trying to get away or urge him to move his hand farther up her leg.

He'd told Grace he wanted to talk to Daniel, which was true, but he'd also hoped to talk to Beth again. Unfortunately, Beth and Drew were nowhere in sight. When he'd asked about them, Nicole said they'd cut out early because they both had to work in the morning. Considering they couldn't have been there more than an hour, Alexander wondered if it had more to do with Drew's comment than them having to work the next day.

Nicole and Jeff excused themselves and headed upstairs to play, leaving Alexander, Grace, and Daniel alone. Daniel was in real estate and Alexander wanted to get a feel for what was out there in respects to office buildings he could use to set up a practice. Even though it could take up to a year for his license to come through, he didn't want to wait until the last minute to start looking for a space to rent.

"I was wondering if you could put together some numbers for me for commercial buildings."

"Did your license come through already?" Daniel asked before taking a sip of his drink.

Alexander shook his head. "I just want to stay on top of things and see what's out there. Besides, it will take a while to get things up and running before I can start seeing patients. I can get all the back end stuff out of the way in the meantime."

"You're thinking ahead." Daniel grinned. "I wish more of my clients thought like you did. You'd be amazed how many come in needing something yesterday."

"I prefer to have a game plan. I can improvise when I have to, but things go much smoother when there's a plan in place."

Daniel lifted his glass in a mock salute. "I couldn't agree more." He took another sip of his drink. "Did you want to stop by tomorrow and take a look at the listings?"

"Sure. What time?"

"Around noon? We could make it a working lunch."

With plans made, Alexander decided it was time to get Grace home. She had to be at work early tomorrow and she needed her rest.

When they arrived at her house, he got out and walked her to her door. Unlike the night before, he followed her inside.

Grace placed her keys on the side table and removed her coat. She barely got it off before he backed her against the wall and covered her mouth with his.

Her response was immediate. She circled her arms around his neck and kissed him back for all she was worth. His little kitten was worked up.

Alexander pushed her skirt up and tugged her panties down, letting them fall to the floor. He wasted no time touching her pussy. All his teasing earlier had him hard as a rock, but what he wanted more than anything was to touch her, and lucky for him that seemed to be what Grace wanted as well.

She bucked her hips, pushing against his hand, and he slipped two fingers inside. They slid easily in and out as he mimicked the rhythm with his tongue. It felt so good to finally be able to touch her like this after he'd been dreaming about it for weeks.

He cupped her breast with his free hand and felt her pebbled nipple press against his palm. As much as he loved her shirt, it needed to go. "Take your shirt off. It's in my way."

Grace grabbed the hem of her top—no hesitation at all in her movements—and wiggled it up her torso and over her head. He wasted no time palming her tits and teasing them with his fingers. In the not too distant future, he imagined spending hours paying homage to them.

For now, though, he contented himself with being able to touch her freely. He squeezed one of her tits, lifting it, and brought his lips down, sucking it into his mouth. Feeling her flesh on his tongue had him groaning. He felt as if his cock were going to explode out of his pants.

She rode his fingers while he licked and sucked on her lovely tits. It seriously didn't get much better than this. He could feel her arousal coating his fingers as he continued to pump in and out of her. Grace's head was thrown back, her mouth open slightly, and her chest rose and fell with her rapid breathing. He wanted to take a picture so he could keep the sight of her like this with him forever.

"Sir?" Her voice was breathy.

He eased his fingers in and out of her a few more times before answering. "Yes?"

"Sir, may I come?" He could hear the pleading in her voice. She was close.

Alexander took her nipple between his teeth and tugged slightly. "Not quite yet, *gattina*."

She dug her nails into his shoulders as if she were trying to hold onto something to keep herself from coming.

He licked her nipple, easing the pain he'd inflicted, before lowering himself down to his knees. It wasn't as easy a position for him as it used to be, but for her it was worth it. He placed his free hand over her abdomen and used his fingers to spread her open. Without preamble, he went in.

A whimper left her lips as he circled her clit with his tongue. Grace fisted her fingers in his hair, looking for purchase but couldn't seem to find it. Her legs began to tremble, and then a shudder went through her entire body. He knew she wasn't going to be able to hold on much longer no matter how hard she tried.

Alexander gazed up at her from his perch between her legs. Her eyes were unfocused, glassy, and her skin was flushed, not from embarrassment as it so often was, but from how turned on she was. "You may come, *gattina*."

Unlike before at the club where it had still taken her several minutes to fall over that peak, this time it was as if he'd flipped a switch. A scream came from deep in her throat and a shockwave rippled through her body until she slid down the wall onto the floor beside him.

He twisted around and positioned her onto his lap. The floor wasn't the most comfortable place in the world to sit, but he couldn't carry her with his leg and he didn't think she would be able to walk at the moment.

She burrowed against his chest, her fingers outlining the buttons on his shirt as her breathing returned to normal. His erection pressed against her thigh, demanding attention, but he did his best to ignore it. Tonight was about her. He'd get his pleasure, just not now.

"How are you feeling?" he asked once he was sure she was fully aware of her surroundings again.

She snorted, which made him smile. "Spent."

Alexander laughed. "That's good. It means you should sleep tonight."

"Yeah." Then she looked up at him through hooded lashes. "But what about you?"

"Don't you worry about me. I'm fine."

"But—"

He placed a finger over her lips. "I'm fine. Nothing a cold shower won't cure."

The look on her face told him she didn't understand. In a way, he didn't either, but something was holding him back. He kept telling himself it was her that he was waiting on, but was it really? He didn't know the answer and that bothered him.

Instead of delving into the whys, he lowered his head and captured her lips with his once more. This time the kiss was soft and deep, and he hoped conveyed a fraction of what he felt for her. Something might be holding him back but it had nothing to do with his feelings for Grace.

She sank into the kiss, holding tight to his shirt as they let their tongues explore.

As much as he didn't want to, eventually he had to break the kiss. "You need to get to bed. You have work tomorrow."

"I know." She looked up at him and worried her bottom lip with her teeth.

"What is it?" he asked.

Grace averted her gaze, choosing to look at the hardwood floor instead of at him. He was about to demand she tell him what was wrong when she asked, "Will you stay?"

It took him a moment to process what she said. "You want me to spend the night?"

She nodded and met his gaze.

"Grace, I don't—"

"Please?"

He looked into her eyes and knew he couldn't say no even though he wasn't sure it was the best idea, not when his cock was straining against his pants as it was. Would he be able to keep his hands to himself if he was lying beside her all night? He didn't know the answer to that. And more importantly, did he want to?

Alexander took her face in his hands and placed a chaste kiss on her lips. "Okay. I'll stay."

Chapter 15

Grace grabbed her shirt and panties from where they'd been discarded on the floor, and they headed upstairs to her bedroom. Inviting him to spend the night wasn't something she'd thought through. She hadn't wanted him to go. That was all she knew.

As they walked up the stairs, she could tell his leg was beginning to bother him but she didn't say anything. Every time she did he shrugged it off and told her not to worry about it. But wasn't it her responsibility as his sub to take care of him? She wanted to care for his needs and that included easing his physical pain if she could.

"You take the bathroom first," he said when they entered her room.

She nodded and padded into the bathroom. As she readied herself for bed, Grace couldn't help but wonder if the reason Alexander was holding back was because he thought she wasn't ready. And while she could understand that given the conversations they'd had in the past, after tonight she realized she was. More than ready. Even after two orgasms her body was humming.

When she reentered her bedroom she was naked. Alexander was sitting on the end of her bed. She saw how his gaze roamed over her curves and how his pants were still tented with his very obvious erection. He stood, but he didn't approach her. Instead, he made his way into the bathroom.

He seemed to be attracted to her. So what was the problem?

The thought occurred to her that maybe she needed to make the first move, but that didn't sit well with her. She didn't like to be the aggressor in the bedroom. That was the whole point of being submissive. She wanted her partner to take the lead, to take control.

Images of Alexander hovering over her had her blood pressure spiking again. What was she going to do if he didn't take her soon?

"Do you want to put some pajamas on?" She jumped a little, not realizing he'd walked back into the room.

Grace figured this was a good time to push things without actually doing anything. The decision would still be his. "Do you want me to?"

He seemed to contemplate it for a moment, and then said, "I think that might be best."

Disappointment filled her as she went to her dresser and pulled out a T-shirt and some shorts. If she had any lingerie she would have worn that, but Kurt hadn't liked her in anything when he was home, and since he'd been gone she'd reverted back to her old standby.

Alexander waited for her to climb into bed before stripping down to his boxer briefs and joining her. He wrapped his arm around her waist and pulled her close.

Grace lay there for several minutes listening to their breathing. He was still awake. She could tell. And even though she could no longer see his erection, she imagined he was still worked up. He hadn't been in the bathroom long enough to take that cold shower he'd mentioned.

"Sir?"

"Yes?"

She scraped her teeth along her bottom lip, anxiety gnawing at her stomach. "I want you to know that I'm ready for us to have sex." Grace blew out a shaky breath. "I didn't . . . I didn't want you to be holding back because you thought I wasn't."

He combed his fingers through her hair. "I'll take that under advisement. Now get some sleep."

Grace frowned, but knew it wouldn't do any good to try and change his mind. At least not tonight. She closed her eyes and tried to enjoy the fact that she'd won one battle tonight. He was there, in her bed.

The next morning she woke up alone. After glancing around the room, she noticed Alexander's shirt was still folded neatly on the dresser. Grace didn't think he would leave without saying goodbye, but for a moment doubt had crept in. She immediately felt guilty.

Alexander came strolling into the room, carrying a tray of food. He'd put his pants back on from last night. "You're awake."

"Yeah." Grace looked toward the window. It was still dark out. At least she hadn't overslept. "What time is it?"

"Five thirty. I was just coming to wake you up." He placed the tray on the nightstand beside her bed.

She sat up, resting her back against the headboard. "You made me breakfast?"

He grinned and his eyes lit up, pulling her in as they so often did. "Did you miss the part about me insisting you eat three meals a day?"

"No, Sir."

His gaze softened and he brushed the tips of his fingers along the side of her face. "As much as I love hearing you call me *Sir*, you don't have to when we're not playing. Alexander is fine."

She picked up the half a bagel he'd brought her. "Sorry. I guess it's habit. I always called Kurt *Sir* or *Master* unless we were around others who weren't in the lifestyle."

"We're still feeling things out. It takes time. But I wanted you to know I don't expect it or require it unless we're playing."

Grace nodded and took a bite of her bagel. "Thank you for breakfast."

He kissed her forehead and stood. "Anytime."

She watched him put on his shirt, socks, and shoes. "Are you leaving?"

"You need to finish getting ready for work and I want to get a workout in before I meet Daniel," he said as he finished tying his shoes.

"Okay."

Alexander walked back to her side and tipped her chin up until she was looking at him. "I'll see you tonight." He ran his thumb over her bottom lip then turned and left, leaving her to finish her breakfast alone.

Tommy was his usual perky self when Grace arrived at the café. He prattled on about the club he and his girlfriend went to the night before, going on and on about how great the DJ was. Grace was only half listening. Beth had smiled at her when Grace first got there, but other than that she'd been fairly quiet. Then again, Tommy hadn't really stopped talking.

It wasn't until several hours later when Tommy was busy manning the front register that she found herself alone in the back with Beth. The morning rush was over and they still had some time before people began coming in for lunch. Beth poured herself a cup of coffee. "Want some?"

"No, thanks." Grace bit the inside of her cheek to keep from adding *ma'am*.

Beth nodded, brought her coffee over, and sat down. She tilted her chin in the direction of a nearby stool. "Might as well take a load off while you can."

Grace took a seat.

"You know, there's no need to be nervous or uncomfortable. I'm still the same person I was two days ago and so are you," Beth said.

Grace thought she should be honest. "I feel like I should start calling you *ma'am*."

Beth snorted. "I wonder what Tommy would think of that."

"Does Tommy know?"

"About our lifestyle?" Beth kept her wording vague in case they were overheard. "No. And to my knowledge he and his girlfriend lead a very vanilla life."

Grace hadn't met Tommy's girlfriend, so she'd have to take Beth's word for it.

Beth placed her coffee mug on the counter and met Grace's gaze. "Nothing has to change. At least while we're at the café. I'm still Beth, your boss, and you're still Grace, my employee."

"I guess I wasn't sure if . . . how . . ."

"We're just two people sitting here having coffee." Beth smirked. "Or one person having coffee and the other keeping her company."

Grace grinned. "It's not weird for you at all?"

"Not really," Beth said, picking her mug back up and taking a sip. "And it shouldn't be for you either. You have nothing to be ashamed about. It's part of who you are just like it's part of who I am."

"You don't think any less of me?" Grace felt guilty asking it, but she needed to know.

"Do you think I think less of Drew?" Beth asked instead.

"No."

"Then why would I think less of you?" Her boss leaned forward and placed a comforting hand on Grace's arm. "I've known you had submissive tendencies since the day I met you. It didn't bother me then and it doesn't bother me now. In fact, I'm glad to see you embracing who you are."

Grace never got the chance to respond since Tommy burst through the doors, holding up a piece of paper. "We've got a large order and they need it ASAP."

Without a word, she and Beth hopped off their stools and got to work.

***

Daniel's office was downtown near the Arch, which would have made it easy to find even if Alexander hadn't had GPS. When he walked in, all the desks were empty and there was not a person in sight. He checked his watch. It was eleven fifty-six. "Hello?"

A few seconds later a young man who looked to be right out of college popped his head out of a room on the left. "Hello. Can I help you?"

"I'm looking for Daniel."

The young man opened his mouth, but at the sound of someone else entering the room, he turned, leaving his words unsaid.

Daniel strolled into the main room with a folder tucked into the crook of his arm. "Right on time."

"Years of being made to run miles for being even a minute late is a hard habit to break."

His friend chuckled. "One of the many things I don't miss about the military." Then he addressed the young man. "I'll be gone for a couple of hours. If the Robinsons call, let them know I still haven't heard anything back."

"Will do."

Daniel plucked his jacket from the coatrack near the entrance and they headed out. "There's a nice bistro around the corner that recently opened up."

"Sounds good."

The bistro was close enough to walk to, so Alexander left his car in front of Daniel's office. It was a little windy, but at least the sun was shining. Considering the amount of times he'd been deployed in the desert, the change in temperature was still a bit of a shock to his system.

Once they took their seats, Daniel handed Alexander the folder he'd brought with him. "I spent the morning putting together some listings I thought might interest you. All of them have easy access to the highway. I figured accessibility would be important."

"Yes. Very." Alexander took his time going over the locations Daniel had put together. There were close to a dozen, but only two piqued his interest. They were both the right size, in great locations, and the prices were reasonable.

Their server brought their food, and Alexander set the paperwork aside to dig in.

"What do you think? Is there anything in there you think could work?" Daniel asked.

Alexander wiped his hands, flipped the folder around, and pushed it across the table toward Daniel. "I think these two might work."

Daniel gave the listings a casual glance. "Would you like me to see if I can set up a time where you could take a look at them in person?" he asked before going back to his food.

"That would be great."

The two of them concentrated on their meal for several minutes. Alexander had to admit that the food was good. He was going to have to bring Grace.

"How did Grace like the club last night?" Daniel asked. "She seemed a bit unnerved around Beth."

"Beth's her boss and she wasn't expecting to see her there." Alexander shrugged. "You know how it is."

"I do. And I also know it's usually a much harder transition for subs than it is for us."

Alexander nodded, but didn't say anything more. All things considered, Grace had done extremely well. She hadn't run, so that was a plus. He also had confidence that Beth would try and smooth things over with Grace. The conversation he and Beth had in regards to Grace reassured him that Beth felt almost as protective of Grace as he did.

"This isn't only an arrangement for you, is it?" The question came out of the blue and when Alexander looked at his friend he realized that he must have let his mind wander for longer than he thought.

There was no reason for him to lie, but for some reason he didn't want to talk about his feelings for Grace. Not even with Daniel. "Grace and I are still feeling things out. In many ways she's still mourning her husband."

Daniel studied him for a long moment, and then dropped the subject. They spent the rest of their meal talking about the two listings Alexander indicated he wanted to take a look at. It was a nice way to pass the time on a Saturday afternoon.

After leaving Daniel's office, Alexander went back to his apartment. The temptation to drop by the café to see Grace had been great, but he'd resisted. He didn't want to crowd her. Especially since he had his own shit to figure out. Like why he hadn't made love to her last night.

Thinking about lying in bed with her—her soft body curled next to his—had the muscles in his groin tightening. He wanted her. There was no doubt about that.

He kicked off his shoes and tossed his keys onto the counter. Desire was not what was stopping him. That much he knew.

For a month he'd contented himself with being her friend. Now he had the green light for more and he was getting cold feet. It made no logical sense, but as a doctor Alexander knew that often emotions weren't logical. In fact, most of the time they were downright illogical. He'd told Grace as much on more than one occasion.

Alexander sat on his couch and turned on the television. Some woman came on the screen. She was talking, but his mind was elsewhere.

Without even thinking about it, he pulled his phone out of his pocket and checked it to see if Grace had texted him. She hadn't. He could only hope that meant things had gone well and she hadn't run out on Beth and her job.

Unable to sit still, Alexander turned off the television, shoved his phone back in his pocket, stood, and scooped up his keys before heading toward the door. If he had time to kill, he was going to use it for something productive. Even if he couldn't wrap his head around what exactly was stopping him from claiming what was now by all rights his, he could at least be her Dom.

With the help of his phone, he found a store nearby that carried lingerie and club attire. The place was full of leather, lace, and satin, as well as a wide variety of sex toys. As tempting as the toys were, he steered clear of that section for the moment and focused on what he'd come there for: an outfit for Grace.

"Can I help you find something?" a woman in her twenties asked from behind the counter.

"I wanted to see what kind of club wear you carry."

She walked around the counter. "Our club line is back here."

Alexander followed her to the back of the store. There were skirts, tops, and even high heels that would make Grace almost as tall as he was. "Thanks."

"Anytime. Let me know if you need any help." She gave him a long look that made him think she was talking about more than help with clothing choices, and then made her way to the front of the store again.

He found a few items he thought looked interesting. One was a red dress that had a similar neckline to the top Grace had worn the night before only it dipped even lower. Alexander was already fantasizing about pushing the draping fabric out of the way to free her tits so he could play with them.

Slinging the dress over his arm, he continued looking. Although he had every intention to see her in that dress, it wasn't exactly what he wanted her to wear tonight.

It took him a while longer before he came across the outfit he wanted. He ran his fingers along the barely there hem and imagined Grace's ass poking out from beneath.

Taking the outfits he'd chosen to the front, he swiftly paid for them and was on his way. He needed to get home, shower, and change before picking up Grace. Thinking about Grace in the clothes had Alexander needing to adjust himself several times during the drive home. He couldn't wait to see her in the little skirt and top he'd picked out. The question was how long would she stay in them.

Chapter 16

Grace had to admit she was feeling a little better about things by the time she said goodbye to Beth and Tommy in the parking lot. She figured she'd most likely see Beth at the club later. Their talk had helped ease a lot of Grace's fears.

As soon as she arrived home, Grace raced upstairs to her bathroom and stripped. Last night she'd been full of nervous energy, still afraid on some level that she'd embarrass her new Dom. Tonight she was thinking more along the lines of seduction.

She reached for a towel as she stepped out of the shower and began mentally cataloguing what she had in her closet. There was a midnight blue dress that was kind of sexy, and a green and black skirt she could pair with a corset. The skirt wasn't overly short, but it did hug her curves.

Wrapping the towel around her torso, she headed into her bedroom. It would be so much easier if Alexander was there. He'd tell her exactly what she should wear and she wouldn't have to be worrying about it.

Thinking about Alexander had her picking up her cell to see how much time she had before he was due to arrive. It ended up being a good thing she checked her phone because he'd sent her a text fifteen minutes ago.

Wear something comfortable tonight. You will be changing

at the club. – Alexander

Well, she guessed that solved that problem. She quickly typed back to let him know she'd gotten his message.

Yes, Sir. – Grace

So instead of worrying so much about finding the right club outfit, Grace spent a little extra time making sure everything else was perfect. She shaved and trimmed her pubic hair, did a swift pass over her legs with a razor, and plucked some unruly hairs from her eyebrows.

When she was satisfied with her grooming, she went back to her closet and selected her favorite jeans. They fit her like a glove and made her backside look really good. She hoped he liked them.

At six she opened her door to Alexander and let him inside. He closed the door behind him, and then raked his gaze over her figure before making eye contact. "Have I seen you in those jeans before?"

"Once, I think."

He motioned with his finger that she should turn around.

Grace obediently faced away from him, secretly pleased at his reaction. She sucked in a breath when she felt his hand cup her ass. He massaged the soft flesh before going lower. With gentle pressure that only made her want more, he ran two fingers up and down the seam between her legs.

His breath ghosted over her ear as he leaned in. "I like these jeans a lot. You should wear them more often."

She swallowed as the ache inside began to build. "Yes, Sir."

Then his hands and his breath were gone. "We need to get going. I want to get to Serpent's Kiss by seven."

He removed her coat from the closet and held it out for her while she put it on. Kurt used to do that for her as well. It was something so small and she hadn't realized she'd missed that part of being taken care of, but she did. He even pulled her hair out from the collar for her. "Thank you, Sir."

Alexander grinned and opened the door.

They ended up having dinner at a Mexican restaurant. Neither one of them had ever been there before, but it was good. Nothing out of this world amazing, but it had the usual standard fare.

Dinner did, however, take them longer than anticipated and they didn't pull into the parking lot outside Serpent's Kiss until almost seven thirty. She knew he had wanted to be there earlier, but she saw no sign of agitation. He seemed to just accept it.

He came around to help her out of the car before reaching into the back seat to retrieve his cane and a bag. She guessed the bag contained whatever she was to wear.

There was a different girl manning the coatroom tonight. She greeted them when they entered and took their coats. "Enjoy your evening."

The first thing Grace noticed when they walked into the club was that there were a lot more people there tonight than there had been last night. She wondered if it was like that everywhere—where Saturday nights were busier than Friday nights—or if this was an anomaly.

Grace didn't get a lot of time to contemplate that before Alexander handed her the bag. "You know where the locker rooms are?"

She nodded. "Katrina . . . Mistress Katrina showed me during my tour."

He didn't seem overly bothered by her slip. It was playtime. Titles mattered. "I'll be at the bar getting us some waters. Come find me when you've changed."

"Yes, Sir."

The locker rooms were at the back of the club, which meant she had to maneuver her way through the main floor of the club in order to get to them. A few people nodded in her direction as she weaved her way through the crowd, but no one spoke to her. In any other setting that might seem odd, but here it didn't. Especially if they'd seen her come in with Alexander.

She passed through the bathroom to the women's locker room. Metal lockers lined one wall. Grace placed her bag on a bench in front of one of the empty lockers and began removing her clothes.

"You're Grace, right?"

Grace had already removed her shirt and bra, leaving her standing there topless, but she didn't want to be impolite and ignore the woman. "Yeah." Grace cleared her throat, resisting the urge to cover up. "Yes. I'm Grace."

The woman held out her hand. "I'm Ali. We met last night." At Grace's confused look, the woman added, "I was in the lobby. I took your coat."

At that, it clicked. "Oh yes. Yes. I remember."

"Anyway, I just wanted to say hi and welcome you to the club. I know it can be somewhat overwhelming at first, but it really is a great place. Mistress Katrina makes sure of it."

"Thanks."

"I'll let you get back to changing. I wouldn't want to get you in trouble with your Dom." Ali winked.

Her reference to Alexander had her wondering. "Does everyone already know I have a Dom, then?" Not that she minded, but they'd only been there one night.

Ali chuckled. "Pretty much. You'll find that word travels fast around here." With that, Ali was off.

Grace shook her head and went back to what she was doing. She finished removing her clothes and went to see what was inside the bag.

There was a blue skirt—if it could be called that. Grace held it up against her waist. It barely teased her thighs. There was no way it could cover her butt, at least not completely. The top wasn't much better. It was a lace corset. She already knew her nipples would be visible.

Trying not to think about it, she put on the outfit. It was what Alexander wanted and she would be a good sub and do as he asked. Besides, she had said she wanted to seduce him.

Taking a look in the mirror, she figured this might do it. She'd been right about the skirt. The bottom curve of her ass was exposed. He hadn't given her any panties and knew better than to put on the ones she'd been wearing. That meant anytime she bent over her pussy would be on display.

Thinking about that did the opposite of what she'd expected. She could already feel herself getting wet.

Grace pressed her thighs together, giving herself a little friction, but it did nothing to ease the ache she was experiencing. She knew better than to do more than that. Her Dom would not be pleased if she made herself orgasm.

Placing her things, along with the now empty bag, into the locker, Grace took the key and headed out into the club to find Alexander. She tried to ignore the looks she got as she made her way over to the bar. It made her want to pull her skirt down, but then she remembered there was nothing to pull down.

Alexander sat at one end of the bar, chatting with someone.

Their backs were turned, so she was a few feet away when he spotted her. A smile that was full of pride graced his features. As uncomfortable as she was, Grace was happy she'd pleased him.

The man turned and she realized it was Justin. He gave her a once-over and she didn't miss the male appreciation in his eyes.

"Grace." Alexander held out his hand, beckoning her to his side.

She took his hand and he nudged her between his thighs, her ass pressed against his groin, as he resumed his conversation with Justin. They were talking about cars. From the sound of it, Justin ran or owned his own mechanics shop. Grace knew nothing about cars, as was evident in her having to call Alexander when her battery died.

As time went on, Alexander's hands began to creep. At first it was a brush of her leg. Then it was more deliberate as he dipped his fingers up under her skirt and began playing with her right there in front of Justin.

***

Grace had marked exhibitionism as a soft limit on her paperwork, but after getting her off the night before, Alexander had a feeling she was more into other people watching than she thought she was. He'd been teasing her for the last twenty minutes as he talked to Justin, priming her, and Justin was enjoying the show.

She let out a soft purr when he finally touched her and tilted her hips up toward his fingers. Alexander used his other hand to steady her hips. He wasn't ready for her to come quite yet.

"How long have you had your shop?" Alexander asked, acting as if he wasn't fingering his girl's wet pussy.

"It'll be eight years in March." Justin kept glancing down. "I'm thinking about opening up a new location about an hour outside of the city, but I haven't found the perfect location."

"I understand. I've recently started looking for an office building. Once my license processes through the state I want to get a practice up and running. Pushing papers all day isn't my idea of fun."

Justin lifted his glass. "I hear that. I detest paperwork, but unfortunately it's a necessary evil of being a business owner."

Alexander curled his fingers upward, grazing Grace's G-spot. She dug her nails into his thigh, causing him to harden more than he already was. "Why don't you hire an office manager? Help take some of the pressure off." At the word pressure, he shifted his hand again so with each stroke he was applying pressure to her clit. He heard her suck in a breath and her chest began to rise and fall rapidly. She was getting close.

"I may have to look into that, but for now I'm focused on expanding."

"Daniel's in real estate. Have you spoken to him?" Alexander asked as he continued to torture the woman in his arms. The sounds coming out of her were making it difficult to concentrate on anything but her.

"No, but that's a good idea."

Grace's nails were digging holes in Alexander's jeans and her nipples looked as if they were hard against their lace confines. He wanted to take them between his lips and suck on them until he heard her scream.

He ran the tip of his tongue along the rim of her ear, and then gave it a playful bite. "Would you like to come, *gattina*?"

"Yes. Yes, Sir," she said, her chest heaving.

Alexander inched her skirt up a little more, exposing her completely to Justin before continuing his assault on her clit. "Justin's going to watch your pretty pussy come for me, so don't hold back. Show him how much you like it when I fuck you with my fingers."

Grace sucked in a harsh breath as he gave up any pretense of teasing. She bucked her hips and threw her head back against Alexander's shoulder. He felt her inner muscles clench and release several times before a whine rose from her throat as she came.

Justin wasn't the only one to witness Grace's orgasm, but other than a smirk or two from a few Doms and an envious look from a couple of nearby subs, everyone else in the club continued with what they were doing. It wasn't as if a sub being made to come on the main floor of the club was unusual. Serpent's Kiss was a kink club after all.

Alexander removed his fingers and reached for a napkin from the bar. As he was wiping the evidence of Grace's orgasm from his hands, Brandon placed a fresh bottle of water in front of him. "I figured the lady might be thirsty."

Grace heard Brandon and opened her eyes. It was clear by the look on his face that he'd enjoyed the show. Alexander saw the blush begin to rise on her cheeks.

"There's no reason to be embarrassed, Grace," Justin said. "That was lovely to watch."

"He's right," Brandon assured her. "There isn't anything better than watching a woman truly lose herself in pleasure."

Alexander twisted the lid off the water bottle and handed it to Grace. She took it and brought it to her lips, not responding to Justin or Brandon's comments. He could tell they were both highly amused by her shyness. He had to admit it was extremely appealing. Even more so since minutes ago she'd been coming on his hand, not caring who was watching. It was only when the haze of her arousal faded that her timid nature took hold again.

Eventually Brandon got called away and Justin excused himself, leaving them alone. She continued to sip her water, her eyes downcast.

"Talk to me."

"You like making me come when others are watching." She spoke the words so softly he barely heard them.

He made her stand up and turned her to face him. "Yes, I do. And you like it, too." Alexander dared her to deny it.

She picked at the label on her water bottle. "I've never . . . before."

"You've never been made to orgasm in front of other people before or you've never wanted to?" he asked.

It took her a moment to answer. "Both."

Alexander took the bottle of water from her hand and placed it on the bar before pulling her against him. He slipped his hand under her skirt and palmed her ass. "I've never made a sub come before an audience either before last night."

Her eyes widened. He'd shocked her. Well, there were a lot of things she didn't know about him just as there were many things he didn't know about her. They had time to figure it out. He didn't plan on going anywhere.

"Then why . . ."

"Last night was an experiment of sorts. You'd put it on your list as a soft limit and it was something I was curious about. Seeing you so worked up watching that couple made me want to test the waters. I'd half expected you to use your safeword." He'd been almost certain of it. How wrong he'd been.

"It didn't even cross my mind." He could tell how hard it was for her to admit that.

He grinned and rubbed his thumb along the side of her face. "I know."

Her blush, which had been fading, bloomed once again.

Alexander chuckled. She was too adorable when she was like this. "Go to the locker room and get your things. I'm taking you home."

He released her and she took a step backward. "Do you want me to change?"

"No. Leave your outfit on. I'll remove it later."

She nodded and hurried off to the locker room. It was only a little after nine. The night was still young. He'd thought about staying, taking her upstairs and getting a room, but he figured he'd pushed her enough for one night. Besides, he was ready to have some alone time with her. He had some boundaries of his own that needed pushing.

Chapter 17

Grace still couldn't believe she'd done that. And even more amazing was that she'd enjoyed it. The embarrassment had only kicked in later. It hadn't even occurred to her to use her safeword. Not once.

That didn't, however, make it any easier exiting the club and knowing everyone had been watching her. Even Ali, the woman who'd introduced herself to Grace in the locker room, waved goodbye to her from across the room with a knowing smile.

Alexander helped her into his car, making sure she was covered. Not only would it be indecent exposure, but it was also quite chilly. She huddled in her coat as he drove through the downtown streets toward her house. A few miles from their destination, he turned the heat on full blast.

"Thanks." She held her hands up to the vents, trying to warm up.

He reached over and squeezed her knee in response. The gesture had her body beginning to warm in a complete different way. It didn't matter that there had been nothing sexual about it. Her body reacted to his touch.

Like the night before, Alexander waited for her to unlock the door and then followed her into her house. It didn't feel odd at all for him to be there, and the way he casually hung up both their coats spoke to how comfortable he was as well. Realizing that brought her up a little short.

"What is it?" he asked when he noticed her staring.

"Sorry. I was just thinking how comfortable it feels having you here."

He closed the small distance between them and ran his hands up and down the outsides of her arms. "Does that upset you?"

"It should," she whispered. Then she met his gaze and asked, "Shouldn't it?"

Alexander brought his hands up to cup her face. "There's no wrong answer here, Grace. You feel how you feel."

They didn't appear to be playing now. This wasn't a Dom talking to his sub. This was Alexander being there for her and helping her deal with the complicated emotions that kept bubbling up inside like he had from that first day. She had no idea why he put up with her. Without thinking about anything else except what she wanted in that moment, Grace rose on her tiptoes and pressed her lips to his.

Her eyes fluttered open to meet his gaze as she pulled back. Alexander eased his palms up her arms, following the curve of her neck until he bracketed her face with his hands. He rubbed his thumbs along her cheeks several times before bringing his mouth down to cover hers.

Unlike her chaste peck on the lips, his kiss was firm and demanding. Her Dom was back. He held her face in the exact position he desired as he took what he wanted. Grace forgot about everything else and allowed herself to get lost in his kiss.

It ended as abruptly as it had started it. He released his hold on her so quickly she struggled to keep herself upright. "Upstairs. Now."

Grace only paused for a moment to catch her breath before scurrying up the stairs. She didn't waste any time upon entering her bedroom before taking up position on the floor, making sure her legs were spread wide so he would know she was ready and willing for whatever he had in store.

Several minutes passed. She heard him moving around downstairs, most likely making sure everything was locked up tight. Grace hoped that meant he planned on spending the night again. When she finally heard him on the stairs, her heart began pounding in her ears. She focused on taking deep, calming breaths, trying to get herself in the correct mindset.

The sound of his footfalls stopped when he reached her bedroom. She knew he could see her kneeling there, waiting for him, but he didn't approach her. Not right away.

Right when she thought she wouldn't be able to take it anymore, he walked up to her, gathered her hair into one of his large hands, and tilted her head back, forcing her to look up at him. The sensation sent tingles all the way down to her toes.

He traced the outline of her lips with his free hand before reaching for the snap on his jeans. Within seconds his pants were down around his ankles and he was stepping out of them. Something flashed through his eyes for a split second, and then it was gone. He didn't give her time to contemplate it before moving forward and pressing his cock to her lips.

Grace relaxed her jaw. Her mouth fell open, inviting him in.

As he pushed inside, Alexander closed his eyes as if what he was doing took great concentration. She ran her tongue along the underside of his head and she heard a sound she didn't quite understand come out of him. She looked up to find him staring down at her.

He brought his hand up to her mouth, cupping her face. It was a very loving gesture—in contrast to the emotions she saw racing across his face.

Then he spoke, his voice raspy. "Tap on my wrist if you need me to slow down."

It was all the warning she got before he thrust his hips, sending him deeper. His cock bumped the back of her throat before retreating. She had to remember to relax her throat and breathe. It had been a long time since she'd done this for a man. He repeated the motion over and over again as she massaged her tongue along his salty flesh, wanting to increase his pleasure.

The closer he got, the more his fingers flexed in her hair. He was watching her with an intensity that had every muscle in her lower half pulsing with anticipation and satisfaction. In that moment her only focus was on serving him, and that brought her a peace she hadn't known for a long time. It was absolutely freeing.

He stopped moving and for a second she thought maybe she'd done something he didn't like, but he was still buried inside her mouth. Thoughts were swirling around in her head as he just stood there, his cock filling her mouth. She could taste the saltiness of his pre-cum as it gathered on his tip, but he remained where he was, in some sort of holding pattern.

"You look breathtaking like this," he said out of the blue.

She didn't know what to say—couldn't say anything given their position—so she gave his cock a long slow lick instead.

Alexander closed his eyes once again as if savoring the sensation. Then he looked down at her with a fire in his eyes. "You are too tempting for your own good, *gattina.*" He removed himself from her mouth and dropped his hand from her hair. "Get on the bed with your ass in the air."

Hurrying to her feet, she crawled onto the bed facing away from him on all fours, her ass in the air as instructed. Given how short her skirt was and that she wasn't wearing any panties, she knew her pussy was on full display for him.

Grace didn't get a chance to think much about it or anything else before he was sliding his hand between her legs, his fingers going straight for her clit. She couldn't stop the moan that escaped. It felt so good to have him touch her like this.

"Do you like that?" he asked.

Before she could answer, he landed a solid blow with his free hand to her backside. She let out a little yelp. "Yes, Sir."

He switched to the other side. The sound of his hand meeting her flesh bounced off the walls of her tiny bedroom. The sting left behind only added to the heat between her legs, driving her closer and closer to orgasm.

The assault on her bottom continued, warming it and sending her into an almost floaty state. His hands left her body, and then she heard the sound of a wrapper being opened. Only vaguely did it register that he must be putting on a condom.

Before she knew it, his hands were back. This time his thumbs spread her wide before she felt the head of his cock nudging her entrance.

"Please," she begged. "Please . . ."

Grace gasped as he plunged forward until his balls pressed against her.

"You all right?" he asked, his voice sounding as if he was in pain.

She nodded. "Yes. Yes, Sir. I'm more than all right."

With her enthusiastic reply, Alexander placed one hand on her hip as he began to move. She closed her eyes, letting the sensations racing through her body take over. This was what she'd wanted. Everything else in the world fell away until there was only him.

***

Alexander gritted his teeth as he pumped in and out of Grace. She felt better than he could ever have imagined. Her walls hugged his cock and welcomed him as if he belonged. It was both pure pleasure and absolute torture all in one.

Right before she'd taken him into the warm recess of her mouth it had occurred to him that guilt was what had been holding him back. It was one thing to give her pleasure, to provide her what she needed. To take from her was an entirely different animal. Kurt had been his friend—the best friend he'd had since joining the Army. A part of him felt as if he was somehow betraying him by being with her like this, but heaven help him, Alexander couldn't resist anymore.

The sound of their bodies coming together echoed in his ears and the smell of sex invaded his senses. Then there were the sounds coming out of Grace herself. It was intoxicating. He wanted more.

He reached forward to cup her breast, but it was still covered by the corset she wore. With more hatred for the material in that moment than he should have, he tugged at the hooks until he felt them release. It wasn't pretty, but pretty wasn't what he was going for.

Once her tits were free, he found her nipple and placed it between two of his fingers, twisted, and pulled. A cry erupted from Grace's lips that had him increasing his pace. He dug his fingers into her hip, slamming her back against him with every forward thrust of his pelvis.

A pain shot down his leg and Alexander knew whether he wanted to or not he was going to have to change their position. This time when he retreated, he slipped out of her completely. He thought he heard a soft whimper from Grace.

"Don't worry, *gattina*. I'm not nearly done with you yet." He smacked the right cheek of her ass. "Take that corset off and turn over."

Grace rose up, removed the corset, tossing it onto the floor as if she wanted to be rid of it as much as he did, and lay down on the bed facing him this time. Her hair was in disarray from him having his hands in it, and her skin had a beautiful pink hue from their activities.

Alexander shed the rest of his clothing and crawled onto the bed to hover over her. He wasted no time capturing her lips in a searing kiss. This woman made him burn in the best possible way.

Taking his time, he kissed and touched what was his. Grace ran her hands along his back and shoulders. It had been years since anyone had touched him like this and it was almost his undoing. He wasn't even inside her and he felt as if he was on the verge of coming. Alexander needed to slow things down.

He licked his way down her neck and collarbone until he was staring at her tits. Her nipples were hard and asking to be sucked on. Who was he to deny them?

Grace arched her back and tangled her fingers in his hair as he took one of her breasts into his mouth and sucked as if his life depended on it. Her nails scraped against his scalp when he added his teeth to the torture, alternating between pain and pleasure, hard and soft. He remembered thinking how he could spend hours worshiping her tits. It wasn't far from the truth.

She began squirming beneath him, looking for friction, but he didn't give her any. Instead, he held her hip down with one hand while he moved to torture her other breast.

"Sir?"

"Yes?"

"May I come?" He felt her still trying to move beneath his hand, but he held her still, not giving her what she wanted.

He took a moment to meet her gaze. Her eyes were hooded and darker than usual from her arousal. "Can you come from me playing with your tits?"

Grace blinked. "I don't . . . I don't know."

A sly smile crossed Alexander's face. "Let's find out, shall we?"

With that, he went back to what he'd been doing, sucking and licking and biting her very delectable tits. He'd heard of women who could come solely from breast stimulation, but he'd never witnessed it. Grace was very worked up, however, and the way she was straining for friction made him think she was close.

Alexander readjusted their position so he could use his lower half to keep her hips still, freeing one of his hands. He cupped her other breast and began kneading it in his hand. Every now and then he'd bring his fingers together to pinch her nipple or tease it with the tip of his finger. Then he'd switch breasts and start the torture all over again.

He had no idea how long he spent playing with her breasts, but the little mewling sounds coming from Grace told him she was both enjoying it and hating it at the same time. Her breathing had become increasingly labored and with more and more frequency she dug her nails into his shoulders. He'd probably have marks. The thought only drove him on.

Grace bent her leg, and then let it drop back down onto the bed. She did this several times before she began thrashing her head back and forth. A gasping sound came out of her moments before she arched her back and clung to his head, holding him in place. A ripple went through her body as more moans and pants released from deep inside her.

With a final lick of her now very abused nipples, he pushed himself up until he was face-to-face with her. He didn't even try to hide the satisfied smirk on his face. "I guess we answered that question."

She tried to bury her head in his shoulder. "I can't believe that just happened."

Alexander chuckled, making him even more aware that his cock was inches away from her pussy. It wiped the smile from his face as his own need took over. "I'm going to fuck you now. You're not to come again until I say. Understand?"

"Yes, Sir."

With a slight adjustment of his hips, the tip of his cock was once again at her entrance. "Bend your legs."

As soon as she was spread open for him, he tilted his hips forward and let himself sink into her warmth once more. She was so wet he slipped inside easily.

He leaned down and captured her mouth with his. Grace parted her lips, allowing him to take whatever he wanted, and he took. She wrapped her arms around his neck and held on as he moved in and out of her, steadily increasing his pace. He felt her body begin to tighten, her fingers begin to flex against his skin, but she didn't ask for permission to come. She bit down on her bottom lip and rode it out like the good little sub that she was. His sub.

The memory of her on her knees, sucking his cock, had Alexander barely holding on. He could feel the surge of energy getting stronger. He wasn't going to last much longer.

Propping himself up on one elbow, he took her hand and brought it down between them. "Touch yourself."

She didn't hesitate. He could feel her rubbing circles over her clit, driving her closer to orgasm. Still she didn't ask to come.

He placed his hand over her neck possessively and looked into her eyes. "You're mine and your orgasms are mine. You only touch yourself if I tell you that you can."

Her internal muscles spasmed and released around his cock, telling him more than her words. She tried to nod, but his hold on her neck prevented that. "I'm yours and my orgasms belong to you. Only you."

He barely let her get the words out before he kissed her again. "Come for me, *gattina*."

Grace moved her fingers faster over her clit as he continued to drive in and out of her. She clung to his shoulders, digging, scraping her nails. Her pussy clamped down on his cock a split second before a strangled cry left her lips and her body began to shake.

Knowing she'd reached her climax, Alexander let go and it didn't take him long before he felt his orgasm roll over him. All the pent-up passion he'd kept inside for this woman exploded all at once, leaving him completely spent.

He tumbled to the side, making sure not to crush her, and gathered her into his arms. The emotions that had been scratching the surface for over a month were there in front of him, plain to see and unable to be pushed back into the box he'd had them stuffed in.

He was in love with Grace.

It was too bad he didn't know if she would ever be able to love him back.

Chapter 18

Grace wasn't sure she could get more relaxed. Every bone in her body felt as if it had been turned into flexible rubber. She sighed and cuddled closer to Alexander, enjoying the moment and not thinking about much of anything.

He sat up a little to pull the edge of the blanket over her, flexing his stomach muscles. She recalled him mentioning working out, but somehow she thought his injury would make it difficult for him to maintain the same level of fitness that had been required when he was on active duty. Granted, he might not be able to run or climb, or do all the things he used to that required the full use of his legs, but his upper body was beyond impressive. Unable to resist, she traced the outline of his abs with her index finger.

Alexander seemed unaffected by her exploration of his body until he noticed her gaze had lowered to his legs. There were scars along both legs, but one had a long angry one that ran almost the entire length of his limb. She could only imagine the kind of pain he must have been in to have that type of damage.

"I wasn't awake for most of it." He seemed to sense the direction of her thoughts.

"But after? When you woke up?" Grace tilted her head up to look at him.

He shrugged. "I'm told I briefly regained consciousness during the transfer in Germany, but I don't remember it. The first conscious memory I have is waking up stateside and by then I was being pumped full of morphine."

The tough guy act wasn't going to work with her. She knew better. "Still, eventually they had to take you off the morphine."

Again, he downplayed it. "It wasn't anything I couldn't handle."

He wasn't looking at her, but she could see the muscles in his jaw clenching. She thought back to the look on his face earlier. Things began clicking into place. They'd talked about it before, at least her side of things, the guilt, the confusion. But all that had been before they'd begun their agreement. Before they'd begun to have a physical relationship.

Grace rested her head on his shoulder, her gaze once again going to the scars on his legs. She worried her bottom lip and debated whether or not to say anything about the thoughts going through her head. She'd always been able to talk to him about things . . . things she couldn't talk to anyone else about because he understood. But they were lying in her bed, naked, after having sex. Could she really ask him if he was feeling guilty about sleeping with her?

"You're tensing up. Something's bothering you." It wasn't a question.

"Just thinking." She was hoping he wouldn't press her, but of course she knew better.

"What are you thinking about?"

She hesitated a little too long.

"Are you having second thoughts about our arrangement?" He kept his tone even, but that only told her there was more emotion behind his question than he was letting on.

"No. I'm not having second thoughts."

"Then what is it?" he asked. "And don't tell me it's nothing."

Grace couldn't help but grin. She hugged him tighter, some part of her fearing his reaction to what she was about to say. "I was thinking about the look on your face earlier when I was kneeling. You looked as if you were in pain."

He didn't bother trying to contradict her.

"And I was thinking about how I'd told you I was ready and still you waited for us to have sex."

Again, he remained quiet.

Grace wasn't sure how she felt about having a one-sided conversation, but she pressed on. "I was wondering if you were feeling guilty. About being with me. Physically, I mean."

His body beneath her turned to stone. She'd obviously hit a nerve.

"This is what Kurt wanted. You shouldn't feel guilty." She paused. "Neither of us should."

Grace lay listening to his breathing, letting what she'd said sink in. She had no idea if it would make any difference in his mind. Guilt was a funny thing. She knew that well.

Time dragged on with neither of them saying anything. The stiff set of his body hadn't eased and she was beginning to regret saying anything. She should have let it go and changed the subject. That was if he would have let her.

"You're right," he said out of the blue. "A part of me does feel guilty, like I'm betraying him somehow."

She squeezed her eyes shut as a wave of emotion hit her. "You're not."

He didn't answer.

Grace was torn. They needed to have this conversation, get it out in the open, but everything was so raw. She pressed her lips against his throat. "I'm glad if I was going to do this that it was with you."

With that he relaxed a little and circled his arms around her, holding her tighter. His lips grazed the top of her head, lingering. "You should get some sleep."

"Will you stay?"

There was a long pause before he spoke. "Sure."

They each took a turn in the bathroom before climbing into her bed, this time under the covers. She wondered if Alexander would put his boxer briefs back on, but he left them on the floor.

Grace rolled over on her side to face him. He noticed. "Do I need to order you to go to sleep?" It was meant to be teasing, but she knew he was doing it to deflect. Why did men always have to run away from feelings?

"No, Sir. I'll go to sleep."

When she didn't move or close her eyes, he raised an eyebrow at her in question. "But?"

"But I wanted to ask you something first."

He looked wary. "And what's that?"

"Do you regret our arrangement? Having sex with me?"

"No," he said. "I don't regret our arrangement."

She didn't miss that he'd only really answered half her question. "And sex?"

Alexander sighed and turned toward her. "It's complicated. But no, I don't regret that either."

"Why is it complicated?" She knew she was pushing and it shocked even her. Normally she wasn't so brave.

He looked down the length of the bed, and then at Grace. "Do you really want to have this conversation here? Now?"

While she understood the awkwardness of their current position given the topic, she needed to know. "Yes." She pressed her lips together and met his gaze. "I think we need to. Don't you?"

Alexander searched her face for a long moment and then nodded. "Maybe we do."

She fumbled beneath the covers until she found his hand and laced their fingers together. He'd been there for her so many times and it seemed as if he was struggling.

"It didn't feel right to take pleasure in your body," he admitted.

Thinking back to their first scene, and then the club, things began to make more sense. "It was okay to give me pleasure but taking it for yourself . . ."

"I felt guilty as hell." He paused. "Still do."

"Why?" He gave her a look that said he couldn't believe she was asking that question, so she clarified. "I mean we talked about it and you knew me moving on, finding another Dom, was what Kurt wanted. He may not have envisioned it would be you who would be my Dom, but I have to assume he'd be okay with it. You were his friend. He respected you. Trusted you enough to deliver that letter to me."

"Don't you see that's why I feel so guilty?" He must have seen her confusion written plainly on her face. "Kurt trusted me. He trusted me to find you and give you his letter. He didn't expect me to start fucking his wife."

If she hadn't been so used to Kurt's cursing, Alexander's words would have bothered her. As it was, Grace realized them for what they were. "Is that what you're doing? Fucking me?" Using that word felt strange. She could only imagine what it sounded like to him. She never cursed.

He looked at her as if maybe she'd lost her mind, giving they were currently lying in her bed, naked after doing exactly that. "Did you forget about the last two hours?"

"That's not what I mean." She brought their hands up and studied the way they were entwined together. "I know what we have isn't normal or traditional, or whatever, but it's more than just sex. You're my Dom and my friend."

There was something else that flashed in his eyes, and then it was gone. It wasn't quite the same as before and it was gone before she could analyze it. He scooted closer, drawing their linked hands up to his mouth. "It doesn't change the fact that what I want to do to you is anything but friendly."

As he kissed a line down her arm, Grace's eyes rolled back in her head and she forgot what she was going to say. "Alexander?"

He lunged forward, pushing her onto her back, and pinned her to the mattress. The look in his eyes was heated and her body reacted. "What do you call me while we're in this bed?"

Grace moistened her lips. "Sir."

Alexander grinned. "Much better." Then he kissed her. Everything Grace had been about to say was thrown out the window as he reached between them and began making her body sing again.

***

He stared at the popcorn ceiling in Grace's bedroom. It was around three in the morning and Grace was sound asleep beside him. After he'd ravished her again she'd barely been able to keep her eyes open. That, of course, had been the plan.

Tossing the covers to the side, Alexander got out of Grace's bed and walked into the bathroom, making sure to wait until the door was closed before turning on the light. He didn't want to wake her. Grace needed her sleep.

There was a little bear sitting on the back of the toilet, holding an American flag, which seemed to be watching him as he relieved himself. Alexander had noticed several bears positioned around her house and wondered if she collected them. He'd have to ask. It wasn't something he'd thought about before.

He flushed and went to the sink to wash his hands. His leg was aching, but considering he could hear the rain outside hitting the windows, he wasn't surprised. It was par for the course with an injury like his.

Opening Grace's medicine cabinet, he found some ibuprofen and tossed two in his mouth, chasing them down with a handful of water from the tap. He was reaching to turn off the water when there was a soft knock on the bathroom door.

"You can come in. I'm decent." Which was a total lie. He was standing there in his birthday suit, but it wasn't as if she hadn't seen all of him earlier that evening.

She slowly pushed open the door and edged her way inside as if she wasn't sure of herself. Maybe she wasn't. After their talk, he wasn't sure about much of anything.

"Everything okay?" she asked.

He turned off the water and dried his hands. "Yeah. My leg was bothering me, so I swiped a couple of your ibuprofen."

Grace frowned. "Is there anything I can do?"

"I'll be fine." His limp as he moved toward her only deepened the creases in her forehead.

"I used to give Kurt massages. Would that help?"

The thought of her hands on him had his cock twitching. "I don't—"

"Please, Sir. Let me help you."

It was the pleading look in her eyes that broke him. "All right."

At his agreement, she jumped into action. Grace opened one of the drawers beside the sink and removed a dark blue bottle of what he assumed was lotion. Then she took hold of his hand and led him back into the bedroom. "Lie down."

He gave her a hard look.

She lowered her gaze to the floor, looking utterly submissive and adorable. "Sorry. Sir, would you please lie down on the bed so I can massage your leg for you?"

As tempting as it was, he resisted the urge to touch her. Alexander knew if he did, they'd end up having sex again, his leg be damned. Instead, he stretched out on the bed and placed his hands behind his head. That was the only way he could be sure he'd keep them to himself.

Grace squeezed some of the lotion into her hands, and placed the tube on the nightstand before rubbing her hands together. With the gentlest pressure, she began massaging the lotion into his leg. As she grew more confident she wasn't hurting him, Grace used her fingers more, pressing against his muscles. She glided over his scars as if they didn't bother her at all.

Alexander closed his eyes as the ache in his leg began to fade. He didn't know if it was the ibuprofen kicking in or what Grace was doing or both. Either way, he wasn't going to complain. Besides, even if it was the pills, Grace's fingers were heavenly.

The more she worked her magic, the more his mind began to move in a different direction. He was less focused on the discomfort and more on how Grace's hands felt pushing and pulling on his skin—and how they would feel gliding along another part of his anatomy. He groaned as the picture formed in his head.

Grace heard him and halted her movements.

He looked down, meeting her gaze. "Don't stop."

"I don't want to hurt you," she said.

Alexander shook his head. "You're not. It feels amazing. Thank you."

It took her a minute to resume what she'd been doing.

Once she was finished with one leg, she moved on to the other. That leg didn't pain him like his left one did, so his mind was much more aware of her touch. Especially as she inched higher toward the top of his thighs. The closer she got to his groin, the more his cock began to sit up and take notice.

Grace noticed, too. She grazed her fingers along the inside of his thigh and his cock jerked in response. He'd already come twice tonight, but apparently a certain part of his anatomy hadn't gotten the message.

She lifted her hand then lowered it before meeting his gaze. "May I, Sir?"

The part of him that was still riddled with guilt about taking pleasure from her screamed at him that he should refuse—that he should thank her for the massage and order her back to bed—but there was something in her eyes that told him this was what she wanted. As usual, he couldn't tell her no. He nodded his agreement.

Instead of touching him right away, she reached for the lotion again. After coating her hands, she gripped his length. Her slick hands glided along his flesh, drawing a delicious moan deep from within his chest. He gritted his teeth as she used one hand to pump his cock and the other to caress his balls.

She ran her thumb along his head, circling the tip, before sliding back down to the base, and then returning to do it all over again. He pressed his head farther into the pillow to keep himself from reaching for her. Who knew a hand job could be this good? It sure wasn't when it was his own hand, and he couldn't recall it ever being like this. Even thinking back to when he was younger, the last time a woman had given him a hand job that hadn't only been a prelude to her going down on him, he couldn't remember it ever being like this.

Grace didn't let up, and soon he was doing his best to control his breathing. He was going to come and it was going to happen sooner rather than later if she kept it up. There was no way he was going to make her stop, though. Not now.

She seemed to know he was getting close. "May I swallow your cum, Sir?"

The innocent look on her face belied what she was asking. It was beyond hot. "Yes, *gattina*. Swallow my cum. Swallow every last drop."

Given the look on her face, one would have thought he'd offered her a prize. Then again, maybe he had. It was considered an honor for a sub to take her Dom's cum into her body.

Most of the lotion she'd used had long been worked into his skin, making it easy for her to wrap her lips around the head of his cock and suck as she continued to work his length with her hand. She used her tongue to coax him on almost as if she were licking the most delicious lollipop.

At the last minute, moments before he came, Alexander reached down, grabbed the back of her head, and pushed himself deeper into her mouth. He felt his cock hit the back of her throat. It was the final straw. He emptied his cum down her throat and, good girl that she was, Grace didn't miss a beat. She breathed through her nose and swallowed several times, making sure she got it all. Every last drop. Exactly as he'd instructed.

When she lifted her head, she had a satisfied look on her face, which helped with the still-present guilt he felt.

Alexander sat up, took her by the arms, and brought her so she was lying on top of him. He raked his fingers through her hair and kissed her, plunging his tongue inside her mouth.

When he released her, they were both breathing hard. "Thank

you, *gattina*."

She smiled back at him. "Anytime, Sir."

Chapter 19

The next morning Grace didn't wake up alone. Alexander was still in bed beside her, his back propped up against the headboard, reading. It took her a few moments to realize that he had the romance novel she'd been reading in his hands.

Before the anxiety could really take hold, he looked over and met her gaze. The expression on his face was unreadable. "You're awake."

She sat up, holding the blankets to her chest, which was kind of silly considering what they'd done the night before. "Morning."

Alexander closed the book and placed it on the nightstand before facing her again. He moved closer, bringing one hand up to cup her face. "How did you sleep?"

"Good." In truth, she'd slept better than she had in a long time, most likely due to the multitude of orgasms he'd given her. "How about you?"

"Very well, thank you." He grinned, although there was still something there in his eyes she couldn't put her finger on, and brushed his thumb along her cheekbone. His touch had all her nerve endings coming alive. "Do you have plans with your mom and sister today?"

Grace swallowed. Her mouth was really dry all of a sudden and it had nothing to do with his question. "Yes. Dinner."

He hummed. "What time is that?"

"Noon." She was whispering, but she had no idea why. It wasn't as if anyone could hear them.

"Anything you need to do before then?" His voice had this sensual tone to it that had her pressing her legs together under the covers, seeking friction.

"No."

The smile on his face got bigger. "Good."

Her breath hitched as he began to move. But instead of coming toward her, he went in the opposite direction and placed his feet on the floor before easing himself into a standing position. She hadn't missed how he'd favored his leg, making sure he was steady on his feet before turning to her and holding out his hand.

Grace blinked several times then took his offering and let him help her up. He led her into the bathroom, stopping right inside the door. "Do you need me to give you a minute?"

Grace was grateful he'd asked. She didn't think she could go to the bathroom in front of him. "Yes, please."

"Open the door when you're done." He stepped out of the room, pulling the door closed behind him.

She swiftly did her business, and after washing her hands, she gave her teeth a once-over with her toothbrush. A glance in the mirror told her that her hair was standing on end, but she let it go for now.

Alexander was waiting right outside the door when she cracked it open. He strolled inside and wrapped his arm around her waist, giving her a hard kiss. "I figure we both need a shower after last night."

A blush stained her cheeks at the reminder. She'd had no shame last night, begging him to come in her mouth.

Without a word, Alexander turned on the shower and adjusted the temperature. Once he was satisfied, he helped her step into the tub and followed after her.

The water was warm, filling the room with steam. He took his time washing her hair for her before grabbing her body wash and working his way down her body, making sure every inch of her was clean. Nothing he did was overly sexual, but her body didn't seem to get the message. By the time he turned her so she could rinse off, she was primed and ready.

He didn't touch her, though. Not the way she wanted him to. He grabbed the body wash and went to work cleaning himself from head to toe. She was left standing there vibrating with pent-up sexual energy while he washed away the evidence of their night together.

Grace was caught a bit off guard when the water shut off. She'd been so focused on watching the movements of his body that she hadn't realized he was done.

They both stepped out, drying their feet on the mat she kept on the floor.

"Towels in here?" he asked, tilting his head toward the linen closet.

She nodded, words seeming to leave her as she watched the muscles in his thighs flex as he moved. He really was in great shape considering he'd spent six months in a VA hospital recovering from his injuries.

He removed two large towels, placed one on the counter, and unfolded the other. She went to reach for the one he'd set on the counter, but before she could, he began drying her off with the towel in his hands. It was a caring gesture, but all it did was make her want him more. Since when had she become such a horny mess?

When he was done, he wrapped the towel around her torso.

"Thanks."

He sent her a panty-dropping grin that had her clenching her thighs together again, and picked up the towel he'd laid on the counter. She thought about asking if she could dry him off as he'd done for her, but before she could, he was done. He secured the towel around his waist and they headed back to the bedroom.

"Would you like to go out to breakfast?" He gathered his clothes from where he'd discarded them on the floor. Considering he had nothing else with him, he was going to have to put his dirty clothes back on. She wished she had something else to offer him, but she didn't think the few things she had left of Kurt's world fit Alexander.

Much to her surprise, thinking about her husband didn't have her feeling as if she were going to fall into some sort of abyss as it had in the past. Grace still missed him and she probably always would, but the prospect of going on without him wasn't as scary as it had been. She was moving on exactly how he wanted her to.

She slipped on a pair of pink panties and some jeans. "I can cook."

They ended up sitting at her kitchen table twenty minutes later eating bacon and eggs. It felt comfortable, natural, to have Alexander sitting there beside her, eating his breakfast. She liked having him here even though there were still those moments of guilt that would pop up. Grace kept having to remind herself that this was what Kurt wanted.

The thought had her pausing mid-bite. Had it been what Kurt wanted? Not the moving on part, but Alexander. Was it Kurt's plan all along for Alexander to become her Dom? Was that why he'd asked Alexander to deliver the letter to her in person? Had he known about Alexander's lifestyle? These were questions she would probably never know the answers to.

"Everything okay?" Alexander had noticed she'd stopped eating.

She tried to smile. "Yeah. Just thinking."

He gave her his full attention. "Anything you want to talk about?"

While she knew she could tell him her thoughts, they were too fresh. Instead, she told him the other worry on her mind. "Gabby stopped by Friday night. She saw me all dressed up and wanted to know if I had a date. I told her you were taking me to a club." Grace paused. "I didn't tell her what club, of course."

"Of course." Alexander wiped his mouth and took hold of her hand. "And you don't know what to tell her about us."

Grace nodded.

He turned her hand over and pressed his lips to her open palm. It sent tingles up her arm in the most delicious way. "Would it be easier if you told her we were dating?"

"I don't know," Grace admitted. "She's going to question me either way."

"True. But I'm sure she'd have a lot more questions if you told her I was your Dom." He winked at her, trying to lighten the mood.

It worked. A tiny giggle escaped her lips. "You'd be okay with that?"

Alexander didn't answer right away. He seemed to be debating how to respond to her question. Unease began to fill her gut.

The look on her face must have tipped him off to her thoughts because he moved closer and placed both hands on her face, drawing her in. She could smell her soap on his skin from their shower. He searched her eyes before pressing his forehead against hers. "You are more than my sub, Grace. Much more. I . . ." He swallowed. "I don't have a problem with you telling your sister we're dating."

"You're sure you don't mind?"

He kissed her forehead, and then leaned back in his chair and resumed eating. "I'm sure." He motioned toward her plate. "Your food's going to get cold."

Still somewhat concerned over what he obviously wasn't saying, Grace picked up her fork and began to eat.

Several minutes passed before he spoke again. "How would you feel if we were dating?"

She had to force the food in her mouth down her throat. "I don't know. I mean . . . we're friends . . ."

"Grace, what I feel for you is much more than friendship." There was no misinterpreting his words. He wasn't talking about their play arrangement. "Besides, it only seems right if I'm going to defile my best friend's widow that I at least be dating her."

"So you want to date me because of some sort of sense of honor?" She wasn't sure how she felt about that.

"No." The look in his eyes gave her no reason to doubt him. "I want to date you because you deserve more than just me coming over every weekend to fuck you."

Blunt. But she wouldn't have expected less. "So what would that mean? Us dating?"

Alexander pushed his chair back and reached for her, pulling her into his lap. He nipped his teeth along the side of her neck and ran a hand up her leg. Her heart beat faster, anticipation coiling in her belly. "It would mean you'd be my girlfriend."

"Your girlfriend?" She was only half paying attention to his words. Most of the blood in her brain was going south. "That sounds kind of cheesy, doesn't it?"

"Hmm." He nuzzled his nose along her collarbone. "Lovers?"

Grace sighed and tangled her fingers in his hair. "Better."

"I'm not sure I like that. *Lovers* still implies our relationship is limited to the bedroom."

"Relationship?" The words were barely out of her mouth before he pressed his lips to hers, cutting off anything she was going to say. It was the last word either of them spoke for a while.

At a little after eleven Alexander said goodbye, promising to call her later. He gave her a kiss that left her breathless and wanting more, even after their intense make-out session in her kitchen. The man could kiss. It took her a full ten minutes after he walked out her front door before her heart rate returned to normal.

The drive to her mom's felt as if it took no time at all. She made every traffic light between her house and her mom's, which in and of itself was some sort of miracle, or maybe it was a curse. She hadn't decided which. Grace had kind of hoped she'd get stuck in traffic or something, anything to postpone the inquisition from her sister. If only Gabby hadn't stopped by Friday night. Or if Grace hadn't opened the door.

Grace groaned. If she'd thought it'd been bad before . . .

Luckily, Grace got a small reprieve. Her sister didn't come out to greet her when she pulled up. That was probably in part due to the fact that they were experiencing a cold snap. St. Louis didn't get as chilly as places farther north, but it wasn't uncommon for it to get down into the thirties at night in November. Unfortunately, they hadn't been above forty-five for the last three days. She, and almost everyone else in the city, was ready for it to warm up a little.

A high-pitched shriek greeted her as she opened the door to her mom's house, followed by the sound of a little girl giggling. Taylor.

Hanging up her jacket, Grace followed the sound into the kitchen. The sight tugged at her heartstrings. Gabby had Taylor in her arms, half upside down, a huge smile on her face. Grace and Kurt had been talking about starting a family, but they'd wanted to wait until his deployment was over. He didn't want to miss the doctor's appointments and the birth because he was stationed half a world away.

"Hey," her sister said when she noticed her standing there.

Grace buried her melancholy feelings and headed into the room. At least she had her niece. "Hey."

Their mother strolled into the room. "It's about time."

"I'm on time." Grace even double-checked with the clock hanging on her mother's wall.

"Barely." Caroline stirred something on the stove and then removed two dishes from the oven. "Grab some extra napkins, and let's eat."

Dinner conversation mainly centered around the upcoming

holiday. Taylor's father had asked if he could have his daughter for Thanksgiving. "I told him I'd think about it, but I don't know how I can say no. I mean he finally seems to be taking an interest and wants to spend time with his daughter."

"What's changed?" their mother asked, although the same question had been on the tip of Grace's tongue.

"I have no idea. I just hope it lasts. I'd hate for Taylor to get attached and then he takes off again."

Both Grace and Caroline nodded. It was a real concern. He'd been involved in the beginning, but shortly after Taylor was born he said he got a job out of state and took off for over a year. To his credit, he'd sent Gabby money every month to help with bills, but he'd never called or come to see Taylor. The only way her sister had known he was back in town was because of the postmark on the envelopes.

"I gots a new toy, Aunt Grace."

"Did you?" All talk of Taylor's father ceased and they gave their attention to the little girl.

"Uh-huh. Mommy says we have to eat first and then I can show you."

Grace smiled. "I can't wait."

The toy ended up being a stuffed animal. Apparently the dog was from a cartoon. Grace stood there grinning and nodding her head as Taylor went on and on. It had been years since she'd watched a cartoon and this wasn't one she'd ever heard of.

Gabby came into the room and made a beeline for her daughter. "Did you want Skye to take a nap with you?"

Taylor held on to the toy in a death grip and nodded.

Grace watched as the two disappeared down the hallway in the direction of the bedrooms.

"It's too bad you and Kurt couldn't have had any little ones." Her mother went to the couch and sat down.

This wasn't something Grace wanted to talk about. "Do you want anything to drink?"

Her mom shook her head and patted the spot next to her.

Reluctantly, Grace took a seat.

Caroline placed an arm around Grace's shoulders and gave her a one-armed hug. "I know this is hard for you, but things will get better. You'll find someone else. He may not be the same as Kurt was, but that's okay. You deserve to be happy, sweetie."

Moisture formed in Grace's eyes, but she willed it away. She didn't want to cry. She'd cried enough for a lifetime already.

But her mother's words brought back the conversation she'd had with Alexander. "I've started seeing someone."

Her mom sat up and turned to face her. "Really, Grace? That's wonderful. Who is he?"

Gabby walked into the room and took a seat a few feet away, the smile on her face saying it all. "He's a doctor. Right, Grace?"

"You knew about this?" their mother asked, the hurt in her voice evident. Grace could already feel the blush starting.

"I stopped by Friday night and she was all dressed up for a night on the town. He was taking her dancing."

Caroline turned her attention back to Grace. "That sounds like fun."

"Yeah." Grace tried not to think about Friday night. It wasn't the type of thing one wanted to relive when sitting in front of your mother.

"So tell us about him. What's he like? Where did you meet him?"

Grace spent the next half hour answering questions about Alexander. When she told them he'd served with Kurt, her mother had admonished her for not inviting him to join them for dinner. And then her mother had floored her with her next suggestion. "You should invite him to Thanksgiving. If he's new in town he probably doesn't have any family here. It's not right for him to spend it alone."

She also heard what her mom didn't say. Bringing him to Thanksgiving dinner would mean they'd get to meet him. Was she ready for that? "I'll ask."

Chapter 20

Gabby had kept her questions about Alexander fairly tame while they their mother was present, letting their mom set the tone of the conversation. But when Caroline excused herself, saying she needed to make a phone call, Gabby got up and plopped herself down on the couch beside Grace. "Okay, out with it."

"Out with what?" Grace wasn't going to make this easy. Why should she?

Her sister rolled her eyes. "Your date, silly. And why didn't you tell me? This is big news."

"It's not."

Gabby snorted. "For months I tried to get you out of your house. All you did was go to work and come home. You kept telling me that you had no desire to put yourself out there again. Now here you are dating a doctor no less." Her sister gave her a once-over. "And you're obviously sleeping with him."

Grace ducked her head, trying to hide the red in her cheeks.

It was no use, of course. Her sister knew her too well and she wasn't going to let it go. "I knew it!"

"Gabby, I—"

"Oh, no you don't. You don't get to tell me you don't want to talk about it." Gabby grabbed hold of both Grace's hands and waited until she looked up. "I'm so happy for you."

"Thanks," Grace said. "I think?"

Gabby chuckled. "So how is he in bed?"

Grace wanted a hole to open up in the floor and swallow her. "Can we please change the subject?"

Her sister released an overexaggerated sigh. "Fine."

"Thank you."

Gabby squeezed Grace's hands, causing her to glance up again. "You look happy."

That surprised her a little, although sitting there thinking about it, Grace had to admit she'd been doing a lot better over the last month or so. That was due in no small part to Alexander. He'd made her feel as if there was still hope. Hope for a life—a real, meaningful life—after losing Kurt.

Their mother ambled back into the room with a sleepy-looking Taylor. The little girl was leaning her head against her grandmother's shoulder, clutching her toy in one hand and rubbing her eyes with the other. "This little one wanted to see her mommy."

Gabby abandoned their conversation and stood to take her daughter. "Did you have a good nap with Skye?"

Taylor nodded. "She was really tired, Mommy."

Gabby brushed some damp hair away from her daughter's face. "Are you thirsty?"

The little girl nodded.

Again, the scene between mother and daughter tugged at Grace's heart. Her mother sat down beside her, taking up the spot Gabby had vacated moments before. They watched as Gabby carried Taylor into the kitchen.

"You know it's not too late," Caroline said.

Grace looked at her mother a bit confused.

"To have kids of your own, I mean."

"I don't think—"

"How about this doctor? Does he want kids?" her mother asked.

"Um. I don't know. We haven't talked about it." Other than their play arrangement and their brief conversation that morning about telling her family they were dating, they hadn't talked about the future at all. He was her Dom. And maybe her boyfriend? Even that was unclear. They'd kind of gotten sidetracked.

"Might be something to think about. You aren't getting any younger." Her mother's words hit their mark. She was going to be thirty-four next month. Her biological clock was ticking.

Shortly after Gabby and Taylor reentered the room, Grace said she needed to go, making some excuse about needing to get things situated before Taylor's visit the next day. She didn't think her mother or her sister were fooled.

Once she was back home, Grace worked mindlessly to tidy up, not wanting to have lied. She made sure anything that was breakable or potentially dangerous was either put away or moved high enough Taylor wouldn't be able to reach them. It didn't take her long. There wasn't much on her first floor outside of her kitchen anyway.

Next she headed upstairs to change the sheets. The moment she stepped foot in her bedroom the reminders of her and Alexander's night together were everywhere. The sheets were still twisted from their bodies and the air had a heavy musky scent. With every breath she relived the memory, her body already wanting more.

She held the sheets up to her face, inhaling as she stripped the bed. Alexander didn't wear cologne, so his scent was more subtle. It was still there, though, and she found even that comforted her. She almost didn't want to change the sheets.

An hour or so later her phone rang. She set the basket full of clean clothes on the table before she answered. She knew from the caller ID it was Alexander. "Hi."

"Hi." There was a pause. "How did things go with your sister?"

Grace pulled out a chair and sat down. "She asked if we'd had sex."

He laughed. "Direct and to the point."

"Yeah. That's Gabby." Her sister did not know the meaning of tact. At least not when it came to Grace. Gabby was always pushing Grace's buttons. But maybe that was a sister thing.

"I'm assuming she doesn't know about your lifestyle choice?"

"No." Grace knew her eyes were probably bugging out of her head at his suggestion even though there was no one there to see. "I'm pretty sure she thinks I've only ever had sex in the missionary position."

His amusement came through the phone. "If she only knew."

The color in her cheeks was back. "Yeah."

"You're blushing, aren't you?"

She touched her face, as if doing so would somehow stop her reaction. "I can't help it."

"That's okay. I think it's rather cute." He lowered his voice an octave. "Especially when I'm doing things to your delectable body."

That certainly didn't help cool her down. She needed to change the subject. "Um. My mom wants me to ask you if you'd like to join us for Thanksgiving dinner. You don't have to, but when Mom found out you were new in town and most likely didn't have any other family, she—"

"Grace, I'd be honored to have Thanksgiving dinner with your family."

She swallowed. "You would?"

"Of course." He paused. "Unless you don't want me there."

"No. It's not—" She blew out a breath. "I just don't want you to be uncomfortable. My family . . . they think we're, you know, together. A couple."

He didn't answer right away. "I thought we covered that this morning."

"That we would tell my family that we're dating." So did that mean . . .

"Not only your family."

"Oh." She guessed that answered her question.

Alexander gave her a minute. "Does that scare you?"

She couldn't lie. "A little."

"Grace, nothing has to change. We can let things happen naturally. We can go as slow as you want."

She didn't respond.

"Stop worrying about what you might not be able to give, or have, or whatever is going through that head of yours."

That had the corners of her mouth tipping up. "Habit."

"Do I need to come over there and spank you again?" She could hear the smile in his voice.

"Maybe." She was being sassy, which wasn't like her at all.

There was a rumble through the line. "I'm tempted to take you up on that, but if I come over there right now I won't just be spanking your ass."

Her body heated and this time it had nothing to do with embarrassment.

"But we both need to be up early in the morning and I want you to get some sleep. If I'm there, I'll most likely wake you up again."

"I didn't mind," she whispered into the phone.

Alexander groaned. "Not helping, Grace."

She giggled. "Sorry."

"No, you're not, *gattina*, but that's okay. I'm sure I can think of several ways you can make it up to me."

"I'm sure you can, Sir." Her words sounded breathy and faint.

"I want you to do something for me tonight." There was something in his voice that did nothing to calm her desire.

"Yes?"

"I want you to plug yourself for me."

Her ass clenched as if it already knew where he was going with this.

"I saw several butt plugs in your toy chest. Use the smallest one since it's been a while. I want you to start preparing yourself for me, which means every night before you go to bed I want you to plug yourself."

"I don't think I have any lube."

He paused. "It's getting late. I'll stop by the store tomorrow on the way home and drop it off to you. You can start tomorrow."

"Yes, Sir."

"And Grace?"

"Yes?"

He made her wait. "I'm very much looking forward to fucking your ass in the near future."

She sucked in a breath, her body tingling.

"Good night, Grace," he said. "Sweet dreams."

Lowering the phone, she pressed her hand to her forehead and tried to breathe. Something told her any dreams she would be having tonight wouldn't qualify as sweet.

***

Alexander chuckled as he hung up the phone. By the end of their conversation, he doubted she even remembered talking about where their relationship was going. He had so much fun playing with her, which was a definite plus in his book. So far, they seemed to be very well matched in the bedroom.

Of course, they were a good fit in other ways as well. She was easy to talk to once she got past her shyness. And because she'd been an Army wife for so long there were things she understood about him many civilians didn't. She was a great companion as well as a lovely sub.

The issue was to get her to see that. Sometime Grace concentrated so much on where she was lacking that she missed all the things she was good at.

He'd spent a good portion of his day catching up on some reading. There were years' worth of medical journals full of new technology he needed to brush up on. In the Army everything was about triage—patch 'em up and send 'em on. From time to time he would have the opportunity to sit down and go over the latest and greatest in the world of medicine, but for the most part if it didn't have to do with how to stop someone from bleeding out, removing shrapnel from wounds, or amputation, he skimmed over it.

Things were different now. When he'd finished medical school, Alexander had every intention of serving his six years and then starting his own practice, but he hadn't been able to abandon his comrades. That, and by the time his six years were up, his parents had both passed away. There was nothing calling him back home. At least in the Army he had a place.

It was the hardest part of the transition—the being alone. There wasn't much alone time in the Army, especially when you were deployed. If you wanted to be alone, you pretty much had to lock yourself in one of the latrines.

When he'd woken up in the VA hospital it was late at night. One of the first things he noticed was how quiet it was. Oh, there were noises, lots of little beeps and clicks, but nothing compared to what he'd been used to. It had frightened him at first, the lack of noise, until he'd realized he was in a hospital and he was stateside.

The microwave dinged and he removed his bowl of soup, carrying it into the living room where he could continue his reading. Before he knew it, the sun had gone down and it was time to get ready for bed.

He removed his clothes and tossed them into the basket he kept beside the door in his bedroom. Grace had never been to his place, a problem he thought maybe he should solve in the not too distant future. He wanted her to warm to the idea of them being a couple, and maybe being in his space would help with that. It wasn't much, but for now it was home.

His bathroom wasn't as nice as hers. It was pretty basic. But considering he used to share a shower with a hundred or so guys, it could have been a pipe sticking out of the wall for all he cared.

After washing up and taking care of business, Alexander made his way over to his bed. He'd spent the last two nights with Grace, her warm body pressed against him. His bed felt cold in comparison and he questioned his wisdom to stay there tonight instead of with her.

He hadn't wanted to crowd her, though. That and he needed a little perspective as well. He was still dealing with the guilt of pursuing his best friend's widow even though he knew that in some ways they were doing it with Kurt's blessing. Or at least that's what Alexander was telling himself. Kurt wanted Grace to be taken care of and he could do that. He would do that if she would let him.

Rolling onto his side, he ran a hand over the cool sheets and imagined her lying there beside him. He knew she was okay with their D/s relationship. She'd embraced that part. It was the rest that had her wavering and he wasn't sure exactly what it was that kept her holding back. She said it was because she didn't know if she could give him what he needed, but that didn't make sense to him. Not really. He didn't know how to help her get past it. All he could do was hope and pray that time would get her to see they could be good together, and not only as Dom and sub.

The next morning dawned way too soon. He stretched before lowering himself to the floor to do his morning sit-ups. Before his injury he was able to do one hundred easy, but lying in a bed for months had destroyed that.

He'd had to work his way from doing tiny crunches in his hospital bed to finally being able to do sit-ups again. After seven months, he could manage fifty before his muscles began to protest. Still, it was good to feel his strength returning, even if he had little hope of ever recovering the full function of his leg again.

Sweat rolled off him as he made his way to the shower. He placed his hands against the wall, leaning forward, letting the water trail down his back. It felt good, but not as good as Grace's hands.

Alexander tipped his head back, letting the water hit his face. He couldn't stop thinking about her. Even the simplest things brought her to his mind.

His cock began to harden, and he knew he needed to change the direction of his thoughts. Alexander reached for the soap and began to lather his body, ignoring the ache in his groin. He would see her tonight when he dropped off the lube and maybe she could relieve his growing problem.

As he was getting dressed for work, his gaze drifted back to the bed, then to his closet. Before he could overthink it, Alexander stuffed a change of clothes in a black bag, and went to find some breakfast. He knew it probably wasn't the best idea for him to stay overnight during the week, given they both had to work, but last night he had missed having her beside him. It was insane considering he'd slept alone his entire life with very few exceptions, but there it was and he wasn't going to fight it.

His day went by faster than he expected. He'd been sure it would drag since he was anxious to see Grace again, but the two meetings he'd had to attend had helped. There hadn't been time to do much of anything beyond answer question after question regarding various medical procedures, their uses, and their effectiveness. It was a good thing he'd been reading up on all the latest techniques and trials.

By the time he stopped by the grocery store to pick up some coconut oil and the adult store for a few other things, he was desperate for some stress relief. Alexander pulled up outside Grace's house, grabbed his black bag, his recent purchases, and his cane. He walked up the stairs to her front porch and rang the doorbell.

Several minutes passed and no one answered.

He'd told her he would be stopping by. Had something come up and she'd forgotten to call him?

Alexander tried again.

Before he was able to remove his finger, the door swung open to a very harried looking Grace. "Alexander."

"Grace? Is something wrong?"

"No. No. I—"

"Grace, who is it?" The sound of a woman's voice floated in from the other room.

"Umm."

"If you need me to tell them to go away—" The woman appeared behind Grace. She was a little taller with a few more curves, but there was no mistaking these two had to be related.

Grace met his gaze. She looked almost apologetic. Then she half turned to her sister. "Gabby, this is Alexander. Alexander, this is my sister, Gabby."

Gabby stepped forward, thrusting her hand out for him to take. "It's good to finally meet you, Alexander."

He took her hand and gave it a firm shake. Grace's sister was a lot more outgoing than Grace, that was for sure. "Very nice to meet you, Gabby. I've heard a lot about you."

"Well, that makes one of us." She dropped her hand and backed farther into the house. "Are you going to invite him in? Or are you going to make him stand out in the cold?"

Grace mouthed the word 'sorry', and opened the door more to allow him to step inside. He wanted to say more, to tell Grace it was all right, but Gabby was right there, not taking her gaze off him. He'd have to wait until later. When they were alone. For the time being, he tried to let her know as best he could that it was fine. He was going to have to meet her family sooner or later.

Chapter 21

Grace waited for Alexander to remove his coat and hung it up for him. Her hand was still on the hanger when she felt his hand on her lower back. He bent to place his bag on the floor inside the closet. It was only then she realized he'd been carrying three bags. One looked to be an overnight bag. The other two were plastic—one of which looked like the kind they gave you at a novelty store. Given their conversation the night before, Grace had to assume somewhere in one of them was the lube he promised to pick up. She only hoped her sister hadn't seen it.

She met his gaze.

He grinned and gave her back a gentle rub. "Relax."

The sound of something falling on the floor caught their attention and they all turned in the direction the sound came from. Without missing a beat, Gabby headed toward the noise. "Taylor, what are you doing that you're not supposed to?"

As soon as her sister was out of earshot, Grace faced Alexander. "I'm so sorry. I thought she'd be gone by the time you got here."

He turned her to face him and pressed his lips against her forehead. "It's fine. I was going to meet her eventually."

This was true. Still, she hadn't meant to spring it on him. Gabby could be a little . . . much.

They made their way into the kitchen, not wanting Gabby to

come looking for them. When they walked in, her sister was on the floor cleaning up the yogurt Taylor had managed to drop. It had gone everywhere. Gabby looked up. "Yogurt, anyone?"

Alexander chuckled beside her. "No, thanks. I think I'll pass."

Gabby shrugged. "Suit yourself." She threw the paper towels she'd been using to clean up the mess into the trash, and went to the refrigerator to grab another yogurt. Within seconds, she'd removed the foil lid and placed the new container in front of Taylor along with a spoon. "Eat your yogurt. You can play with your toy after."

It was almost six o'clock, so Grace wasn't surprised her niece was hungry. They'd had lunch hours ago.

"So tell me about yourself," Gabby said to Alexander as she took a seat beside her daughter, not seeming to be in any hurry to leave.

Grace cringed at what she knew was coming, but there wasn't much she could do other than kick her sister out, and she knew how well that would go.

Alexander seemed unfazed. He pulled out a chair, offered it to Grace, and sat down beside her. "What is it you'd like to know?"

Gabby wiped some yogurt from her daughter's mouth. "How old are you? Where are you from? Are you planning to stay in St. Louis?"

"I'm thirty-five. A lot of places. And yes."

Her sister leaned back in her chair, crossing her arms. "Define a lot of places."

Alexander placed his hand on Grace's leg before responding. She hadn't even realized she'd been bouncing it. "My father was an Army officer, so we moved around a lot."

"I see," Gabby said. "Did you have a favorite?"

"Probably Alaska. Although, I'm not sure I could take the winters anymore." Grace had known he'd lived all over the place. He'd told her how hard it had been to make friends growing up.

Her sister shifted gears. "Grace told us you're a doctor."

It wasn't exactly a question, but Alexander answered anyway. "Yes, that's right."

"What kind of doctor?"

"My specialty is in pediatric medicine," he said.

That surprised Grace. She wasn't sure why. Doctors with all sorts of specialties went into the military for various reasons. It also struck her that she'd never thought to ask him. What a great girlfriend she was turning out to be.

"So you like kids?" Her sister probed deeper. Grace thought about saying something, trying to change the subject, but didn't figure it would do any good. Even if Gabby went with the flow and dropped her current line of questioning, she'd find a way to bring it up again—today, or heaven forbid at Thanksgiving.

Alexander didn't seem to mind her question. "I love kids. One of these days I'd like to have several of my own." This was also news to Grace. In all their conversations, they'd never discussed children. But why would they have? It wasn't as if they were a couple.

But now they were. Sort of. The reality of what they were was still a bit fuzzy.

Her sister's eyes sparkled at Alexander's assertion. "That's good to know. Isn't it, Grace?"

Grace couldn't believe her sister was doing this. "Yeah."

Alexander squeezed her leg, offering comfort. It was Grace who should be comforting him. She couldn't believe her sister.

He tilted his head toward Taylor. "If I remember correctly, Grace told me your little one was three, correct?"

This seemed to please her sister. "Yes. She'll be four in March." Her sister ran a hand over the top of Taylor's head. "She's growing up so fast."

"They do that," he said.

Taylor was almost finished with her yogurt, so Grace thought this was as good a time as any to try and get her sister out the door. "Did you need me to help you take any of Taylor's things out to the car?"

"Trying to get rid of me?"

"I—"

Her sister waved her hand in front of her face in a dismissive gesture and stood. "No, it's fine. I'll get out of your hair. I'm sure you want to spend some quality time with your man." She scooped her daughter up and walked to the sink to wipe her face and hands before addressing Alexander. "It was nice to finally meet you."

"Likewise."

"Walk me to my car?" Gabby asked Grace.

Grace nodded, and then to Alexander she said, "I'll be right back."

Gabby didn't say much on their way outside. She waited until Taylor was secured into her booster seat before drawing Grace in for a hug. "I like him."

"Thanks." What else was she supposed to say?

Her sister looked her in the eye, her face serious. "I know this last year has been hard, but you seem to have found a good man. Don't push him away because you feel some sort of obligation to Kurt. He's not coming back. And you've got a living, breathing"— she grinned—"hunk of a man in there who seems to adore you. Don't mess it up."

Grace's throat constricted as a flood of emotions washed over her. She couldn't speak even if she wanted to.

Gabby gave her another hug and left her standing on the sidewalk as she got in her car and drove away. Her sister's words were fresh in her mind. *Don't mess it up.* Grace looked back to the house knowing Alexander was inside. He wanted them to be a real couple. At least she was fairly sure he did.

Could she do it? Could she let go of her doubts and just let things happen naturally, as he'd suggested?

A cool breeze came from the north and she pulled her coat tighter around her as she headed back inside. She didn't know if she could be what Alexander needed, but she knew one thing: she was going to try. Gabby was right—Alexander was a good man, and for good or bad she wasn't willing to let him go.

***

Alexander made his way into the living room when he heard the door open. From what Grace had shared with him about her sister, he'd known Gabby was direct and she hadn't disappointed. Gabby's line of questioning had made Grace uncomfortable, but it hadn't bothered him. She had a right to know about the man who was dating her sister.

He'd been reluctant to talk about the future when it came to him and Grace, but it wasn't as if he was hiding it either. Alexander just didn't think it was something Grace was ready for. She seemed content to live in the moment for now and he was okay with that. He could wait.

Grace stopped when she saw him standing there. It was as if she didn't know what she should do or say. He had to wonder what her sister had told her because he had no doubt, given what little he knew of Gabby, that she would have given her opinion, good or bad.

He crossed to where she was standing a few feet from the door. She still had her coat on, so he reached for the zipper and helped her remove it.

"Thanks," she muttered as he hung her coat up for her.

"Do you want to talk about it?"

Grace took a step closer to him and placed her hands palm down on his chest. It was a bold move for her. "I didn't mean to ambush you."

Placing his hands on her hips, he pulled her against him. "I know you didn't."

"She doesn't have a filter sometimes." Grace gazed up at him through her lashes. It was such a submissive look.

"I didn't mind her questions." He wanted to ease her mind. "She was feeling me out to see if we're a good match."

Her jaw flexed as if she was going to say something then thought better of it.

He brushed his thumb against the side of her face. "What is it?"

She averted her gaze, staring at his chest. "She told me not to mess it up."

Alexander couldn't help but chuckle, which brought Grace's head up. She was surprised by his reaction. "How exactly does she think you'll mess it up?"

"By pushing you away." It sounded as if she were admitting to some heinous crime.

He brought her closer, letting his lips linger an inch away from hers. "Is that what you want? For me to go away?"

The muscles in her throat moved beneath his hand as she swallowed. "No."

"Good." He smiled and figured this was as good a time as any to bring up their sleeping arrangements for the night. "I brought a change of clothes with me."

She had no problem following the shift in conversation. "You're spending the night?"

"If that's okay with you."

Grace licked her lips, drawing his attention back to her mouth.

"I'd like that."

He hummed as he closed the distance between them. As much as he wished otherwise, Alexander tempered his kiss and kept it fairly chaste. "Have you eaten dinner yet?"

"No. Not yet."

"Me either." He kissed her again.

"I could make something," she suggested.

Alexander didn't release her. "Or we could just order in."

She circled her arms around his neck and pulled him closer, letting him know she was in the moment as much as he was. "Sounds good."

It would have made more sense for them to put things on the back burner until after they ate, but he couldn't seem to stop kissing her. Alexander began walking backward toward the kitchen. She followed him step for step, not allowing any space to come between them.

When they reached the table, he used one hand to push the napkins that were lying in the way onto the floor. He'd worry about picking them up later. All he could think about at the moment was Grace and getting inside her.

He lifted her until she was sitting on the table and spread her legs so he could position himself between them. She was warm and inviting, and the little moans coming out of her were going straight to his cock.

"Lift your arms," he muttered between kisses.

She didn't hesitate and neither did he. Alexander reached for the hem of her shirt, worked it up her torso, and threw it on the floor, not caring where it landed. He went for her bra next and it soon joined her shirt on the floor.

"I love your tits," he said, cupping one of her breasts, feeling the weight of it against his palm. "They fit perfectly in my hand."

Her fingers pressed into his scalp when he brought his fingers together and pinched her nipple. He loved playing with her breasts, but that wasn't what was at the forefront of his mind. The need to feel her surrounding him was too strong to deny.

He removed his tie, letting it fall to the floor, before unbuttoning his dress shirt. She met his gaze and held it. This felt different. At least it did to him. He hoped she felt it, too. There was no playing, no protocol. It was just the two of them. Being together. Connecting.

Grace helped him push the shirt off his shoulders, running her hands back up his arms. Her fingers left a trail of heat in their wake. He picked up one of her hands and pressed his lips to the inside of her wrist. "You are so beautiful."

Almost immediately he saw the color rise in her cheeks. "Thank you." Then she surprised him by using her free hand to draw a line from his collarbone to the top of his slacks. "You're not so bad yourself."

Something passed between them, a moment that had him thinking that maybe his feelings for her weren't all one-sided. That maybe, just maybe, she might be able to feel the same way about him someday.

"My bed was rather cold last night." It was a way to say he'd missed having her in his bed. He was afraid if he came out and said it that it might scare her, which was the opposite of what he wanted.

She pressed her lips together and looked down, her gaze on the hand with which she was fingering the top of his pants. "I'm glad you're staying tonight."

It wasn't exactly as good as saying she'd missed him, but he'd take it. He released her wrist and went for the button on her jeans. She watched as he popped the button and eased the zipper down. "Lean back a little."

Grace placed her hands behind her on the table, leaned back, and lifted her hips. He worked the material down her legs, removing her shoes in the process. She stared at him with such trust in her eyes that he couldn't help but react. His heart beat hard in his chest and his erection pressed impatiently against the seam of his thin dress slacks.

Alexander placed his hand on her chest, letting her know he wanted her to lie back. He hooked his fingers into the sides of her panties and got rid of them as well, leaving her completely naked before him.

Taking his time, he knelt down and spread her open with his fingers. He leaned in, allowing her musky scent to fill his senses, before taking a long leisurely lick. There was something about going down on a woman that Alexander loved.

He did it again and again, circling her clit, sucking her labia into his mouth, and dipping his tongue inside every now and then to taste even more of what she had to offer. Grace's hand came off the table as if she wanted to reach for him, but then she let it fall again. He realized she wasn't sure if that's what he wanted or not.

Shifting a little, he took hold of her hand and placed it on top of his head, giving her permission. Grace laced her fingers through his hair. He loved when she touched him. She didn't try to control his movements. It was more tactile—another point of connection, grounding.

He felt the trembling of her limbs and knew she was close. But suddenly he didn't want her to come this way. He wanted to be inside her when she fell off that cliff.

When he stood, her hand fell away and she opened her eyes, worry in them. He swiftly put to rest any concerns she had that she'd done something wrong by removing his pants and rolling a condom down his length.

Alexander didn't waste any time once he was sheathed. He nestled himself between her legs once more and pressed his cock against her entrance.

Holding her gaze, he pressed himself home, feeling her walls contract around him. It took everything he had not to close his eyes to savor the sensation, but he hadn't wanted to break eye contact.

He reached for her and she came willingly, sitting up and wrapping her legs around his waist. While he had no issues making love to her spread out on the table, she was too far away.

They kissed and touched while they moved. There was no hurry, nothing that required their attention outside the two of them. He'd never felt anything like it before and he knew why.

I love you was on the tip of his tongue, but he bit it back. She wasn't ready. He knew that. Instead, he chose different words. Words that expressed how he felt, but that she could take in a number of different ways. He grasped the back of her head, forcing her to look at him as he reached between them and began massaging her clit. "Mine."

Grace gasped as her orgasm approached and he gripped her head tighter. She dug her nails into his biceps as he pumped in and out of her, driving her higher. His signs of dominance were making her hot.

"Say it," he demanded.

Her breath hitched and he felt her muscles contract around his cock in response. "Yours."

"Damn right," he muttered before crushing his lips against hers. "Now come for me."

He thrust into her harder, faster, not relenting until he heard her muffled screams into his mouth.

Only then did he let go and join her, allowing his release to flow through him as he held her.

Chapter 22

Grace pulled her ponytail tight and took a final look at herself in the mirror before leaving the house. She was running a little later than usual but she couldn't bring herself to be sorry. Alexander had woken her up in the most delicious way. She could still feel his hands ghosting over her body . . . his teeth nipping at her skin. He seemed to know exactly how to touch her.

"You look happy this morning," Beth said when she and Grace were alone a few hours later.

She had no reason to deny it. Besides, if Beth hadn't already heard about what had happened at the club Saturday night, she probably would. Especially since she was part of Alexander's circle of friends. Grace grabbed several bottles off the shelf next to her and began filling them. "I am."

"I'm glad. You deserve it."

Grace didn't respond.

Unfortunately, Beth picked up on her silence. "Something wrong?"

"No. Everything's good. Great, even."

"Why do I sense a *but* coming?"

"It's nothing." She focused on what she was doing and Beth didn't pry. Thing was, Grace wanted to talk to someone about what she was feeling and her options were limited. There was no way she could tell her sister, and Alexander wasn't an option either. Not about this. She needed someone that was unbiased but who understood. At least in part. "Do you think it's too soon?"

Beth carried on as if there hadn't been a break in the conversation. "Too soon for what?"

This was the hard part. Finding the words to explain. "Alexander. He's . . . he's more than—" She searched for the right words. "What I feel . . ."

Beth placed a bowl in the large industrial sink and selected two clean ones from the shelf. "You're falling for him."

Direct and to the point. In some ways Beth was a lot like Grace's sister. But Beth seemed to pick her words a little more carefully.

"Shouldn't it be too soon?" It was an honest question and one she'd been struggling with for a while. With every passing day her feelings for Alexander grew. He'd become important to her.

Beth eyes softened as she met Grace's gaze. "Only you can answer that. Do you think it's too soon?"

"My sister doesn't think so."

"That's not what I asked." The Domme in Beth was coming out a little and hit its mark.

"I don't know. A part of me says it is, but then when I'm with him I just . . ."

"Forget about everything else but him?"

Grace nodded. "Yeah."

Beth grinned. "Then I think you have your answer."

"I know Kurt wants me to move on."

It was said more to herself than to Beth, but her boss heard it nonetheless. "He wants you to move on?"

"What?" Grace asked, confused.

"You said Kurt wants you to move on. Not that you know he'd want you to move on." Beth paused. "You can tell me to butt out if it's none of my business."

Right then Grace made a decision. If it was anyone else, she would probably have made something up or said she'd said it wrong, but she didn't think Beth would judge her. Or Kurt.

She took a deep breath and released it. "Kurt wrote me a letter. Before he died. He asked Alexander to deliver it to me if anything happened to him."

"I see." Beth said, wiping her hands on a nearby towel. "So this letter . . ."

"Kurt said he wanted me to move on. To find another Dom."

Beth took Grace's hand and squeezed, offering her a bit of comfort. She knew this wasn't easy for Grace to talk about. "That's why you came to the club."

"Yes." Grace used the back of her free hand to wipe the moisture from her eyes. "Kurt had done some research and found out about the club and Katrina. He'd . . . he'd known I would come back to St. Louis to be near my mom and sister."

"Sounds like he was a good husband and master. Very prepared."

Grace smiled despite the heaviness in her heart. "He was."

"And now you seem to have found another man who wants that place in your life." It wasn't a question and Grace had to wonder how much Beth had picked up on in the little time she'd seen Alexander and her together.

"He wants a relationship. Outside of play." They were slow at the moment, the morning rush over. Otherwise there was no way they'd be able to have so much uninterrupted time to talk. Grace was actually surprised Tommy hadn't burst through the double doors yet.

Beth propped her hip against the counter. "And that's not what you want?"

The way she said it gave Grace the impression that Beth didn't believe that for a second. Considering the smile she'd strolled in with that morning, it was the obvious conclusion. "I do."

It only took a moment for Beth to connect the dots. "So what's the problem?"

"I guess it's insecurity. I mean I was with Kurt for ten years. I don't know how to be someone's girlfriend anymore." Grace lowered herself onto one of the stools. "Stupid, right?"

Her boss' eyebrow rose and she gave Grace a look she was all too familiar with. Did all Dominants get pulled into a room and shown how to give a sub that look of disapproval?

"Sorry. Poor choice of words."

"Yes." Beth went to the big walk-in refrigerator and retrieved a bag of lettuce. She placed it on the counter and tore it open. "I won't tell you I know what you're going through because I don't, but your husband went out of his way to let you know he wanted you to find someone else who could meet your needs. If Alexander is that man, why not embrace it and let things happen naturally?"

"You sound like Alexander."

Beth grinned. "Wise man." She pointed to the counter a few feet away from Grace. "Can you hand me those cucumbers over there?"

Grace hopped off her stool and brought the cucumbers to Beth. "It's easier to do when I'm with him. It's only when I'm alone that I can't get my brain to shut off."

"Give it time. If it's meant to be, it will all work out. Look at what happened with me and Drew. I wasn't exactly looking for a relationship when we met, but he was persistent. Eventually, I had to give in." She said the last part with affection.

Every time she'd seen the two of them together, the love between them was there plain as day. Then Grace had seen them together at the club. They had a connection, a bond. She'd had that once with Kurt. She wanted it again.

That afternoon as they were leaving, Beth pulled her aside. "If you ever need to talk, call me. It doesn't matter what time."

"I couldn't—"

"Yes, you can." Beth took hold of both her hands this time. "I may be your boss, but I'm also your friend. I know you have Alexander, but sometimes it's good to have another female to talk to. Especially one that understands the lifestyle you've chosen."

She hesitated and Beth raised her eyebrow again.

"All right. Okay," Grace said.

"Good. Now that we have that settled, do you have any plans tonight or would you like to grab some dinner with me? Drew's working, so I'm going to be stuck at home by myself unless I can convince you to join me."

Grace was tempted to roll her eyes, but she didn't. Dominant types didn't tend to like that. And even though Beth wasn't her Dom, it still felt as if doing so would be very bratty behavior. "I don't have any plans."

"Great. I need to swing by my house to shower and change. How about we meet at Imo's in an hour?"

"Sounds good."

As soon as Grace walked through the front door of her house, she hung up her coat, kicked off her shoes, and reached for her phone to text Alexander. She had no idea if he was planning to come by tonight, but she didn't want to worry him if he did stop by and she wasn't home.

Beth invited me to dinner. Drew is working. – Grace

While she was waiting for his response, she trotted up the stairs to take a shower. Working in a restaurant, no matter what, at the end of the day you smelled like food. It was inevitable.

By the time she stepped out of the shower ten minutes later, she felt much cleaner and she had a message from Alexander.

I'm still stuck at work. Have fun with Beth. – Alexander

Grace bit her lower lip as she considered her response. Should she ask him to come over tonight? That was an acceptable thing for a girlfriend to do, right?

Would you like to come over later? – Grace

Several more minutes passed that had her second-guessing herself. Given he'd be coming over after dinner, it was clear she was asking him to spend the night. Again.

It might be something a girlfriend would ask, but she wasn't only his girlfriend. She was his sub. Had she overstepped some sort of boundary?

I'll have to stop by my house for some clothes. Around 8? – Alexander

She breathed a sigh of relief. It had been years since she'd had to navigate the dating waters, even if it was with Alexander.

I'll see you then. – Grace

Several more minutes went by and she wondered if maybe it was taking him so long to respond because he was in a meeting. That would make sense.

I'm very much looking forward to it. – Alexander

And Grace, make sure you eat well. You'll be burning off a lot of energy tonight. – Alexander

Two sentences and her body temperature rose by at least ten degrees. She blew out a loud breath and glanced over at her bed— the bed she and Alexander had shared several times now. A smile pulled at her lips. She was sure the guilt would keep cropping up now and then, but she wasn't going to try and pretend this wasn't what she wanted anymore.

She sent him a quick text back before she headed out to meet Beth.

I'm looking forward to it, Sir. – Grace

***

Fucking lawyers. They were the thorn in his side these days. Why they didn't get medical degrees of their own if they were going to try cases involving malpractice he didn't understand. They certainly thought they knew better than everyone else, including those who actually had a medical degree.

He'd been stuck in that conference room for six hours. Six fucking hours, attempting to explain to that pompous jackass of a lawyer that the scenario he was proposing was not only absurd but downright impossible. But the idiot had been convinced he was right. Even Alexander's boss agreed, but still the man persisted. In fact, after a while Alexander began to think the man dug in his heels *because* of Alexander's boss backing him up. Janet might not be a doctor, but she'd been in this business for close to twenty years. She wasn't stupid.

Alexander tried to shake it off. What he needed was something to get his mind off the idiot he'd left up on the fourth floor. What he needed was Grace.

After climbing into his car, he drove home. He had some time to kill since it was still early. When Grace had texted him to say she was having dinner with Beth, it had given him a moment to catch his breath and not strangle a certain lawyer. He was glad she and Beth were forming a deeper relationship. Grace didn't have many friends. Any, that he knew of actually. Hopefully going to the club would change that. She could connect with other subs and not have to worry about them judging her.

After showering and changing out of his suit into something a bit more comfortable, Alexander swung through a drive-thru before making his way to Grace's. He was a little early, but he had no problem waiting.

Grace pulled into her driveway around seven forty-five. The sun had already set, but the lights from the streetlamps bounced off her blond hair, drawing the eye of anyone who was watching.

She turned toward the noise when she heard him get out of the car. The look on her face morphed from concern to joy as she realized it was him. He would never get tired of seeing that look. It had been appearing more often the last few days. Alexander hoped that meant she was getting used to the idea of them being a couple.

Based on the conversation they'd had the night before, he was hopeful.

"Have you been waiting long?" she asked as she came toward him.

He grabbed his overnight bag and his cane and locked up his vehicle. "Not too long." In truth, he'd been there since a little after seven. It didn't matter. He pulled her against him and gave her a swift kiss before they went inside. "How was dinner?"

"Nice." She removed her coat and hung it in the closet before taking his and doing the same. "Did you know Beth grew up in Ohio?"

"Can't say that I did."

"She moved here to go to school—"

He crushed her against him and cut off her words with a bruising kiss. When they came up for air a few minutes later, her breathing was labored and her lips were swollen. "As much as I want to hear all about your evening, there are more pressing matters I want to attend to first." Alexander took her hand and placed it over his erection.

She cupped him and rubbed her palm up and down, causing him to groan. It felt good, but it wasn't exactly what he wanted.

Before all thought went out the window, he removed her hand. The cooler air hitting his groin brought back a little sanity. "I want you in your room, kneeling on the floor, waiting for me when I come upstairs."

Her pupils dilated a little more. "Yes, Sir."

Alexander dropped his hands, releasing her. He waited at the base of the stairs while she ascended and turned the corner toward her bedroom.

The time it took him to check the downstairs and make sure everything was locked up for the night gave him the opportunity to settle himself. After the day he'd had, what he needed more than anything was to let it all go and sink into the dynamic he and Grace had. The thought of seeing her gazing up at him with those expressive eyes of hers while she waited for his command had him hurrying up the stairs as fast as his bum leg would take him.

When he walked into her bedroom, he found Grace exactly as he'd requested. She was naked, kneeling by the end of her bed, her knees spread wide. Her breathing told him she was as excited as he was for what was to come. She was such a beautiful submissive, and she was his. The internal voice inside his head telling him he should feel guilty for the thoughts running through his head was almost nonexistent. He wanted Grace and she wanted him. They weren't betraying anyone.

He closed the distance between them, using his cane to steady himself. It had been a long day. She kept her gaze on the ground as he approached, but that wasn't what he wanted. He wanted to see her eyes, to see the emotion in them staring back at him.

Reaching out with his left hand, he threaded his fingers through her hair, letting the silky strands run through his fingers. Even such a simple gesture brought him some much needed peace. He heard her sigh and knew she felt it, too.

Alexander gathered her hair together and tilted her head back so she was looking up at him. There was complete trust in her eyes, and he decided to take a chance. He lifted his other hand, his cane dangling from his fingers, and rubbed his thumb and index finger along the line of her jaw. "I missed you today. I had a horribly long meeting and all I could think about was how much I would rather be here with you." He paused. "Or anywhere with you."

There was a slight shift in her eyes and he could tell she wanted to avert her gaze, but she didn't—her years of training evident. He waited for several minutes to see if she would bolt or use her safeword, but she didn't.

When he was satisfied she wasn't going to abruptly end their scene, he continued. "We're going to enjoy some impact play tonight. I want you to lie on the bed facedown, legs spread. I'm going to have some fun."

Chapter 23

Grace could feel the warmth from her shoulders to her knees. Alexander had worked her over good with several different floggers. She'd forgotten how good it felt to drift into subspace as the flogger kissed her skin.

A contented sigh left her lips as she snuggled closer to Alexander. He tightened his hold, giving her breast he held in his palm a little squeeze. "All right?"

"Hmm. More than all right. I think I'm still in subspace."

His chest vibrated beneath her cheek. "You did seem to enjoy your flogging quite a bit."

"Yes, I did." She placed a kiss on his chest and skimmed her hand down the length of his torso. "Are you feeling better?"

It hadn't taken her long to realize he'd had a bad day and had needed to work through some of his frustrations. He hadn't been rough with her, not really. But as the scene went on, she felt his mood shift as he let go of whatever it was that had been bothering him. She'd been pleased she was able to help.

"Much better. Thank you, *gattina*." His lips brushed against the top of her head.

They fell into a contented silence as they lay there touching. Everything felt right. Peaceful. She thought about what her sister and Beth had said. She knew they were right. It was time she fully embraced whatever this was between her and Alexander and stopped living in the past.

Making that decision took a huge weight off her shoulders. "Are you staying?"

She felt his lips turn up into a grin. "Unless you're kicking me out."

"Nope. No kicking."

He continued to play with her breast as they talked, and her lady parts were starting to wake up again even though he'd already given her three orgasms tonight. She knew she needed a distraction. "Can I ask you a question?"

"Anything."

"What does *gattina* mean? I'm assuming it's Italian?" She absentmindedly traced a circle around his nipple, memorizing the dips and bumps.

"It is." He lowered his hands to her waist and shifted her so she was lying on top of him. "It means kitten."

She could feel his erection growing against her belly and wondered if her playing with his nipple had a similar effect on Alexander as his massaging her breast had on her. Still, she tried to focus on the conversation at hand. "Do you call all your submissives *kitten*?"

An amused smirk appeared on his face. "No."

So it was only her. For some reason she liked that he'd reserved that name for her alone.

Alexander cupped the side of her face with one hand and reached between them with the other, finding her clit. He circled it slowly as he held her gaze and whispered, "My sweet *gattina*."

She heard his words, but more than that she felt the emotion behind them.

He increased the pressure on her clit, driving her higher, yet he made no move to change their position or reach for a condom. Instead, he cradled her face in one hand with the gentlest pressure while he drove her toward another orgasm.

Her body was still buzzing from earlier, so it didn't take long before she was teetering on the edge. "Sir?"

"Yes, *gattina*?"

"Sir, I'm so close. May I come? Please?"

He pulled her face down to his. "Let go. Come for me."

His words were barely audible, but she'd heard them. More importantly, her body heard them and responded. He caught her gasp with his lips, plunging his tongue inside her mouth to devour every moan she had to give while she rode out her fourth orgasm of the night.

As she was coming back down to earth, she heard him rip open a condom. Moments later, he lifted her hips and placed his cock at her entrance. There was no talking, no sounds other than their kisses as he lowered her down onto his erection.

He held onto her hips, guiding her movements. Time slowed and all her nerve endings felt as if they were right below the surface of her skin. She could feel the air around them brushing against her flesh. It was so much cooler than the heat, the fire, she felt inside.

She had no idea how long they rocked back and forth, grinding against one another. He kept her on the brink without allowing her to fall over the cliff for what felt like forever, but she didn't mind. He seemed to need this as much as he'd needed to flog her earlier. And to be honest, she needed it as well. Things were shifting between them. It had been happening for a while, since the beginning really, but she'd been resisting it. But this. Here. Now. There was no way to pretend. Somehow, Alexander had pushed past all her walls.

Eventually, he flipped them over so he was pressing her into the mattress, but he refused to pick up the pace. He hiked her leg up over his hip, changing the angle. The new position had her digging her nails into his shoulders. She wasn't going to be able to hold on much longer.

He must have been able to read her mind because he reached between them and pinched her nipple. Hard. "Don't you dare come. Not yet."

A whimper escaped her. Grace gritted her teeth, hoping she could stave off her orgasm. She didn't want to disappoint him.

The exquisite torture went on until she saw sweat beading on Alexander's temples. It was obvious he was trying to hold his own climax at bay. "Sir, are you okay?"

He met her gaze, took hold of the side of her head, and kissed her. "I'm fine. Just enjoying fucking my submissive. I can't seem to get enough of her no matter how many times I'm inside her. Or for how long."

Her pussy liked that and responded by tightening around him, trying its best to hold him deep.

Alexander propped himself up on one elbow, but didn't stop the gentle torture as he continued to move his hips in and out. He ran his index finger along the curve of her neck and her mind immediately went to what was missing. His gaze locked with hers. "I want you to wear my collar. The next time we go to Serpent's Kiss, I want my collar around your neck, letting everyone there know you're mine."

She swallowed, a flood of emotions surging through her body. He watched her face and waited for her answer. The answer was easy. Despite her back and forth, her uncertainty that whether or not what she felt for him was right, this thing between them was real. She felt it every time he touched her—every time she thought about him. "I would be honored to wear your collar, Sir."

He took hold of the side of her face, tilted her head back, and kissed her hard. "I will make sure you don't regret it, *gattina*. I promise."

Alexander didn't give her a chance to answer as he continued to kiss her with abandon. As his tongue danced in her mouth, his hips increased their rhythm. She held on, lifting her hips to meet each of his thrusts.

Snaking his hand down over her breast and along her side, he splayed his hand on her hip. He eased his thumb between them, placing it over her clit. The sensation was too much to bear. Her head fell back and her muscles contracted around him in a vise grip. She was panting, desperate to come. Her heart felt as if it would beat out of her chest.

"Do you wish to come, *gattina*?"

She could barely get the words out. "Yes, Sir."

"I do like seeing you like this, so close and trying not to come without permission."

He brushed his thumb over her clit again and she jerked. Not because she didn't want him to touch her, but because he was right. She was about ready to blow whether she wanted to or not.

Alexander scraped his teeth against her neck as he placed gentle pressure against her clit once more. "Come for me."

As he offered his permission, he bit down on her neck, sucking the skin into his mouth. At the same time, he picked up his assault on her clit and began pistoning in and out of her deeper, harder. It was too much. She screamed as her climax hit her like a freight train.

Seconds later, while she was still riding out her own orgasm, she heard Alexander grunt as he reached his own climax. His entire body shook as he emptied himself inside her, letting her know that his reaction to their extended joining had been as powerful for him as it had been for her.

He peeked up at her through his lashes, a satisfied smile on his face. "We will definitely be doing that again."

Maybe it was the look on his face or maybe it was the fact that her emotions were still so close to the surface after what they'd done, but she started laughing. A concerned look crossed his face for a moment before he decided to join her.

***

Alexander woke up drenched in sweat. After he'd regained consciousness in the hospital, he'd suffered from frequent nightmares. They were vivid and terrifying. It was always the same. He was trapped, his leg pinned down, preventing him from moving more than a few inches, while he watched his buddies get picked off one by one. He could see all their faces—the look in their eyes the moment they realized their fate—and there was nothing he could do to stop it.

As his body recovered, he'd also worked on healing his mind as well. He'd talked to one of the VA shrinks a few times and wrote down everything he could remember in a journal. It had been one of the most difficult things he'd ever done in his life, but he knew that if he didn't face it head on that it would slowly destroy him. But dealing with the realities of PTSD was a lot different than reading about it in a medical journal.

He took several deep breaths, trying to calm his heart. It had been months since he'd had one this bad. And usually he could take a few moments to center himself and he'd be okay. For some reason, that wasn't happening this time.

Careful not to wake Grace, he climbed out of bed and made his way into the bathroom. He felt hot and cold at the same time. It was unsettling, but rationally he knew it was most likely the difference in his internal temperature and the cooler air hitting his sweat-covered body.

The logical part of his brain forced him to turn on the shower and get under the spray. As the warm water fell against his skin and the steam filled his lungs, he began to breathe a bit easier. He reached for the soap and began working the latter between his hands, taking his time washing his body.

By the time he turned off the water and reached for one of Grace's towels, he was feeling somewhat normal again. Or as normal as he ever felt these days.

Alexander threw his wet towel into the hamper and turned off the light before heading back into the bedroom where Grace was still sleeping. She was lying on her side, her arms tucked up under her chin. A light from outside streamed in through the windows, landing on her hair. It almost looked as if it had flecks of gold in it the way the light was hitting it.

His chest clenched with a surge of emotion. It was so powerful it nearly sucked the air out of his lungs. It was a combination of overwhelming love mixed with the weight of responsibility he felt to do right by her.

A sigh escaped her lips as she rolled over. The movement caused the sheet to pull away from her chest, leaving most of her upper body exposed. Although his libido wouldn't balk at going another round, he knew she needed her sleep. They both did.

With that in mind, he slipped back into bed as gently as he could. Alexander closed his eyes and tried to relax back into sleep. He listened to Grace breathing beside him, the soft inhale and exhale relaxing him.

The feel of her fingers against his arm made him open his eyes. He looked over at her, but her eyes were still closed. She sucked in a breath and scooted a couple of inches closer to him. "You okay?" Her words were mumbled, barely audible.

He gathered her in his arms and turned them so her back was against his chest. "I'm fine. Go back to sleep."

A sleepy grin appeared on her face. "Yes, Sir."

Alexander smiled and placed a kiss on the back of her head before closing his eyes again.

It took a while, but he did eventually fall asleep again. Holding Grace had helped ward off the nightmares.

Her alarm went off at five thirty. Neither one of them seemed all that anxious to get up, but they both had work. He pulled her to him and gave her a lingering kiss. "Why don't you grab a shower while I go downstairs and make the coffee?"

She stretched. "Okay."

He waited until she was out of sight before he got out of bed. Last night his adrenaline had been pumping, so he hadn't paid much attention to his leg. This morning he was paying for the neglect. It took him several minutes until he felt comfortable putting his full weight on it.

The sound of the shower turning on told Alexander he needed to get a move on. He'd brought his cane upstairs the night before and he reached for it without hesitation. Last night was amazing, but it had taken a toll on his body.

Alexander was pouring their coffee into mugs when Grace strolled into the kitchen. He handed her one before taking a seat at the kitchen table.

"Thanks." She took a sip and set the mug down on the table. "We had some muffins left over yesterday."

"Sounds good." He wasn't picky. At this point he probably would have eaten just about anything she put in front of him. They'd both burned off a lot of calories last night.

Grace brought a plate of five muffins to the table. "There's cranberry, banana nut, and one blueberry, I think."

They spent the next several minutes devouring the muffins. To be honest, he probably could have eaten all five himself.

As they were cleaning up, Alexander felt he needed to broach the subject of her collar again. Although he was fairly sure she did want to wear his collar, it was always better to address these things when hormones were not in play. This was a serious commitment for both of them.

He wrapped one arm around her waist and tugged her flush against him. Grace came willingly, circling her arms around his neck. She looked almost angelic as she smiled up at him.

"I thought we could go shopping tonight."

The look on her face told him she hadn't been expecting that.

Alexander pressed on. "I know some Doms like more traditional collars for their submissives, but I want something you can wear everyday as well."

He felt her muscles tense, but she didn't comment.

"Have you changed your mind?"

Grace stared back at him with wide eyes. "No." She swallowed.

"I just . . . Kurt picked out my collar himself. I figured . . ."

"I can pick something out on my own if you'd prefer, but I'd rather have your input." He cupped her ass and pressed her pelvis against him in a suggestive way. "The final decision will be mine, of course."

She smiled up at him. "Of course."

He placed a kiss on her lips and released her. "I'm hoping to get out of work on time today. How about I pick you up at five thirty? We can get something to eat and then go look for your collar."

Alexander's day went much smoother than the previous one. The idiot lawyer was nowhere in sight.

After lunch his boss stopped by his desk. "I was wondering if you have a minute."

He glanced at the stack of folders to his left. It wasn't as if they were going anywhere. "Sure."

Once they were inside Janet's office, she walked behind her large wooden desk, sat down, and invited him to take a seat. "I wanted to talk to you about the meeting yesterday."

His good mood went out the window. "What about it?"

"I wanted to let you know I was impressed by how you handled yourself. Gregg is an ass and more than once I've wanted to drop-kick him into next week."

Alexander chuckled. "You won't get any argument from me."

Janet grinned. "He likes to goad people. It's how he's made his reputation. You didn't bite."

"After having drill sergeants shouting in your face, Gregg Bowers isn't all that scary."

"I imagine not." She laughed. "Anyway, I wanted to talk to you about your future here. You're a great asset and I'd hate to lose you. I know when we first talked you were hoping to start your own practice."

She left the sentence unfinished, giving him an opportunity to take it wherever he wished. "At the moment, that's still the plan."

Janet leaned back in her chair. "What can I do to change that?"

Chapter 24

Grace was surprised to find her sister sitting on her front steps when she got home from the café. It was the middle of the day, which meant Gabby should have been working. "Hey."

Gabby looked up as Grace approached. "Hey."

She took a seat on the steps next to her sister. "Shouldn't you still be at work?"

"I took the day off." Her sister shrugged like it wasn't a big deal, but she could tell something was off. Especially since Gabby wasn't asking Grace the latest details regarding her relationship with Alexander.

"Want to talk about it?" Grace asked when Gabby didn't say anything more.

It took a moment for her sister to respond. Gabby stared down at her hands, twisting them nervously in front of her. "I did something stupid. Really, *really* stupid."

Grace was almost afraid to ask. "What did you do?"

"I slept with Jax."

"When?"

Grace tried to keep the shock out of her voice, but she didn't know how well she succeeded. Her sister looked as if she wanted to crawl into a cave and disappear. "Last night."

When Grace remained silent, her sister continued. "He wanted to take Taylor to the park after work, so I arranged for him to pick her up at the babysitter. By the time I got to his place to pick her up at seven thirty, she was already passed out on his couch."

"How exactly does that translate into you two . . ."

Gabby cracked a bit of a smile at Grace's reluctance to go on. "Having sex?"

"Yeah." It was stupid. Grace had no trouble talking about all sorts of kinky things with Alexander, but with her sister she felt like she was a bumbling teenager again discussing her first kiss.

"I don't know exactly. One minute we were talking about how he wanted to see Taylor more, and the next we were kissing." Gabby dropped her head into her hands. "Before I knew it, our clothes were on the floor and we were in his bedroom. We didn't even make it to the bed."

"Was it good?"

Gabby snapped her head up to meet Grace's gaze. "What?"

"The sex. Was it good?"

Her sister looked at Grace as if she's lost her mind. Maybe she had. This wasn't the type of thing Grace normally talked about. "That's not the point. It shouldn't have happened."

"Maybe not. But it did."

"I know." Her sister lowered her head into her hands again. "What am I going to do?"

"What do you want to do?"

"Hide."

Her sister's honest answer made Grace laugh. "I'm serious."

"So am I. All I want to do is curl into a ball and hope no one finds me."

Grace could see this conversation wasn't going anywhere fast. It was warm out by November standards, but there was still a nip in the air. "Do you want to come inside?"

"Do you have anything harder than pop in your fridge?"

"I think I may have some wine." She was pretty sure she still had an unopened bottle in the back of one of her cabinets.

Gabby pushed her hair away from her face. "Unless you have a whole vineyard in there, I don't think it's going to be enough."

"Come on, it can't be that bad." Grace rubbed a hand up and down her sister's back.

"Yeah, it can."

Grace felt as if she was missing something. Sure, Gabby sleeping with her ex wasn't ideal, but this seemed like overkill.

They sat there for a while, not speaking, the cool concrete they were sitting on slowly seeping through her jeans. Her sister seemed to be thinking about something and Grace didn't want to interrupt her thought process.

Eventually, her sister sighed. "I think I'm falling for him again."

Grace waited.

"He's been so nice lately—wanting to spend time with Taylor, asking if I need help with anything." Gabby glanced in Grace's direction. "The last time he took off he broke my heart and left me trying to raise a newborn on my own."

"I know." Grace pulled her sister in for a hug.

After a few minutes, Gabby pulled back. "I should go. I need to pick Taylor up soon."

"Do you need someone to watch her tonight?" Grace wasn't sure how Alexander would feel about it, but her sister needed her. If it cost her a sore bottom, she'd take it.

"No. That's all right. I've had all day to wallow. Besides, I don't want to mess up your evening."

Her sister stood, brushing the dirt off her jeans, so Grace did the same. "You wouldn't."

Gabby ignored her. She gave Grace a peck on the cheek and turned toward her car. "Thanks for listening."

Her sister was halfway to her vehicle before Grace could respond. "Call me if you need me."

"I will." Her sister opened her car door and slid inside.

Grace stood at the base of her front steps and watched as Gabby drove away.

Once her sister was out of sight, Grace ascended the stairs, unlocked her door, and went inside. Gabby had always been more spontaneous than Grace. Which, all things considered, was a little ironic. As far as Grace knew, her sister wasn't into kinky sex.

After hanging up her jacket and kicking off her shoes, Grace checked her watch. It was a little after four, which meant she had about an hour and a half before Alexander came to pick her up. More than enough time to shower and put in a load of laundry.

Alexander knocked on her door at five twenty-seven. She snatched her coat from the closet and opened the door, ready to leave. But before she could cross the threshold, he stepped forward, pushing her back into the foyer, and shut the door behind him. He gripped her waist with both hands and jerked her closer. Her heart pounded in her chest as his lips found hers and she melted against him, letting her tongue tangle with his.

Alexander rested his forehead against hers, but didn't let her go. "That's better."

She hummed. "Did you have a bad day again today?"

"No. Actually, it went well." He didn't seem surprised that she'd picked up on his mood the day before. "I even got a job offer."

"Really? Where?" Maybe it should have seemed odd that they were standing in her foyer, foreheads still pressed together, having this conversation, but it didn't feel awkward.

"Same company I work for now." He brushed his mouth against her forehead and let his arms fall down to his sides. She didn't miss that he still had his cane. Nor had she missed how much he'd leaned on it that morning. "But my position was always meant to be temporary, until my license came through and I could open my own practice."

She knew how important starting his own practice was to him. They'd talked about it a lot over the last two months. "What are you going to do?"

He picked her coat up off the floor and helped her into it. "I don't know. The money's good. Benefits. Vacation. 401K."

"But it isn't what you want." She could hear it in his voice.

"Shuffling papers around isn't exactly how I saw my future." He opened the door for her and followed her outside. "Then again, up until a year ago I figured I'd be spending at least another ten years in the military."

She nodded, not feeling as if words were needed. Plans changed. Circumstances changed. They both knew that.

Over dinner Grace told him about her sister's visit. "If you needed to take care of your sister tonight, all you had to do was let me know."

"Thanks." Knowing that made her feel a bit better. They were still feeling things out, especially the relationship part. "Her relationship with Jax has always been complicated. The chemistry was always there, but I think she was looking for something more permanent than he was."

"And now?" he asked, swiping a fry from her plate and popping it into his mouth.

Grace shrugged. "I don't know. He seems to be more invested in Taylor, wanting to spend time with her . . . be her dad. But I'm not sure Gabby's willing to open herself up again. He really broke her heart when he took off the first time."

"Hopefully they'll be able to figure it out. It's never easy when kids are involved. Too often they get stuck in the middle." The way he said it made her think he was speaking from personal experience, but as far as she knew his parents had a happy marriage. He seemed to know where her thoughts were going. "My best friend in junior high. In the two years I was there, his parents had split, gotten back together, and then split again. Last I heard, he was living with his mom and spending weekends with his dad. It was hard on him."

"I'm sorry."

Alexander stole another fry. "It was a long time ago."

They finished their dinner and walked hand in hand down the block to a jewelry store. Grace had passed by it several times, but she'd never been inside. She'd never had reason to.

He held the door open and gestured for her to go first. "After you."

***

A woman behind the counter looked up as they entered. She smiled. "Welcome. Anything particular I can help you find today?"

Alexander placed a hand on the small of Grace's back and guided her forward. "We'd like to look at your selection of necklaces."

"Right over here."

She directed them to a long glass case full of necklaces. Most of them he immediately discarded. They were too flashy. He wanted something she could wear every day and to the club.

"I'll give you a few minutes to look. Just holler if you need anything," the woman said before walking to the other side of the store to help another customer.

He moved closer to Grace, his chest pressed against her back as he peered over her shoulder. "See anything you like?" Alexander could feel her hesitation. "I want it to be something you're comfortable wearing."

She glanced up at him, and then back to the case. "I like these two."

The two necklaces she pointed out were in line with what he was looking for, but neither was quite right. One had two circles, one inside the other. The other had a single circle with a small jewel hanging from the center.

Then he spotted something a little farther down. It was almost hidden because it was at the end of the row, next to the bracelets. He moved them closer to get a better look.

"What do you think?" he asked once they were standing in front of the necklace.

"It's pretty."

He brushed her hair back away from her neck with the tips of his fingers and leaned in to whisper in her ear. "Do you like it?"

She sucked in a breath. "Yes, S—"

"Did you find something?" the sales woman asked, reappearing with a flourish from around the corner.

Alexander pointed to the necklace. "We'd like to see that one."

"Of course." The woman removed the necklace from the case and placed it on top of the counter. "It has a simple elegance to it."

"That it does." He picked it up, letting it drape over his fingers. "You'd be able to put a small charm on at the back?"

The saleswoman leaned in slightly, taking a look at the clasp. "That shouldn't be a problem. What did you have in mind?"

"A heart. And I'd want it engraved." He turned to face Grace. "Turn around and lift up your hair. I want to see what it looks like on you."

Obediently, she turned so her back was to him and lifted her hair away from her neck. It only took a few seconds to secure the necklace. As soon as it was in place, she faced him, letting her hair fall. The three linked circles rested just above her collarbone.

He ran a single finger along the black chain down to the gold circles. Seeing it around her neck confirmed it was the one.

Grace's gaze met his. The look in her eyes matched what he was feeling inside: pride, joy—and, he dared to hope—love. "We'll take it."

The sales woman said something, but he didn't catch it. His focus was on Grace.

"Sir?"

Alexander tore his gaze away from Grace and turned to address the sales woman. He had no idea what she'd said, but it didn't matter. "How long to get the charm and have it engraved?"

"As long as we have the charm in stock, we should be able to have it to you in a few days. A week at most."

It took them another half hour to finish things up. He'd looked over the charm options carefully, trying to find one that would work with the necklace and be big enough for what he wanted to have written on it. In the end, he'd settled on a gold heart about the size of Grace's thumb. He filled out the form for the engraving, making sure every letter was legible.

As they were leaving, a sharp pain shot up his leg and he stumbled. Grace reached out to steady him. "Do you want to stay here while I get the car?"

He breathed through the pain and waited for it to subside. "No. It's not that far."

Grace didn't argue, but she did stay close to his side. He hated having to lean on his cane so much, but it was that or he was going to fall flat on his face.

It took a bit longer, but they made it back to the vehicle. He sat down behind the wheel and breathed a sigh of relief as the aching in his legs eased some. Grace watched him, her brow furrowed. He reached for her hand and brought it up to his lips for a kiss. "I'm all right. My leg just gets a little testy when I've been standing on it for too long."

"Can you take anything to help with the pain?" she asked.

"I have some pills at home, but I try not to take them."

"Why not? If they help—"

"Because it's not that bad. Really." He kissed the inside of her wrist and released her hand. "I just need to stay off it for a while and rest."

She didn't comment as he maneuvered into traffic and began heading toward her house. It wasn't until they turned onto her road that she shifted in her seat. "Are you staying tonight?"

He'd been debating that the entire drive. As much as he wanted to stay, having her lying beside him and not being able to have her would be torture. Still, if he had to lie there and do nothing, he'd rather be with her than alone in his apartment. "If that's all right with you."

"Of course." She smiled. "I can massage your leg like I did before, if you'd like."

Memories of the last time she'd massaged his leg, as well as other parts of his anatomy, had a whole new type of ache beginning. He put the car in park in front of her house, unbuckled his seat belt, and turned to face her. Tucking a strand of her hair behind her ear, he leaned in and brushed his lips against hers. "Now, that's an offer I can't refuse."

She grinned.

The walk inside was full of discomfort. Getting up the stairs was the worst and he knew he had an entire flight of them to conquer in order to reach Grace's bedroom. He didn't object when she took his coat and hung it up for him. The only thing he could think about was sitting down and getting the pressure off his leg.

"I think I have some wine in the kitchen."

"That sounds great."

She nodded and hurried down the hall, leaving him alone.

He made his way into the living room, albeit slowly, and lowered himself onto the couch. Grace appeared a few moments later with two glasses of wine.

"Thanks," he said, taking one.

"You're welcome." Grace sat down beside him, folding her legs up beside her.

Alexander placed an arm around her shoulders and hugged her against his side as he took a sip of his wine. It wasn't his preferred drink, but it would do well enough to take the edge off the pain. Hopefully enough that he'd be able to get up the stairs and into her bed.

They sat there quietly, drinking the wine and talking until Grace started to yawn. "We should probably get you up to bed."

She smiled up at him. "And I still owe you a massage."

He drew her face closer, bringing her in for a kiss. "Why don't you go and get things ready? I'll be up in a few minutes."

For a moment, he thought she was going to protest, but then she nodded and stood. "I'll be waiting for you, Sir."

Chapter 25

As it turned out, the exact charm Alexander wanted for Grace's collar wasn't in stock, which meant it wasn't ready by the weekend. She wondered if he would forgo going to the club, but in the end they went. For the most part, they socialized. Alexander thought it was important for Grace to get comfortable with the club. She began to understand why when Katrina stopped by their group Saturday night.

"Were you still interested in me doing the demonstration we talked about?" Alexander asked during a lull in the conversation.

"Of course." Katrina glanced over at Grace, an amused glint in her eye that Grace immediately recognized. It was the look Dominants got when they were about to push their sub's limits "Just let me know when and what you'll need. I'll make sure everything's set up and ready to go."

"I was thinking sometime next month. Maybe a week or so before Christmas."

"Perfect."

The rest of the conversation consisted of somewhat vague talk of tables and toys, along with an exchange of emails. Grace had no idea what type of demonstration they were taking about, but she had a feeling she was going to find out. All the demonstrations she'd ever witnessed, which granted weren't many, included a submissive.

Since she was Alexander's sub, Grace imagined she'd be filling that spot. He didn't say anything for the rest of the evening and the conversation shifted to more mundane topics.

On the drive home, Grace expected him to bring up the subject again, but he didn't. He didn't bring it up the next day either. So Sunday night as they were lying in bed, she broached the subject. "Last night you were talking to Katrina about a demonstration."

"Yes." She could hear the smile in his voice even though she couldn't see his face.

"What kind of demonstration does she want you to do?"

He rolled them both over so he was looking down at her. "She's asked me to do a demonstration on medical play."

It only took a moment for Grace to realize what that meant for her. As anxious as she was about it, she could already feel herself getting wet at the thought of him doing things to her while everyone watched. She really was an exhibitionist. "What will I have to do?"

A smirk appeared on his face. "You're going to be my patient." He paused. "My very naughty patient."

She felt her body temperature rise a few degrees.

Alexander skimmed his lips along her jaw to her ear. "Do you trust me?"

That was easy. "Yes."

He reached down between them and glided his fingers over her pussy. "I'm going to have a fun making you come in front of all those people."

Grace moaned as he slid two fingers inside her. She wrapped her arms around his neck, bit her lower lip, and held on tight as he moved his fingers in and out of her in a steady rhythm.

It was so easy to get lost in the sensations as he touched and teased her, keeping her on edge for as long as possible before allowing her to fall. Her body knew what it wanted, what it longed for. She wasn't going to fight it anymore.

The next couple of days flew by. Grace had talked to her sister several times, including at their mom's on Sunday afternoon. Gabby was still beating herself up over sleeping with Jax. To make matters worse, when Gabby had picked Taylor up at the babysitter's Tuesday night, her daughter had asked if Daddy was coming to Thanksgiving. Her sister had danced around the subject and eventually redirected her daughter's attention. "What am I supposed to say if she brings it up again? She's only three. It's not like she's going to understand."

Grace felt sorry for Gabby. She was doing her best. It couldn't be easy. Especially when her own feelings for Jax were all over the place. "Probably not. I hate to say this, but maybe you and Jax need to talk . . . figure out what you're going to tell her. Chances are she's going to ask more questions the older she gets."

A frustrated sigh came through the line. "Not exactly what I want to do at the moment, but you're right. We do need to talk. About a lot of things."

That was probably the understatement of the year.

"Enough about me, though. Let's talk about something happy. How are things going with you and your doctor? Are you still bringing him with you Thursday?"

Thinking about Alexander brought a smile to Grace's face. "Yes, he's still coming."

"I bet." The way her sister said it made it clear she wasn't talking about Thanksgiving dinner anymore.

Grace felt her cheeks heat. "Can we please talk about something other than my sex life?"

Her sister laughed. "I don't understand why you get so embarrassed about it. I mean you were married for almost ten years and I know you tapped that as often as humanly possible."

If her sister only knew. Whenever Kurt had been away, whether on deployment or for training, as soon as he got back they would lock themselves in the house for two or three days. He'd taken her in every way humanly possible and she'd loved it. She'd be sore for several days after.

Recalling that time left her with a sense of loss. She waited for the feeling of a weight pressing down on her chest and the nausea to settle in as it always did whenever she thought back on those times—on Kurt and their life together—but it didn't come.

"Grace? Are you there?"

"Yeah, I'm still here." Grace forced herself to refocus on the conversation. "Sorry."

Her sister grew serious. "I didn't mean to make you sad. I know thinking about Kurt—"

"No, it's fine. I'm fine."

"Are you sure?" Gabby didn't seem convinced.

"Yes." A change in subject was needed. "Now, what are you bringing to Mom's? I was thinking about making some pasta salad."

They talked for a while about food and work, both avoiding the subject of their relationships, past and present. At nine thirty, she said good night to her sister, made sure the house was locked up, and headed upstairs to get ready for bed. Alexander had to drive to Kansas City for work and wouldn't be back until the next day. It was the first time she'd slept alone in almost two weeks and her house felt incredibly empty. It was strange given she'd spent months alone at a time when Kurt was deployed, not to mention the months after his death. She was trying not to dwell on it, though.

Grace burrowed under the covers and reached for Alexander's pillow. The smell of him mixed with sex had her grinning as she recalled how she'd woken up that morning—with his head between her legs. She could still see the satisfied smirk on his face as he'd crawled up her body like a cat on the prowl.

As she was lying there remembering, her phone dinged, letting her know she had a message.

This bed is awfully lonely without you in it. – Alexander

I was just thinking the same thing. - Grace

A few seconds passed before he replied.

I'd call, but I know you have to be up early tomorrow and if I get you on the phone I doubt either of us will be falling asleep anytime soon. - Alexander

He was probably right. As much as she'd love to hear his voice, chances were good that if he called they'd either be up talking until midnight or they'd end up fooling around. Neither of those options sounded terrible to her, but he was right. They both needed their sleep. She wasn't so worried about herself, but she didn't want him groggy driving home.

What time will you be home tomorrow? - Grace

Hopefully by 2:30 or 3. I have a nine o'clock meeting that shouldn't last more than an hour. - Alexander

Grace bit her bottom lip as she contemplated how to respond.

Call me when you get back? - Grace

I will. - Alexander

There was a long pause.

Good night, *gattina*. Sweet dreams. - Alexander

***

To give Alexander a taste of what his job would entail should he decide to stay, his boss had asked him to join her in Kansas City for several meetings. He'd been introduced to the company executives and a handful of lawyers the company worked with on a regular basis. It wasn't as bad as he'd feared, but he still wasn't sure this was something he wanted to do long term.

Their final meeting ended and he began gathering his things. Alexander wanted to get on the road home as soon as possible. He'd received a voice mail this morning from the jewelry store saying the necklace was ready to be picked up. As they had no plans tonight and neither had to be up early tomorrow for work given the holiday, he wanted to go all out and make this special for Grace. That meant he had some planning to do.

"Heading back?" Janet asked.

"Want to beat the traffic."

His boss wasn't fooled. "Sure you do." She shook her head and chuckled. "Enjoy your long weekend."

"Thanks. You, too."

The drive between Kansas City and St. Louis seemed to take longer than it did the first time around. Maybe that was because he was anxious to get home. He turned on some music, hoping that would make the time go faster.

He ran into some traffic about a half hour outside St. Louis. It took him almost thirty minutes to travel less than five miles. Luckily, once he got past the accident, things got moving again. Still, it was later than he'd hoped. So instead of going home and changing first as he would have liked, he drove straight to the jewelry store.

There weren't any other customers in the store when he arrived, so he was able to get in and out quickly. He made a quick pit stop at his apartment to shower, change, and grab enough clothes for the weekend since he didn't plan on sleeping at his place for the next few days.

Alexander didn't even have to ring the doorbell. She was there waiting for him with a shy smile on her face. He scooped her into his arms and gave her a thorough kiss. "Hi."

"Hi."

They separated so he could close the door, remove his coat, and set his bags down.

"Are you hungry?" she asked.

He reached for her again, crushing her against him. "Starving."

Grace giggled. "I meant for food."

"Oh." He leaned down to kiss her neck. "Yeah. That, too."

She tilted her head to the side to give him better access. "I made lasagna and some garlic bread. I figured you'd be hun—"

His lips covered hers as he backed them into the living room toward the couch. He reached between them and began working her sweater up her torso. "Do you have anything in the kitchen that will burn or catch on fire if it isn't attended to in the next fifteen minutes?"

Grace shook her head. "No."

"Good," he said, working his own shirt over his head and letting it drop to the floor. "There's something that needs my attention first."

An hour later, their bellies full of pasta and bread, they curled up on the couch to watch a movie. He ran his fingers through her hair as she rested her head in his lap. It was one of the most relaxing things he'd done in a long time—just the two of them, lounging on the couch. There was nothing requiring their attention. No reason to rush to bed since they didn't have to be up early the next day.

The movie ended, but neither moved. He glanced down to find her looking up at him. There was something in her eyes that had him concerned. "What is it?"

She smiled and reached up to cup the back of his head, drawing his face down to hers. He allowed the distraction, mainly because he didn't want to push her. This thing between them was still so new and they both had baggage.

"I saw you brought a bag," she whispered.

He hummed and lifted her so she was straddling his lap. "I figured I'd need clothes for tomorrow."

Grace averted her gaze and he wondered if this was what had been on her mind a few minutes ago. He wasn't overly concerned with meeting her mother, but maybe she was having second thoughts about it. Meeting her family was a big step. "Do you not want me to go?"

Her eyes widened as she looked at him again. "No. I mean, yes, I still want you to go. If you want." She paused. "I'm sorry. This isn't coming out right."

Alexander took her face in his hands and waited for her to gather her thoughts.

She closed her eyes and sighed. "I just don't want you to feel you have to."

He pressed his lips to hers with the gentlest of pressure, but it was enough to get her to open her eyes. "Grace, you're important to me and if we're going to continue our relationship, I'd like to get to know your family."

"Even after all Gabby's questions?"

"I had commanders barking orders at me for ten years. I think I can handle your sister."

He'd meant to lighten the mood, but Grace wasn't having it. "Just remember you said that."

Deciding it was best to let it go for now, Alexander gave her another brief kiss before letting her go. "Why don't you head on up to bed and I'll be up in a few?"

Something changed in her eyes. She stood and shot him a look through lowered lashes that spoke volumes.

Almost instantly, with that one look, there was less room in his pants. When he'd suggested they turn in, he hadn't been talking about sex, but now it was at the forefront of his mind. "Get undressed and wait for me."

"Yes, Sir." He caught sight of her grin as she turned to make her way upstairs. She was rather pleased with herself since she thought she was getting what she wanted.

Alexander took his time making his rounds downstairs, making sure every window and door was locked. With casualness he didn't feel, he retrieved his bag from where he'd left it by the door and headed up the stairs. His heart rate rose with each step as his anticipation grew. He knew what he'd find when he walked into her bedroom, but even so the sight had his cock begging to be let out of its confines.

Strolling into the room, he set his overnight bag on the end of the bed, removed her collar, and placed his bag in the corner. He wasn't going to need clothing tonight.

The entire time Grace remained in position, waiting. He palmed her collar in one hand and went to stand behind her. One of the advantages of his long drive from Kansas City was that he'd been off his leg for most of the day. Alexander didn't need his cane, which meant that both his hands were free.

He rested the palm of his hand on her head, allowing both of them to take in the moment. Everything was quiet. It was just the two of them, completely at peace.

With a featherlight touch, he petted her hair, letting them both sink deeper into their roles. She released a noise from deep in her throat that sounded almost like a purr.

"Are you relaxed, *gattina*?"

"Yes, Sir." The words came out on a sigh.

Alexander continued to pet her hair. "The jewelry store called me this morning to let me know your collar was ready. I picked it up this afternoon."

She remained silent, but it seemed more as if she was in the moment rather than any sort of discontent.

He moved to stand in front of her. "Look at me."

Grace tilted her head up, meeting his gaze. There was no hesitation in her eyes, no uncertainty.

"Will you accept my collar, Grace?"

"Yes, Sir."

He held the necklace so she could see the charm on the back next to the clasp. On the underside of the heart it said *La Sua Gattina—His Kitten*. "Lift your hair for me."

The love he felt for her filled him as he unclasped the necklace and secured it around her neck. Alexander gathered her hair in both his hands and she released her hold, giving over control. He tilted her head back, admiring his collar around her neck.

Of course it didn't hurt that at this angle he had an amazing view of her breasts as well. He bent to kiss her while reaching down with one hand to toy with her nipple. The sound she made had him wanting to throw her onto the bed and lose himself in her warmth. It was only years of experience that allowed him to remain in control of his baser instincts.

That didn't mean he wasn't going to get what he wanted. Fucking her senseless had its advantages, but so did indulging.

He gave her nipple one final tweak before releasing her and stepping back. "On the bed and spread your legs. I want to taste my pussy."

Chapter 26

Grace was a nervous wreck by the time they arrived at her mother's house. Alexander kept sneaking glances at her as he drove, the frown on his face deepening the closer they came to their destination. He parked along the street, put the car in park, and reached for her hand. "Why are you so jittery?"

"Sorry." She shot him a feeble grin. "It's just been a really long time since I brought a boy home to meet my mom."

Alexander chuckled. "It's been a while since anyone's called me a boy."

He was right, of course. No one in their right mind would call Alexander a boy. "I meant—"

"I know what you meant, *gattina*, but I promise you it will be fine. I can handle whatever your mother—or your sister—throw at me. They aren't going to scare me off." He cradled the side of her face in his hand and brushed his lips against hers. "Relax." The pad of his thumb grazed her bottom lip. "That's an order."

She closed her eyes, leaned into his hand, and concentrated on the feeling of his skin against hers. This wasn't wrong. She had every right to move on, to find happiness again. It's what Kurt had wanted.

This time when Grace looked at him, she was more at peace. The anxiety was still there, but if he wasn't going to worry about it then she would try not to as well. "Yes, Sir. I will try my best."

He smiled. "That's all I ask."

Alexander balanced two casserole dishes in one hand while Grace brought in the pasta salad and a pumpkin pie. If he hadn't needed his cane, she knew he most likely would have insisted on carrying everything. They'd been up late the night before. He'd brought her to the edge time and time again, not allowing her to go over until he was inside her. Her nipples were still a little sensitive from where he'd clamped them and sucked on them to the point she was begging him to allow her to come.

"Everything all right?" he asked as they approached the door.

Grace didn't get a chance to answer before the door swung open, revealing her sister. "I thought I heard voices."

After Alexander and Grace removed their coats and said a brief hello to Taylor as she ran past them, the three headed into the kitchen where Caroline was taking the turkey out of the oven. She looked up when they strolled into the room. Her gaze rested on Alexander for a long moment, allowing herself to get a good look at him.

Grace placed what she was carrying on the counter, and then took the dishes Alexander had and set them down as well. "Mom, this is Alexander Greco. Alexander, my mom . . . Caroline."

Alexander didn't miss a beat. He stepped forward and extended his hand. "It's great to finally meet you, ma'am."

Her mom stared at his offering for a long moment before wiping her hands and accepting his handshake. "Grace says you served with her husband, Kurt."

"Yes, ma'am. We were both deployed at the same base overseas."

Before things could get awkward, Grace decided to act. "Does anything need to be done?"

Caroline picked up a pair of potholders and dumped a pot full of boiling water and cubed potatoes into a strainer she had sitting in the sink. "Just take what you brought to the table. Once I get these potatoes mashed and the turkey carved, we'll be ready to dig in."

Less than fifteen minutes later, they were all seated around the table, filling their plates with food. Even though they were at her mother's, Grace waited for Alexander to start eating before she took her first bite. The simple gesture brought some balance, which turned out to be a very good thing since the questions from her mother started a few minutes later.

"How long were you in the Army?"

Alexander finished chewing and swallowing his food before he answered Caroline. "Ten years."

"Did you like it?" she asked. Grace had no idea where her mother was going with this line of questioning, but considering the alternative, she'd take it.

"I enjoyed the discipline, the order, knowing what was expected of me and of the men I served with."

Caroline grabbed a roll from the basket. "Grace said you were hurt."

"Yes, ma'am. My leg was crushed in an explosion."

"I'm sorry."

He shrugged. "I was lucky."

They all heard what he didn't say, that Kurt hadn't been so fortunate. What her family didn't realize was that the incident that had caused Alexander's injury was the same one that had killed Kurt. It wasn't something she wanted to get into. Especially not at the dining room table.

After several moments of silence, her mother switched to another line of questioning. "Do you plan on staying in St. Louis?" Grace cringed a little. It was almost as bad as her mother asking what Alexander's intentions were.

"Yes. I'm in the process of getting my medical license here in Missouri, but for the time being I'm working as a consultant." It was his way of saying he was putting down roots. Nothing he said was news to her, but for some reason hearing him tell her mother made it sound more definite. As if he really was declaring his intentions.

Her mother kept pressing. "Grace has been through a lot this last year."

He met her mother's gaze across the table. "Yes, she has."

It was as if something unspoken passed between them. Grace waited for her mother to comment, but she only nodded then went back to her food and a new line of questioning. "Do you have any hobbies?"

The first thing that popped into Grace's mind was the feel of his hand on her backside as he'd spanked her the night before. Of course, Alexander didn't mention BDSM. He chose something more mundane to share with her mother. "I enjoy reading when I have the time."

"Grace likes to read, too." Gabby inserted herself into the conversation for the first time.

Alexander looked at Grace with a knowing glint in his eye. "Yes. She's shared some of them with me."

"Wow. You must be special. Every time I ask her about her books she just tells me I wouldn't like them." Her sister narrowed her eyes at her in mock irritation.

Grace stared at her plate, avoiding eye contact.

"Are you an avid reader yourself?" Alexander asked Gabby, redirecting the attention away from Grace. She wanted to kiss him.

"I've been known to pick up a romance novel when I have some downtime." As if on cue, Taylor dropped her fork on the floor. Gabby scooted her chair away from the table so she could pick it up. She placed the dirty spoon out of Taylor's reach, and then took her own spoon and handed it to her daughter. "But I don't have much of that these days."

Alexander nodded. "Children do tend to require a lot of one's attention, but in the end it's worth it. Time is one thing you can't replace."

Caroline took the opening and ran with it. "Do you have any children, Alexander?"

"No, ma'am."

"Ever been married?"

"Mom!" Grace felt her cheeks heat in embarrassment. She was thirty-four years old. She didn't need her mother vetting her boyfriends anymore.

"It's a perfectly reasonable question," her mother insisted.

Alexander didn't seem fazed. "No. I haven't been married. I do, however, hope to remedy that someday soon."

Grace turned to look at him. She could only imagine the look on her face. Was he talking about her? Surely, he couldn't be—they'd only been seeing each other for a few weeks. Granted, they'd been talking and going out to dinner together for longer, but still.

It was too soon.

The conversation continued, although Grace wasn't really paying attention to what was being said. All she could think about was how casually he'd said he hoped to get married soon. He wasn't seeing anyone else. That was part of their agreement. So if he wasn't talking about her, then who?

"Grace, do you want any pie?"

She blinked and looked up at where her mother was standing not two feet away from her, plate in her hand. "What?"

Caroline raised her eyebrows, clearly wondering where her daughter's mind had gone. "I asked if you wanted pie. Gabby's slicing it up."

"Oh. Yes, please."

Her mother walked away chuckling and shaking her head. Grace was sure her mother thought she was daydreaming or something. It was easier to let her mother think that than tell her that what Alexander said had her head spinning. Was she ready to get married again?

***

Alexander had been watching Grace for a while, but as soon as they were alone he placed a hand on her leg, drawing her attention. "Everything okay?"

She nodded, but he didn't miss how she pressed her lips together, a sure sign she was nervous about something. He didn't get a chance to examine it any further, though, since her mom and sister reentered the room.

They weren't alone again until they said their goodbyes and headed home several hours later. Grace's mom and sister had been full of questions, wanting to know about his childhood, his parents, and even if he'd had any pets growing up. For the most part, Grace had remained quiet throughout the conversation, only commenting when someone asked her a question.

"Tell me what's wrong," he demanded as they made their way back to her house.

It took her too long to answer.

He glanced over and saw her fidgeting, pulling at her fingers. "Grace?"

"You said you want to get married." She paused. "Soon."

The wheels started turning in his head, rushing to catch up to what she'd obviously been mulling over for hours already. "Yes. I would like to get married someday."

Alexander waited to see if she would continue. He figured he'd give her until they reached their destination before he took more drastic measures to get whatever it was out of her. Luckily, she didn't make him wait that long. "Is there someone else?"

They were at a stoplight, which turned out to be a very good thing seeing as how her question had caught him completely off guard. "No. Why would you even think that? Have I given you any reason to think—"

"No," she hurried to explain. "It's just that . . . when you told my mom you wanted to get married soon, at first I thought you were talking about us, but then I thought you couldn't possibly. I mean we haven't known each other for that long and . . ."

The light turned green and as there was a vehicle behind them he had to drive. As soon as he saw an opening, however, he maneuvered his car off the road and put it in park. He gathered her hands in his, needing to touch her. His heart was pounding in his chest. He'd known her mother and sister would ask questions, vet him to make sure he was good enough for Grace, and when she'd asked about marriage he wasn't going to lie. And even though he'd known Caroline's questioning could go down this road, he'd been hoping to put off this conversation with Grace for a little while longer. "I was talking about us."

Grace swallowed.

Her lack of verbal response worried him. "Do you not want to get married again?"

"I hadn't really thought about it."

Time ticked by as they sat in the warmth of the vehicle. He held tight to her hands, not letting go. "I know what we have is new and we're still feeling things out, but if war taught me one thing it's that life is fleeting. And if you want something, you need to go after it, because tomorrow isn't a guarantee."

Alexander cupped her face with one hand, massaging her cheek with his thumb. "I want to fall asleep beside you every night for the rest of my life. And when I wake up every morning, the first thing I want to see is you." He let that hang in the air for a moment before he continued. "I love you, Grace."

He could feel her pulse race beneath his palm. For weeks he'd been biting his tongue, knowing she wasn't ready to hear how he felt. Finally putting it out there was one of the most terrifying things he'd ever done. He had no idea how she'd react.

The only thing he could hear was their breathing and the blood pumping through his eardrums as he waited. Although it was no more than a minute, it felt like an eternity. "What about our agreement?"

There was such vulnerability in her eyes as she stared back at him. He wanted to gather her into his arms and never let her go. "There isn't anything in our agreement that says I can't fall in love with my submissive."

"Yes, I know." She looked down at where he was still holding one of her hands. "I'm not saying this right."

He tilted her chin up, meeting her gaze. "There's no pressure here, Grace. When I told your mother I wanted to get married soon, I didn't mean next week or even next month." One side of his mouth tilted up a little. "Although, I wouldn't say no if that's what you wanted."

Her eyes opened wide at his admission.

"What I meant was that one day, hopefully in the not too distant future, you will agree to become my wife. If that's months from now, or years . . ." He shrugged.

"We've only known each other for two months."

"So?" He released her fingers and cradled her face in his hands as if she were the most precious thing in the world to him. "I've been falling in love with you since that moment in your kitchen when you cried in my arms."

"I don't know what to say," she whispered.

"You don't have to say anything." He brushed his lips against hers. "Let's get you home, and then we can talk some more if you want."

"All right."

He couldn't get back to her house fast enough. As the miles passed, he felt her withdrawing again. It made no sense and because he had to keep his focus on the road, there wasn't much he could do about it at the moment.

When they arrived at her house, he waited until they'd brought everything inside and put it away before leaning against the counter and drawing her into his arms. "Talk to me."

"I don't know what you want me to say."

He pressed a kiss to her temple as he held her against him. "Tell me how you're feeling."

"Nervous. Confused."

Alexander wished Grace's mother had never asked him that stupid question or that he had answered it differently somehow. He'd known what she was doing—they both had—but he was positive Caroline wouldn't have anticipated Grace's reaction. At most, Alexander had figured she'd be shocked or maybe even a little uneasy given they had known each other for such a short time. Originally, he'd planned on waiting another month or two before telling Grace he loved her. Then, when the time was right, he was going to ask her to marry him. Her mother's question and his subsequent answer had thrown that plan out the window. Or the first part of it, at least.

He opened his mouth to ask her what she was confused about when she stepped out of his arms and met his gaze. "I think I'd like to be alone tonight."

The urge to make her talk to him was strong, but he decided to give her some space. He wouldn't let her push him away for long. "If that's what you want."

Grace let her shoulders drop as if a huge weight had been lifted. It was obvious she'd expected him to protest. "Thank you."

He pushed himself away from the counter and closed the distance between them once more. Taking hold of her forearms, he placed a kiss on her forehead. "Call me if you need anything."

She gave him a brief smile, which gave him hope. "I will."

Reluctantly, he dropped his arms, retrieved his cane, and headed toward the door.

When he reached for the knob, her hand covered his, stopping him.

"I just need some time to think."

Without giving it too much thought, Alexander turned to face her. He took hold of her face and kissed her.

They were both breathing hard when he let her go. The air around them was charged and heavy. He didn't think it would take much to convince her to change her mind, to let him stay, but he knew that wasn't what she needed. Sex wouldn't fix whatever was going on in her head. If anything, it would only complicate it more.

He backed away. "Good night, Grace."

"Good night."

Before he could talk himself out of it, Alexander walked out the door.

Chapter 27

It was the Friday after Thanksgiving—Black Friday—the first official shopping day of the Christmas season. People were out trying to scoop up all the deals stores were advertising, and all those people needed to eat. Beth had anticipated they would be busy, but even Grace didn't think she'd understood just how many people would come through their doors that day. From the time Tommy opened up there was a steady stream of people.

With all the running around, Grace didn't have much time to think. She smiled and did her job making sure the customers had what they needed.

Her feet were killing her by the time the last customer walked out the door. She gingerly lowered herself into a chair at the back of the dining room. Seconds later, Tommy joined her, two glasses of water in his hands. He pushed one her way.

"Thanks," she said, gratefully taking it and drinking until half the contents were gone.

Tommy sagged in his chair. "I don't think I've ever seen that many people in my life."

Beth pulled out a chair and sat down without finesse. She looked as tired as Grace felt. "I'll have to crunch the numbers, but I'm willing to bet today was our best to date. I must have made five hundred sandwiches during the lunch rush."

Tommy raised his glass before taking another long drink. "And just think, tomorrow we get to do it all again."

"Maybe it won't be as bad," Grace said, sounding hopeful.

Beth shook her head. "Don't bet on it. Tomorrow is small business Saturday. All the shops downtown will be open, trying to entice shoppers. Chances are good that we'll be just as busy as we were today."

Both Tommy and Grace groaned.

They all sat there for several more minutes, sipping their waters and enjoying doing absolutely nothing.

The reprieve was short-lived, however. Beth finished her water, placed her palms on top of the table, and stood. "I hate to say it, but we need to get this place cleaned and set up for tomorrow. Then I'm going home for a nice long soak in the bathtub."

Cleaning up took longer than usual. Some of that had to do with the fact that they were low on everything. Salt and pepper shakers had to be filled. Coffee restocked. Napkins. The list went on and on. It also didn't help that they were all dead tired.

Grace pulled into her driveway at quarter to five, starving, but having no desire to cook. Instead, she called for pizza. She'd barely made it through her second piece before her eyes started closing and she knew she needed to call it a night.

Stripping out of her clothes, Grace slipped under the covers. She didn't bother putting on any pajamas. Her Dom didn't like when she wore clothes to bed. He preferred her naked and easily accessible.

She reached up to touch her collar. The feel of the metal against her fingertips—it symbolized the connection she felt to her Dom and he felt to her. Despite her jumbled thoughts and feelings, she missed him.

Without thinking about it, she grabbed her phone and dialed his number. He picked up on the second ring. "Grace?"

"Hi." Just hearing his voice soothed her. "I wanted to let you know that I'm all right."

There was a long pause. "Thank you. I've been worried about you."

"I'm fine. Just tired. The café was slammed today." Grace knew she was changing the subject, but she wasn't ready to talk about them yet.

At first, she didn't think he was going to follow her lead, but finally he seemed to sense she didn't want to go there. "I should let you get to bed, then."

For whatever reason, she felt a little feisty and she was too exhausted to fight it. She lowered her voice a little, giving it a seductive tone. "I'm already in bed."

"Are you wearing anything?" His husky tone did all kinds of wonderful things to her body. He didn't even have to touch her and already she was getting ready for him.

"No."

The groan that came through the line had her thinking of other needs besides sleep, like feeling him sucking on her nipples while he held her hands above her head. Or him hovering over her while he filled her with every inch of his cock.

Heaven help her, but her body and heart ached for him and it had only been a day.

"You'd better not be touching yourself, *gattina*." Alexander knew exactly where her mind had gone.

"No, Sir." While it was tempting and she could definitely use the release, she would not defy her Dom. Not in this. Her body was his. If nothing else, she knew that to be true beyond a doubt. And she suspected that despite all the confusion going on in her brain, he owned her heart as well.

Alexander cleared his throat, breaking some of the spell. "I'd like to see you tomorrow."

"I have to work." It was a weak excuse.

"After work," he said, refusing to be deterred. "We can go to dinner."

There was a part of her that was disappointed. Of course, that was the horny part and not the rational part. He was right. They did need to talk—sort this out—and figure out where to go from here. She couldn't let him go. That much she knew. "I'd like that."

"I'll pick you up at six."

"Alexander?"

"Yes?"

Grace worried her bottom lip with her teeth. "Thank you for being so understanding."

There was a lengthy silence on the other end. When he spoke again, she could hear the affection he had for her coming through his words. "Good night, *gattina*. I'll see you tomorrow."

"Good night, Sir."

She placed her phone on her nightstand and burrowed under the covers. As tired as her body was, Grace had some decisions to make. Alexander said he wasn't pushing her into anything, and that, while he wanted to get married, he wasn't expecting her to do it tomorrow.

After throwing off the covers, she went to the closet and dug out the box of Kurt's things she'd saved. Most of it was from his childhood. She kept meaning to ask his mom and dad if they wanted them, but kept putting it off. There were also pictures, pictures of her and Kurt, along with her wedding ring and her collar.

Grace brought the box over to the bed and opened it. Everything was exactly how she'd left it, her collar and ring sitting on top being the newest additions to the box. She grazed her fingertips over the silver heart and closed her eyes. A peace fell over her and the weight she'd been feeling lifted from her chest.

She'd always felt as if Kurt was watching over her, even when he was deployed. The connection they had was strong, even from the beginning. It was then she realized that there was a part of her that had resisted truly letting go and moving on. Having an agreement with Alexander was different than giving him her whole self. It would mean that she no longer belonged to Kurt. She would truly and completely be letting him go. Saying goodbye.

The collar felt heavier than she remembered as she lifted it to her lips. The cool metal against her skin brought with it memories of when Kurt had placed it around her neck. Even then he'd known what she needed. He'd been a wonderful Master. Not perfect, but he always made sure her needs were taken care of.

Tears streaked down her cheeks as she returned the collar she'd worn for almost ten years back to the box and closed the lid. It was time for her to truly and with her whole heart obey her Master's last command and move on.

***

Since Alexander had left Grace's house on Thursday evening he'd been worried about her. He was glad she called him Friday night, if only to let him know she was okay. The more they'd gotten to know each other, both in and out of the bedroom, the more intense his feelings for her became.

On his way to pick her up Saturday evening, he stopped to buy her some flowers. Their relationship might not be conventional, but he was treating tonight as a date. This wasn't about their arrangement. This was about them. As a couple. A couple that hopefully had a future together.

It seemed Grace felt the same way about their upcoming evening. She answered the door wearing a fitted red dress that came down to her knees. It was more conservative than what she would wear to the club, but it still made his mouth water. There were strips of lace that gave hints of the skin underneath, skin he wanted to touch and kiss and lick . . .

He had to focus. They needed to talk. Fucking her senseless wouldn't solve anything in the long term and that's what he wanted. Forever. With her.

Alexander held the flowers in front of him, presenting them to Grace. "You look lovely tonight."

"Thank you." Grace blushed and took the bouquet from him. She brought the flowers up to her face and inhaled. "They're beautiful."

She took a few steps back, allowing him to come in. "I should put these in some water."

"I'll wait."

Grace nodded and disappeared into the kitchen. As she walked away, his gaze was transfixed on her ass. He could have followed her, but he didn't want to test his self-control. Last night had proven that even though Grace's mind was confused, her body didn't seem to have the same issue. He didn't want to tempt fate.

By the time she returned, he'd regained control of his libido—or as much control as he was able to manage in her presence. He helped her into her coat and they made their way to his car.

Instead of going to one of their usual places, he decided to head farther out of town. After a little research, he'd found a restaurant about an hour west of the city that overlooked a small stream. The pictures online had made it look cozy and romantic.

"Was the café as busy today as yesterday?"

"No." Grace turned to face him, resting her head on the back of the seat. She seemed more relaxed than she had when he'd left her Thursday night. Or maybe she was just tired. "Things started a bit slower and we had a short break between breakfast and lunch. Beth was still happy, though. She's pretty sure this week will be her best since opening the café."

"That's great."

"It is."

He turned off the highway and continued down a two-lane road that would lead them to their destination. They still had quite a way to go and he wanted to keep the conversation light. "Have you ever been out this way?"

"I think so, but it's been years. Dad used to like to go for long drives in the country sometimes. We'd get in the car and head out with no destination in mind. We found some really cool places. A lot of small towns and parks that we had no idea existed."

"You don't talk much about your dad," Alexander said, leaving it open for her to say as little or as much as she wanted on the subject.

"He died about five years ago. Parkinson's. Kurt was stationed in Texas at the time, so Gabby and Mom had their hands full. One day Gabby called to tell me that I should come home if I could, that they didn't expect Dad to make it more than another month or two."

"I'm sorry." Alexander hadn't meant to go down such a sad path. He'd figured she'd maybe share childhood stories of her dad, not reminisce about his death.

It was almost as if he hadn't said a word. "When I got there, I realized my dad was already gone. His body was still there, but his mind wasn't. He didn't recognize me. He didn't recognize anyone . . . not even my mom. We were all strangers to him."

Alexander knew what Parkinson's disease could do, both to the person and to their family. Hearing about it from Grace's perspective, however, was a lot different than reading about it in a textbook or seeing it in a clinical setting. This wasn't some random person he had no connection with. This was Grace's father.

Purely on instinct, he covered her hand with his.

She laced their fingers together and squeezed. "Kurt and I had gone to see him the year before. We'd talked about going to Hawaii, but changed our minds. I'm glad we did. Dad was still in his right mind then."

Alexander remained quiet, holding her hand and letting her talk. Grace had stayed in Missouri with her mother and sister for the last month and a half of her father's life. She'd helped her mom with the funeral arrangements and helped her get all the legal stuff in order before she'd returned to Texas.

"Was Kurt able to get leave to come to the funeral?" Alexander asked. He really hoped she hadn't had to deal with that alone.

"Yes. It was lucky he was stateside at the time. It wasn't a month after we returned that he was shipped out."

They talked a bit more about her family throughout the remainder of the drive. It wasn't the lightest of conversations, but since it appeared to be the direction Grace wanted to go, he went with it.

"Oh wow," she said when they pulled up in front of the restaurant. There were white lights everywhere—along the roofline, draped over bushes, woven through the trees. They were clearly going for a winter wonderland theme. All it lacked was the snow.

He rounded the vehicle and opened her door, offering her his hand. "Ready?"

Grace placed her palm in his and exited the car, a look of awe on her face. "This is amazing."

"Wait until you see the inside."

As promised, the inside of the restaurant was as spectacular as the outside. Alexander gave the host his name and they were led past the large fireplace in the center over to a bank of windows. The host held out Grace's chair for her while she sat down. "Thank you."

He handed them both a menu. "Your server will be right with you. Enjoy your dinner."

Alexander knew the moment Grace looked outside. The lights lit up a scene that looked to be out of a painting. "How did you find this place?"

"You can find just about anything on the internet these days."

She seemed a bit flabbergasted, which made him smile. It was the exact reaction he'd been hoping for.

"Good evening. My name is John. I'll be taking care of you this evening. Can I get you started with some wine?"

Alexander ordered them each a glass of wine and an appetizer while Grace continued to gaze out the window. He let her drink in the scenery while he scanned over the menu, every now and then glancing her way.

John returned with their wine. "Do you still need a few more minutes?"

That seemed to jar Grace out of her fixation. "Oh." She turned her attention to her menu and began scanning over the items.

Alexander chuckled. "Yes, please."

Nodding, their server left them alone again.

Then Grace surprised him. She looked up, meeting his gaze, and placed her menu facedown on the table. "Will you order for me, Sir?"

He was trying not to read too much into her request. "If that's what you want."

"It is." Her voice was full of conviction.

When their server returned with their appetizer, Alexander ordered for both of them, making sure to get something he knew she'd like. "I'll get this put in for you right away. Is there anything else you need at the moment?"

"No. I think we're fine. Thank you," Alexander said.

John nodded. "Enjoy your appetizer."

Alone once more, Alexander speared one of the stuffed mushrooms and held it up for her. "Mushroom?"

She giggled, leaned forward, and opened her mouth. Her lips closed around the food and he felt a reaction below his waist. Grace was flirting with him. That had to be a good sign.

He ate one of the mushrooms himself, and then stabbed another one and offered it to her. "I want to talk about Thursday."

There was a slight hesitation as she took the mushroom. Grace finished chewing and swallowing before she responded. "I know." She glanced down at her empty plate, and then back at him. "I'm sorry I freaked out. I just . . . I needed time to think about some things . . . to come to terms with how I feel."

Alexander swallowed and it felt as if he had a lump stuck in his throat.

"When Kurt died, I didn't imagine I'd find anyone else that would make me feel the way he did. I thought I'd be alone for the rest of my life and I was okay with that. Or, I'd accepted it, at least. Then, you showed up with his letter. I didn't know what to think, but I trusted Kurt. He knew me better than anyone."

The noise around them faded into the background as he waited for whatever would come next.

Grace lifted her right hand and placed it flat at the base of her neck over her collar. She met his gaze and held it as she spoke. "I'm ready, Master. Ready to be yours.”

Chapter 28

Alexander took his time responding. Hearing her call him Master had him wanting to take her right then and there, to hell with all the people around them. That, however, would most likely get them both arrested. Not exactly how he foresaw the evening ending.

He studied Grace, trying to get a feel for exactly what she'd meant by saying she was ready. She toyed with her napkin as she waited for his response.

Picking up his wineglass, he took a sip. "I'm going to need a bit more than that. What, exactly, are you ready for, *gattina*?" He'd added the term of endearment to let her know he wasn't upset by her declaration.

Grace looked out the window, and then to him. Her eyes held something in them he'd never seen before. "I realized I've been holding back. Emotionally." She paused. "I'm sorry."

He'd known that, but he'd been willing to give her time to work through it. "You were still grieving."

She nodded. "Yes."

Several minutes passed as he waited for her to continue. It would have been so easy to brush this conversation under the rug and go on with their evening, but they needed to talk this through.

"When we started"—she glanced around the room before going on—"seeing each other, I hadn't thought of sharing my life with another man. My heart still belonged to Kurt, and as far as I was concerned that was how it would always be."

He'd known this as well. The love Grace had for her husband wasn't in doubt. Neither was Kurt's love and devotion to his wife. He'd been an attractive man and had numerous opportunities to cheat while they were deployed, but he never had. It had made Alexander long for that type of connection with someone.

Grace gingerly placed her hand over the top of Alexander's where it rested at the base of his wineglass. He twisted his wrist so he could grasp her fingers.

"When you told my mom that you wanted to get married, I panicked. Not because I couldn't see myself marrying you, but because I could. The more I thought about it, the more real it became." She hesitated. "And then you said you loved me."

Grace closed her eyes and shook her head, trying to keep it together. He gave her hand a gentle squeeze, encouraging her to take her time.

"I wanted to say it back," she admitted, "but I couldn't. It felt like, if I did, that I would be betraying Kurt. Giving you my body was one thing. Giving you my heart . . ."

Alexander's own heart felt as if it was going to beat out of his chest, but he waited until she looked at him again. "And now?"

"Now I realize that what I felt for Kurt doesn't mean I can't feel that way for someone else. I don't have to choose. Kurt was my past." Her shoulders rose and fell as she took a deep breath in and let it out. "You are my future."

They stared at each other across the table, holding hands. This was how their server found them when he brought their food. Alexander thanked him, not breaking eye contract with Grace, and sent him on his way.

After brushing his thumb along the inside of Grace's wrist, Alexander let go of her hand so they could eat. She followed his lead and picked up her fork.

They concentrated on their dinners for a while, letting everything that had been said sink in. Alexander was the first one to break the silence. "I never want you to feel as if you have to forget Kurt. His memory lives on as it should. In both of us."

Moisture pooled in her eyes, but she fought to keep the tears at bay.

Nothing more was said as they finished their meals. Alexander paid the check, and then whisked Grace out the door.

Outside, he steered them away from the parking lot to a walking path that led down to the stream. It was lit with the same holiday lights that surrounded the restaurant. He wrapped his arm around Grace's shoulders and she snuggled close.

The sound of the stream became louder as they rounded the corner. It was chilly and there were no other people in sight, which suited him just fine. Alexander led her over to a wooden bench a few feet from the path, sat down, and pulled her into his lap.

Grace leaned against him, her eyes focused on the rambling water in front of them. "Thank you for bringing me here."

He held her close and buried his face in the crook of her neck. "You're welcome."

The sounds of the night surrounded them as they sat. He took the edges of his trench coat and tried to cover some of her legs so she wouldn't get cold.

"You know, I've never been to your apartment."

Alexander grinned against her shoulder. "Is that your way of trying to wheedle an invitation out of me?"

She shrugged. "Maybe."

"Well, since neither of us has work tomorrow, why don't you stay over at my place? It will, however, mean you'll have to take the walk of shame tomorrow since you don't have any clothes there." He hugged her closer.

"I'm okay with that, if you are."

He ran his nose up the length of her neck to her ear. "Anything that has you in my bed is all right by me."

A shiver rippled through her. "Master?"

His cock was already sitting up to take notice. "Yes, *gattina*?"

"I think I'd like to go home now."

Alexander took a deep breath in and released it, letting hot hair blow against her cooled skin. "Your home or mine?" He didn't want there to be any miscommunication.

She turned to face him, circled her arms around his neck, and rested her forehead against his. "Yours. I want to see where you live."

The drive back to St. Louis seemed to take forever. It didn't take any longer than the drive *to* the restaurant, of course. The only reason it felt that way was because he wanted to get her naked. And in order to do that, he first had to get them to his apartment. He'd thought, briefly, about pulling off the side of the road and having some fun, but dismissed it. Not only would it be awkward in the small space, but what he wanted to do to her wouldn't be easy to accomplish in a vehicle.

With every mile they drew closer to the city, the room in his pants decreased. It was a good thing he'd worn slacks otherwise he would have been in quite a bit of discomfort by the time they pulled up in front of his apartment.

He took her hand in his and led her inside. After turning on the lights, he motioned for her to have a look around. "I'll get us something to drink."

Grace appeared torn, as if her want to get on with their evening warred with her curiosity. In the end, however, her curiosity won out. Or maybe it was her submissive nature letting him set the pace. She strolled through his small apartment as he grabbed some glasses out of the cabinet and filled them with water and ice.

Alexander found her in his bedroom, looking out the window. He handed her one of the glasses.

"Thanks," she said, bringing the glass to her lips.

He took a drink of his water and set the glass on the nearby table before moving to stand behind her. "What are you thinking about?"

"I was wondering where we'll live. Did you want to stay in the city?"

Her train of thought surprised him. He spun her around to face him. "Grace, there's no rush. I know I said I want to get married, but I wasn't exaggerating. We can take this as slow as you want to."

She shook her head. "No. You were right. Life's too short. Kurt and I missed out on so much when he was deployed and I can never get that time back. I don't want to do that again."

Alexander held her face in his hands and pressed his lips to hers with the gentlest pressure. "Maybe we should try living together first." She opened her mouth to argue, but he pressed a finger to her lips, cutting her off. "See if you can put up with me."

Grace hesitated before nodding.

He smiled, and leaned in to kiss her again. "See, that wasn't so hard."

As their lips mingled together, thinking became more difficult.

He crushed her against him and ran his hands up and down her back, cupping her ass. Her breathy moans only fueled the fire he'd been trying to bank for the last hour.

"I want you," he mumbled as he kissed his way down her neck.

"Take me, Master. I'm yours."

That was all he needed to hear. Alexander removed the glass from her hand, placing it next to his on the table. He flipped her around and pushed her against the wall, facing away from him. Reaching for the zipper of her dress, he yanked it down. The dress parted, revealing her skin beneath. He pushed it off her shoulders and watched as it fell to the floor at her feet, leaving her in her bra and a pair of stockings.

Pressing himself flush against her back, he ran a hand down her side and over the curve of her hip. "Are you wet for me?"

Without waiting for her response, he slid his hand between her legs.

***

Grace gasped at the feel of his fingers sliding over her pussy, and then plunging inside her. The weight of him against her, pressing her against the wall, keeping her there, only added to her arousal. She could feel his erection pressing into her backside, begging to be let out of its confines.

"It's too bad we didn't go to Serpent's Kiss tonight. I would have made sure to make you come so everyone could watch."

Thinking about it had heat rushing between her legs.

He must have been able to feel her body's reaction because she felt a satisfied rumble erupt from his chest. "You like that, don't you? No worries, *gattina*. Soon I'm going to have you coming in front of the entire club. They're all going to be watching as I make your pretty pussy sing."

His words were barely able to sink in before his hand was gone and he was turning her around. He took hold of her forearms and held her still while he kissed her, his lips hard and demanding. She loved every minute of it. Now that she'd made her decision, she wanted to feel him filling her, surrounding her, making her his.

Before she knew what was happening, he was lifting her into his arms and carrying her to the bed. "What—"

"Hush."

"But your leg—"

Alexander tossed her onto his bed and swiftly removed his clothes. "I will probably never be able to carry you up a flight of stairs, but a few feet to the bed I can manage. Now, where was I? Oh, yes."

She propped herself up on her elbows and watched as he went to his dresser, knelt down, and opened the bottom drawer. When he turned around, he had a rope in one hand and something she couldn't see in the other. Whatever it was, it was small.

"Give me your wrists," he ordered.

Grace held her wrists out to him, palms up.

He flipped them over and began binding them together. By the time he was finished, she felt the beginnings of subspace coming on, that calm, floaty feeling she loved.

After checking to make sure the ropes weren't too tight, he used the loose end to tug her toward him. He leaned down, pressing a kiss to her lips. It wasn't nearly as aggressive as the last one, but still possessive. "I love you."

The look in his eyes left her no doubt that was true. How had she gotten so lucky to find not one but two men in her lifetime that could love her so deeply? She hadn't stood a chance. There was no way she couldn't have fallen for Alexander. "I love you, too."

He cupped the side of her face and brought their foreheads together. "I promise I will make you happy, Grace. I will do everything in my power to make sure you are safe and loved."

"I know you will."

One side of his mouth quirked up as he lowered his hand from her face and ran it down the length of her arm. "I'm also going to make sure you're fucked senseless on a regular basis."

And just like that, the air in the room was charged once more.

"Lie back and scoot yourself toward the pillows."

She followed his instructions, using her legs to wiggle her body up toward the headboard.

"That's good."

Once she stopped moving, he reached above her head and secured the rope to the headboard. He checked her wrists again, and walked to the other side of the room. When he returned, he had a metal wheel with spikes on it in his hand. Grace tensed.

"Have you ever had one of these used on you before?" he asked.

She shook her head. "No."

He spun the spikes around the wheel with his finger. "I figure since we're going to be doing a demonstration, we should probably practice ahead of time with some of the toys."

"Will it hurt, Master?" It wasn't that she didn't trust him. She did. Completely. But she'd never seen one of those things before and it looked painful.

"That depends on its user."

Grace swallowed.

"Ready?"

"Yes, Master."

He started by running it along her abdomen. She could definitely feel the spikes, but she wouldn't say they were painful.

Changing direction, he moved upward, making a circle around her breast before drawing a line down the center and over her nipple. "For those who enjoy edgier play, they can increase the pressure and draw blood." He repeated the process over her other breast. "But I know that's not something you're into and neither am I."

He continued to run the spiked wheel over her body, trailing it down each of her legs and back up again. Each time he got dangerously close to her sex, but at the last minute would change direction. The longer it went on, the more relaxed she became and the more she enjoyed the sensation.

"Spread your legs for me."

It wasn't until he spoke that Grace realized he'd stopped. She did as he asked, spreading her legs wide.

Alexander knelt between her parted thighs and ran his finger from her clit to her ass. "Did you plug yourself the last two nights, *gattina*?"

"I didn't Thursday, Master." She wondered if he would punish her for disobeying.

"Given the circumstances, I will let it slide this time." He brushed his thumb against her clit several times. "Next time, though, your ass will be paying the price."

She heard a noise and looked down. Alexander had put on a latex glove. Given his previous question, she knew something was going to be going up her ass.

He lubed up his fingers and used his other hand to spread her open before inserting his fingers. Grace blew out a breath and tried to relax. She used to enjoy anal play. It had just been a while.

"That's it." He eased two fingers in and out, gradually stretching her. Once he was satisfied she was prepped enough, she felt him remove his hand. Within seconds, it was replaced by something that felt rubbery. The feel of it reminded her of a dildo, which it very well could have been. She wasn't at an angle where she could see exactly what it was.

As the object was inserted into her ass, she took several deep breaths, giving her body time to adjust.

"I would love to fuck your ass tonight, but you're not quite ready for that yet." He gave the butt plug, or whatever it was, a little twist, causing another gasp to escape from Grace's lips. "Soon, though."

Then whatever he'd placed in her ass started buzzing. The vibrations lit up her nerves and had her sex throbbing in no time.

He wasn't finished, though. Something touched her clit, and then it started humming as well. She realized immediately what it was—a bullet vibe. Small, but effective. And it was about to send her spiraling over the edge.

The feel of his cock nudging the entrance to her pussy only added to everything else she was experiencing. "Please, Master. I want to feel you inside me."

Alexander grasped her hip with his free hand and, with a jerk of his pelvis, he plunged inside until his balls were pressing against her sex. She was full, utterly and completely, and she'd never felt better.

He rode her relentlessly, living up to his promise of fucking her senseless. As usual, he drew out her pleasure for as long as possible, until she couldn't stand it any longer. She really hoped his neighbors weren't home, because if they were they'd undoubtedly heard her scream as she'd been overcome with her orgasm.

Afterward, they made their way to the shower, taking their time washing each other, and then curled up together in his bed. As she was drifting off to sleep, she couldn't help but wonder how different her life would have been if Alexander hadn't delivered her that letter. Would she have ever put herself out there again, or would she have spent the rest of her life alone, clinging to her husband's memory?

Luckily, she would never know the answer to that question.

Alexander was now part of her life. She looked forward to what the future had in store for them. Whatever it might be.

Epilogue

Alexander came up behind Grace and pulled her against his chest. "Ready for tonight?"

Grace chuckled. "No. Not even a little bit." She leaned in to him, taking comfort in his arms.

"You'll do fine." He rubbed his hand along her backside. "Did you have any problems with the prep?"

The prep. Cleaning herself out for tonight's play. It wasn't horrible, but it wasn't the most pleasant thing she'd ever done. "I managed."

He ran the tip of his nose along her neck, sending shivers down her spine. "I promise I will make it worth it."

Of that she had no doubt. Almost three weeks had passed since that night in his bedroom where she'd told him she loved him for the first time. It had been a turning point for them. He'd stopped holding back and so had she.

They still hit a few bumps in the road every now and then. Like two nights ago when she'd been putting some of Alexander's things in the closet. He'd been slowly transferring his things to her house, both having agreed that, given the size of his apartment, him moving was the better option. She'd pushed some of her clothes aside and came across one of Kurt's dress uniforms. She hadn't been able to get rid of it when she'd packed up and come to St. Louis, but she'd completely forgotten it was there. Alexander had found her sitting on the floor of her bedroom, holding the uniform in a death grip. She'd been out of it for the rest of the evening.

As usual, Alexander was nothing but understanding. He'd lowered himself onto the floor beside her even though she knew getting down there had to be a challenge because of his injury. No words were spoken as he held her in his arms.

But tonight wasn't about Kurt, or her past, or his. Tonight was about the two of them performing a scene in front of the entire club. She was scared out of her wits, but she was also incredibly excited. He'd been getting her ready by introducing her to all the toys he was going to use on her, letting her ask questions as they went. It had eased many of her concerns.

"We need to get going. I want to look over all the equipment before too many people get there."

It was almost seven by the time they arrived at Serpent's Kiss. They'd barely walked in the door before Ali noticed them. She waved to Grace from across the room where she was standing with a woman Grace didn't recognize.

"Go on over and say hello. I'll be busy for a bit," Alexander said.

"Yes, Master."

Ali smiled as Grace approached. The two had gotten to know each other much better over the last few weeks. It was nice having another sub she could talk to. Beth was great, but there were some things only another sub would understand, and Grace wasn't sure she would ever be that comfortable talking about that kind of stuff with Drew, sub or not.

"Are you ready for tonight?" Ali asked, unable to contain her enthusiasm.

Grace blew out a breath. "As ready as I'll ever be."

"I'm sure you'll have fun. Your Master knows what he's doing."

Yes, he did. He'd proven it time and time again.

The woman she didn't know elbowed Ali.

"Oh. Sorry. Grace, I'd like for you to meet my best friend, Kim. She came here a couple of months ago to check out the club and now she's decided to join. Isn't that great?" Maybe Ali's enthusiasm wasn't all about tonight's demonstration.

Kim started to offer her hand, and then pulled it back. "It's nice to meet you. Ali was telling me that you're fairly new to the club, too."

"I joined a little over a month ago."

"Oh wow. And you're doing the demonstration tonight? I'm not sure I could be that brave," Kim said.

Ali giggled. "Grace is an exhibitionist. We've gotten to see that firsthand a number of times."

Grace felt her cheeks heat. "I didn't used to be."

Kim nodded toward the platform along the back wall. "Is that your Dom?"

Turning to look in the direction Kim was, Grace saw Alexander bent over a small metal tray, examining its contents. "Yes. That's my Master."

"Isn't that a bit unusual?" she asked.

Grace tore her gaze away from Alexander and back to Grace. "Unusual?"

"To find a master so quickly. You said you'd only been a member of the club for about a month."

Ali looked to be about to say something to her friend, but Grace didn't mind the questions. If Kim was new to the lifestyle then it was understandable that she'd want to know as much as possible. "We met before, but didn't realize we were both into BDSM until we saw each other here."

"That had to be awkward."

Grace snorted. "I ran away."

Kim furrowed her brow in confusion.

"When I saw him across the room, I freaked out and left as quickly as my feet would carry me." She frowned. "It was a rash decision, but at the time I didn't see any other option."

"I probably would have done the same thing."

This time Ali was the one who snorted. "No, you wouldn't. Knowing you, you would have marched up to him, your head held high, and demanded to know what he was doing here."

That didn't sound all that submissive to Grace, but then again maybe Kim wasn't a sub. Ali hadn't really said.

Kim laughed. "Maybe."

"There's no maybe about it," Ali said. "I know you."

Katrina made her way over to them. "How are you ladies this evening?"

"Good, Mistress," Grace and Ali said in unison.

Kim's response showed how new to the lifestyle she really was. "Good." Then she seemed to realize her mistake and added, "Mistress."

Katrina didn't seem fazed by the slip. Subs had the choice, or their Doms did, of whether or not to attach an honorific to a Dominant's name at the club. The only exception to this was Mistress Katrina. She was the club mistress and every sub used her title without exception. It wasn't written in the rules or anything, but it was what was accepted and expected. "All ready for tonight, Grace?"

"Yes, Mistress Katrina." Grace glanced once more in Alexander's direction. This time he appeared to be examining the table itself. "Master is making sure everything is the way he wants it."

She followed Grace's gaze and grinned. "I should probably make sure he has everything he needs."

Katrina excused herself, leaving the three alone again.

"Have you been in the lifestyle long?" Grace asked Kim, curiosity getting the better of her.

"Um. Well . . ." Kim shifted her weight several times, hemming and hawing as if she were unsure how to answer. "I've only done it once."

Grace's eyes widened. She'd only had kinky sex once and she'd joined a kink club? Wow. That was . . . wow. Grace couldn't imagine. Maybe Kim really was a Domme.

While Grace was still trying to figure out how to respond, Kim's attention shifted to something across the room. Grace looked to see what had caught her eye. Justin, the Dom who'd shown her around that first night—the one Alexander had made her come in front of—was striding toward the bar. He wasn't looking their way. As far as Grace could tell, he hadn't noticed them yet.

The look on Kim's face appeared to be more than casual interest. "Do you know Sir Justin?"

Ali was the one who spoke up. "He's her brother's best friend. They've known each other for years. Right, Kim?"

It took Kim longer than it should to answer. "Yeah. We've um . . . we've known each other since high school."

As if he knew they were talking about him, his gaze landed on the three of them. Only a second passed before shock crossed his face followed by what appeared to be extreme displeasure. Given there was no reason for him to be upset or even surprised by Grace or Ali's presence at the club, she could only assume that his reaction was for Kim. He clearly wasn't happy she was at Serpent's Kiss.

"I . . . I need to use the bathroom," Kim muttered before making a beeline for the locker rooms.

"What was that all about?" Grace asked.

Ali shook her head, looking in the direction her friend had gone. "I have no idea. Maybe she's afraid he'll tell her brother."

Maybe. But that wasn't the vibe she was getting.

Unfortunately, she wasn't able examine it any further. Alexander came up beside her and placed a hand on her lower back. "Ali."

"Good evening, Sir."

He looked down at Grace. "Meet me on the platform in fifteen minutes. I'm going to get us some waters."

"Yes, Master."

Ali fanned herself as Alexander walked away. "You are so lucky."

Grace couldn't disagree. "I know."

Not wanting to linger, she told Ali she'd catch her later and headed to the restroom. She had no idea how long their scene would last and it was better to be prepared.

She walked into the bathroom, finding an empty stall. At first, she thought she heard a humming sound, as if someone was singing. But then she realized it wasn't singing. It was talking. And considering the low volume, whoever it was had to be talking to themselves.

Grace finished up and exited the stall. Once she'd washed her hands, she waited, but no one came out. She debated whether or not she should go and get someone, but what would she tell them? That she thought someone was mumbling to themselves in the bathroom?

Realizing she had to make a decision, Grace went back to the stalls and found the one the sound was coming from. She tapped on the door of the stall and the noise stopped.

"Are you okay?" Grace asked.

No one answered. Then then door opened to reveal Kim. She looked somewhat embarrassed. "Sorry. I didn't realize anyone could hear me.”

Grace frowned.

Kim stepped out of the stall and Grace moved out of the way. She went to the sink and turned on the water. “Justin has been my brother’s best friend since high school. I guess I wasn’t as ready to see him as I thought I was.”

This surprised Grace. “So you knew he was a member here?”

“Yeah. When I came with Ali a few months ago, I saw him then.”

Grace thought about what Ali had told her. “Are you afraid he’ll say something to your brother?” She highly doubted it. From what she knew of Justin, he was a well-respected Dom at the club. To betray another member’s privacy, friend of the family or not, would be a huge violation and would probably get his membership revoked.

“No. I don’t think so.” Kim smiled, but it didn’t reach her eyes. “Don’t you have to go? I thought you were doing a demonstration or something tonight.”

All the color drained from Grace’s face. She’d been so worried about Kim, she hadn’t been thinking about the time. The last thing she wanted was to start the scene off on the wrong foot. “I—”

“Go. I’ll be fine. Promise.”

Grace had no choice but to believe her. She hurried out of the bathroom and went straight to the stage. When she realized Alexander wasn’t there yet, she breathed a sigh of relief.

“Cutting it close, aren’t you, *gattina*?” Alexander’s voice came from behind her.

She lowered her gaze to the floor. “Yes, Sir.” Later, when they were alone, she’d explain why she’d almost been late, but given their audience, she decided not to go into detail.

He studied her face for a moment, and then nodded before reaching for a white lab coat that was draped across a round stool.

As he put the coat on, Grace saw Kim emerge from the restroom. She stayed along the edge of the crowd.

Alexander moved to stand in front of her, blocking her view of everyone but him. He tilted her chin up, making her look at him. He rubbed his thumb along her jaw as he gazed into her eyes. “Ready?”

For him, she would always be ready. “Yes, Master.”

About the Author

Sherri spent most of her childhood detesting English class. It was one of her least favorite subjects because she never seemed to fit into the standard mold. She wasn't good at spelling, or following grammar rules, and outlines made her head spin. For that reason, Sherri never imagined becoming an author.

At the age of thirty, all of that changed. After getting frustrated with the direction a television show was taking two of its characters, Sherri decided to try her hand at writing an alternate ending, and give the characters their happily ever after. By the time the story finished, it was one of the top ten read stories on the site, and her readers were encouraging her to write more.

Since then Sherri has published several novels, many of which have hit the top 100 in their category on Amazon. Writing has become a creative outlet that allows her to explore a wide range of emotions, while having fun taking her characters through all the twists and turns she can create. You can find a current list of all of Sherri's books and sign up for her monthly newsletter at www.sherrihayesauthor.com.